MR SPARKS

Also by Danny Weston

The Piper

DANNY WESTON

ANDERSEN PRESS • LONDON

First published in 2015 by
Andersen Press Limited
20 Vauxhall Bridge Road
London SW1V 2SA
www.andersenpress.co.uk

2 4 6 8 10 9 7 5 3 1

British Library Cataloguing in Publication Data available.

ISBN 978 1 78344 321 5

Typest in Sabon by Palimpsest Book Production Limited,
Falkirk, Stirlingshire

Printed and bound by
CPI Group (UK) Ltd, Croydon, CR0 4YY

This one is for the two best book bloggers in the universe – Vincent Ripley and Ann Giles, the Book Witch. Thanks for all the kind words over the years.

How ridiculous I was as a marionette! And how happy I am, now that I have become a real boy!

Carlo Collodi, *Pinocchio*

1

OCTOBER 1919

1

The Visitor

'Where in the world have you been?' snapped Aunt Gwen in her broad Welsh accent. 'The time you've taken, you'd have thought you'd gone to Africa for that bread.' She was standing on the steps of the Sea View hotel, her hands on her hips, her black hair tied back in a severe bun.

Owen tried not to look guilty. Earlier that morning, she had sent him over to the bakery to pick up a basket of fresh loaves. Owen knew from bitter experience that it really didn't do to keep Aunt Gwen waiting, but he'd been feeling reckless, so on the way back from the baker's, he'd taken a quick detour onto the pier to watch the Punch and Judy show.

'Sorry, Aunt Gwen,' stammered Owen. 'There was quite a queue at the baker's. I came straight back.'

'I hope so, for your sake,' she said. 'Because if I hear you've been wandering aimlessly around Llandudno again, you and I will have *words*.' Aunt Gwen didn't like tardiness in any shape or form and Owen knew only too well that she wasn't slow to demonstrate her displeasure. She kept a length of cane in her room, which Owen had felt across his backside three times since he'd first arrived here, ten months ago. The first time had been for taking too long to follow instructions, the second, for being unable to finish a portion of Aunt Gwen's famously disgusting mutton pie. There'd been a third occasion, but he couldn't remember now exactly what he was supposed to have done that time. At any rate, he didn't much fancy a fourth dose, so he lifted the basket of bread and started up the steps to the entrance.

'I'll take that,' she told him, yanking the basket from his arm. 'We're expecting a guest at any moment. You stay here to help with the luggage.'

Right on cue, the growl of an engine turned Owen's head towards the street and he saw a motor taxi approaching. It was one of only a few taxis operating around Llandudno. The Great War had ended less than a year ago, so there was a real shortage of motor vehicles and the fuel required to run them. It also made them an expensive choice for travellers.

'He's here already!' said Aunt Gwen, shooting an accusing glare at Owen as though it was somehow *his* fault. She hurried up the steps towards the entrance and shot a final glance at Owen before she went inside. 'Be polite,' she warned him. 'And for goodness' sake, smarten yourself up!'

Owen wasn't sure how he'd do this at such short notice, but he spat on his hand and brushed down his unruly thatch of black hair, then rubbed the toecaps of his boots on the backs of his trousers.

The cab rumbled to a halt outside the Sea View and the driver climbed out and opened the rear door. A single passenger alighted and stood on the pavement, watching as the driver moved to the rear of the vehicle, to unstrap a heavy traveller's trunk that was balanced precariously on the luggage rack. The owner of the trunk looked on in silence, making no attempt to help.

The man didn't look very well, Owen thought. He was ancient, his skinny frame bent with age and somehow swamped by the old-fashioned frock coat and waistcoat that he was wearing. He wore white gloves and had shiny black-and-white spats on his feet. The effect was completed by a black top hat and an ebony walking stick with an elaborate jewelled head, which the man kept tucked under one arm. The wisps of hair that protruded from beneath the brim of his hat were white as a fall of snow.

All this Owen saw in an instant as he ran past the guest. Then he was helping the sweating, grunting driver to ease the heavy trunk down from the rack. They managed to lower it to the pavement and Owen noted – with a hint of relief – that it now rested on four sturdy wheels, which would at least make it a bit easier to move around. The old man came forward and paid the cabbie, waving away any change. Then he looked at Owen, nodded gravely and said simply, 'Bring the trunk.' He had some kind of a foreign accent, Owen thought, but it was hard to place.

The old man headed for the entrance of the hotel and Owen struggled along in his wake, alternately pushing and pulling the trunk, which he now noticed was covered with a multitude of exotic-looking labels featuring scenes from around the world. By the time he'd reached the doorway and was levering the trunk up the steps, he'd noted Zanzibar, Calcutta and Singapore amongst them, but he'd have needed a lot longer to look through them properly. He wished he'd thought to ask the cab driver to give him a hand to get it inside, but the vehicle had already moved away in a cloud of smoke, so there was nothing for it but to struggle along the best he could. He jolted the trunk over the last step and thought he heard a small sound from within it – a kind of grunt of discomfort, but he told himself he must have imagined it.

Once he finally had the trunk inside, he trundled it across the wood-block floor and found the old man standing at the counter, giving his details to Aunt Gwen.

'So it's just the two nights, then?' Owen heard her say. She made no attempt to keep the disappointment out of her voice. The business was entering the annual doldrums known as 'out of season' and Aunt Gwen preferred long residencies; but at the same time, she wasn't one to pass up business of any kind.

'It's just a passing visit,' announced the old man, signing the register with a theatrical flourish. 'Always there is work to be done and always there is travel.'

What *was* that accent? Was it . . . could it be . . . *German*? Owen hoped not. Feelings still ran high in this small seaside town. Owen supposed that he had more reason than most to resent such a man's presence. His own father had died in the War – well, that was the supposition, at least. Officially, he was missing, presumed dead, along with thousands of others. The last they'd heard from him was a brief letter written in July 1918, but it gave no indication of where he had been at the time and said only that he was looking forward to coming home. No body had ever been found and for a while, Owen and his ma had somehow managed to keep alive the hope that he would miraculously reappear. But when the War finally ended in November 1918, and there was still no word of him, the realisation that her husband was never coming home affected Owen's mother badly, causing a rapid descent into madness. She'd finally been deemed incapable of bringing up her only son and had been committed to the North Wales Lunatic Asylum in Denbigh just before Christmas 1918.

That was when Aunt Gwen had stepped up and announced that she had plenty of space and would be more than happy to provide a secure home and a prosperous future for her much-loved nephew, Owen. Aunt Gwen was, if nothing else, a great saleswoman. The authorities had swallowed every word and Owen had been promptly delivered into her tender care.

Right now, she was peering suspiciously at the register, an expression on her face that suggested she had just detected a bad smell.

'The Great Otto?' she read. 'What kind of a name is that?'

'The name under which I have performed for forty years,' said the old man proudly. 'The name, madam, which has graced the residences of royalty all over the world.'

Aunt Gwen sniffed. 'Well, it won't do for me,' she said. 'Your *real* name, if you don't mind.'

The old man bristled and, for a moment, Owen suspected that he was going to walk out in disgust. But his shoulders slumped, his head bowed. Perhaps he was just too tired to put up a fight. He picked up the pen and wrote down something else.

'Otto Schilling,' she read. 'There, that wasn't so hard, was it?' Her eyes narrowed. 'It sounds a bit . . . You're not *German*, are you?'

'No, madam, I'm Belgian by birth. From Liège. Do you know it?'

'No, but of course the Belgians are always welcome here. After everything your people went through in the Great War—'

'I fail to see what was so great about it,' interrupted Mr Schilling. 'And it wasn't so bad for me. I was touring America for most of it. Occasionally there were cockroaches in the hotel rooms, but that's about as bad as it got.'

Aunt Gwen gave him a frosty smile. 'I can assure you, you won't find any cockroaches *here*,' she told him. 'This is Llandudno's *premier* hotel.' She waited as though expecting a response, but when she didn't get one, she continued. 'You are most welcome, Mr Schilling. I'm going to put you in our finest room.' She handed him a key. 'You'll have a lovely view of the sea front and the pier. You can go up in the lift,' she added proudly. 'Do you know, we're the first hotel in Llandudno to actually *have* one.'

'How lovely for you,' said Mr Schilling. It was hard to tell if he was being sincere or taking the mick. Owen suspected the latter.

Aunt Gwen shot her nephew a look. 'Room seven,' she said. 'Help the gentleman up with his trunk. Get him some fresh towels. And don't be all day.'

Owen nodded. He knew only too well why Aunt Gwen had been so quick to offer him a home. She'd been mostly motivated by the opportunity to acquire an unpaid skivvy, someone to take care of all the troublesome little jobs that came up on a daily basis in an establishment like this. Aunt Gwen had never married and therefore had no unpaid little skivvies of her own. Oh, she had to observe the law and allow Owen to go to school five days a week – but as soon as he got home, the chores began and weekends were one long toil of changing beds and making fires and scrubbing bathrooms till they shone. Over the summer holidays she'd really had her money's worth out of him, working him around the clock at her busiest time of year. Now at least, things were easing off a bit.

Owen wheeled the trunk over to the lift, slid back the doors and manoeuvred the thing inside. For all Aunt Gwen's proud claims, the lift was a narrow little affair, not much more than a shoebox on a string. Once Owen had got the trunk in and pushed himself alongside it, there was barely room for Mr Schilling to squeeze his skinny frame into the remaining space, but he somehow managed. Owen got the concertina cage door closed and pressed the button. As the lift began to rise, he heard a tiny voice, speaking from somewhere nearby.

'Are we nearly there yet?' it said.

Owen looked at Mr Schilling in alarm, but it quite clearly hadn't been *him* who had spoken. It had sounded like a little boy. Now Owen heard a muffled bump and the same voice said, 'I'd kill for some fresh air right now.'

'Shush, Charlie,' said Mr Schilling calmly.

The voice seemed to have come from inside the trunk. Owen looked down at it in dismay and then back to Mr Schilling. The old man smiled at Owen.

'So,' he said, 'What's your name?'

Owen stared back at him, open-mouthed.

'Er . . . Owen,' he murmured. 'My name is . . . Owen.'

'Good. We shall be friends, I think.'

And the voice in the box said, 'That goes for me too!'

Then the lift came to a shuddering halt. They had arrived.

2

Here's Charlie!

Owen followed Mr Schilling out of the lift, pushing the trunk ahead of him, not really knowing what to think. What in the name of Lucifer was going on here? Thoughts flashed through his mind in a mad scramble. Mr Schilling was a kidnapper who had a small child locked in his trunk. Mr Schilling was trying to smuggle his *own* child in without paying for him. Mr Schilling was . . .

The old man unlocked the door of the room and walked inside. Owen followed, pushing the trunk more gingerly now, because he thought he was aware of other sounds coming from within. Was it . . . could it be . . . the sound of somebody breathing? Mr Schilling was taking no notice. He stood for a moment, looking around. It was a decent enough room, with a few pieces of well-chosen furniture – a double bed, a wardrobe, a sideboard. It was bigger than average and there *was* the much-boasted view of the pier, though a light drizzle was falling now, making it look rather drab, a straight line of stone jutting out into the gunmetal grey of the Irish Sea. Mr Schilling walked to the window and stood gazing out of it, as though deep in thought.

'Where would you . . . like the trunk?' asked Owen.

The old man waved a hand to his left, as though it was too much of a bother to think about. 'Put it over there,' he suggested. He watched as Owen pushed it into position. Then he returned to his contemplation of the view.

'Otto,' said a muffled voice from within the trunk and Owen instinctively took a step away from it. 'Come on, this has gone on long enough.'

Mr Schilling sighed. He walked over to the trunk, reached out with both gloved hands and placed the tips of his fingers in a complicated pattern on several dark wooden insets that studded the front of it. There was a harsh metallic click and suddenly, magically, the trunk sprang open as if with a life of its own. One section lifted silently upwards, another hinged to the left, a third to the right. And Owen found himself looking into a treasure trove, an interior papered with layer upon layer of colourful handbills and posters, all of them announcing the arrival of an act called The Great Otto and Mr Sparks. The names of the venues listed on the posters seemed impossibly grand. Fritz Schmidt's Party Hall, Berlin! The Pleasure Dome, Siam! The Montparnasse Theatre, Paris! Further down, there were rows of drawers holding who knew what mysteries? Colourful scarves and ropes hung from metal racks, there were chains and strings of bunting, printed in every shade under the sun. Owen was feasting his eyes when that voice spoke up again, a high-pitched childlike tone.

'Are you going to leave me in here all blooming day?' it demanded.

Mr Schilling frowned. He stooped and unlatched a large central drawer, which slid silently open as magically as the trunk had done. Mr Schilling reached inside and when he withdrew his gloved hands, Owen saw to his relief that the old man was holding a ventriloquist's dummy. So that was what he'd heard! Mr Schilling had been throwing his voice into the trunk so expertly, so convincingly, that the explanation had never occurred to Owen. He looked at the dummy and decided that the word hardly did justice to what Mr Schilling had in his arms. This was a character.

'Allow me to introduce you to my old friend, Mr Sparks,' said Mr Schilling. He walked over to a bentwood chair and sat down, placing the dummy on his lap.

Mr Sparks looked at Owen and the boy could feel a

strange thrill go through him, because the intensity in the dummy's bright blue eyes was quite unnerving. He had a large, round head, bright pink in colour with red patches on the cheeks and a smattering of orange freckles across the nose. His hair was an unruly ginger thatch, wearing thin and ratty here and there, as though he had seen better days. But the face was dominated by a wide grin, two rows of evenly spaced teeth with a wide central gap. The teeth stretched almost from ear to ear, impossibly white and framed by ruby red lips that glistened in the light from the window. Mr Sparks' eyes flicked open and shut a few times, making an unpleasant rasping sound. He twisted his head from side to side on his slender neck, as though performing some kind of stretching exercise. His clothes, Owen noticed, were impeccable, a smart black suit with a collar in matching silk and a crimson bow tie.

'Hello, 'ello,'ello,' he said. 'Who have we got here then?' The voice was English, Owen decided, a chirpy Cockney, no trace of Mr Schilling's accent at all.

'Err . . .' Owen felt vaguely foolish talking to a dummy, but he answered anyway. 'My name's . . . Owen.'

'I know that!' snapped Mr Sparks. 'I'm not cloth-eared, I did hear the conversation earlier. What I mean is, what have we *got* here? What sort of a fellow? Good, bad, smart, stupid?' He leaned forward slightly on Mr Schilling's lap. 'Can you keep a secret?' he whispered.

'Er . . . I suppose so.'

'Good. I'm not a dummy. I'm a *real* boy.'

Mr Schilling looked down at him sternly.

'Now then, Charlie, what have I told you about making things up?'

'I'm not making it up!' protested Mr Sparks. 'You know me, Otto, I only ever speak the truth. Cross my heart and hope to die.' He leaned even closer. 'Unlike Otto here, who tells everyone he's Belgian, but *we* know that's not true, don't we, Owen? We know Mr Schilling actually comes from Aachen, which is across the border from Belgium, so technically speaking . . .' He flipped his eyebrows up and down, making a squeaking sound. 'He's a flipping Hun . . . *a German*!'

Owen couldn't help but laugh at this, but Mr Schilling looked genuinely angry. 'Charlie, I've told you before! You mustn't go around saying those things about me. You'll cause me all kinds of problems.'

'Huh. You think you've got problems! Try being squashed in a box all day long and see how you like that.' He

17

returned his attention to Owen. 'So . . . Owen. Have you got a surname?'

'Er . . . yes. It's Dyer.'

Mr Sparks' eyes seemed to light up at this news. He burst into a little poem. 'This is the tale of Owen Dyer. He tried to join a male voice choir. The choirmaster said, "No fear! We don't want no Dyer 'ere!"' Mr Sparks threw back his head and guffawed delightedly. 'See what I did there? Dyer 'ere. *Diarrhoea!*'

Owen had been watching Mr Schilling intently as the poem was recited. It was an amazing performance. There was not the quiver of a lip or the twitch of an Adam's apple to give the game away. 'That's fantastic,' he said.

'Don't be looking at *him*!' protested Mr Sparks. 'I'm the one doing all the hard work. That old fool just smiles and takes the money.' He fluttered his eyelashes. 'So, Owie . . . you don't mind if I call you that, do you?'

'I prefer Owen.'

'But it sounds better, doesn't it? It sounds less . . . Welsh. Not that there's anything wrong with the Welsh. Some of my best enemies are Welsh. What was that poem I used to know? Oh yes! Taffy was a Welshman, Taffy was a thief, Taffy came to my house and stole a leg of beef—'

'I've heard that before,' interrupted Owen, looking accusingly at Mr Schilling. 'That's not very nice.'

'I've told you,' protested Mr Sparks. 'Don't be looking at *him*! You think he controls what I say? I'd like to see him *try*. Now look, maybe we've got off on the wrong foot, *Owie*. Let's be friends. My friends call me Charlie so you can call me . . . Mr Sparks!' The dummy waggled his head from side to side for a moment, before continuing. 'No, seriously . . . I need to ask you a question.'

'Umm . . . right?'

'That steaming old baggage downstairs . . . I'm sorry, I mean that charming lady at the desk. That was your mother, was it?'

'No it wasn't. That's my Auntie Gwen.'

'Ooh! This is the tale of Auntie Gwen, who sat upon a fountain pen. The pen pushed through, her pants so blue. She still leaves ink marks, now and then!' Mr Sparks sniggered at his own cleverness. Then he leaned forward and lowered his voice again. 'Shall I tell you another secret?' he murmured.

'Erm . . .'

'You don't like Auntie Gwen very much.'

'Oh, that's not—'

'You *don't*! I can read you like a book!'

'Don't pick on the boy,' suggested Mr Schilling. 'You'll hurt his feelings.'

Owen looked at the old man, nonplussed. This seemed a bit rich. After all, it was *him* making the dummy say these terrible things.

'She's . . . not so bad,' said Owen, trying to sound matter of fact.

'Not so bad as in not so good? I reckon she's a right old nag. Where *is* your mummy, Owie?'

'She's . . . not around,' said Owen, trying to keep the misery out of his voice. 'She's . . . in a hospital.'

'Oh dear. Hope it's not the Spanish 'flu?'

'No. It's . . . not that sort of hospital.'

'Oops.' Mr Sparks waggled his eyebrows and glared at Mr Schilling. 'Quickly, Otto,' he hissed. 'Change the subject, change the subject!' He turned back to look at Owen and somehow affected a look of sympathy. 'And what about dear old Dad?'

'He . . . died in the War,' said Owen quickly. 'Or at least, he—'

'Oh my goodness. You have been in the wars, haven't you? Well, obviously it was your dad that was *in* the wars.

You're just the innocent bystander. Aww, poor little Owie! What a tragedy. Your poor old dad. Murdered.' He turned to look up at Mr Schilling. 'By the wicked Hun,' he added slyly, and he gave Owen a broad wink.

'Charlie,' snapped Mr Schilling. 'One of these days, you really will go too far and then . . .'

'Then what, *Herr* Schilling? Don't forget who puts the bread on the table. If I decided to stop talking, you'd be in a right old pickle, wouldn't you?"

They gazed at each other for a moment and it seemed to Owen that in the silence, he could feel waves of mutual hatred pulsing between them. Finally Mr Sparks turned slowly back to look at Owen. 'So from what you're telling me . . . you're practically an orphan.' He put his head to one side and fluttered his eyelashes, making a faint clattering sound. 'Aww . . . kind of gets you right there, doesn't it?' Mr Shilling lifted one of Mr Sparks' hands and placed it briefly on his chest. Mr Sparks closed his eyes for a moment as though thinking, then opened them and said, 'You know what I'm thinking, Otto? This could be the one we've been looking for.'

Mr Schilling studied Owen for a moment. He shook his head. 'Don't be ridiculous,' he said. 'He's just a boy.'

21

DANNY WESTON

'Well, *you* were a boy once . . . back in the Dark Ages.'
He gave a hideous little cackle. 'How old are you, Owie?'

'I'm . . . twelve.'

'Oh yes, the golden age. I remember when I was twelve
. . . ah, happy days. Of course, we made our own enter-
tainment then. You could get an old wooden tea chest and
play with it for hours. God, we were bored!' He chuckled.
'How old d'you think *I* am, Owie?'

'Err . . . gosh, I don't know.'

'Take a wild guess!'

'Umm . . .'

'Go on, guess. GUESS!'

'Er . . . thirty-five?'

Mr Sparks' jaws snapped shut with a click. He sat there,
his big blue eyes gazing mercilessly at Owen. 'That's how
old you think I am? Thirty-five? Thirty-flipping-five? Is that
how old I look to you?'

'Well, no, you *look* like a little boy, but I thought . . .
somebody could have made you a long time ago, couldn't
they? Maybe you're older than you look.'

Mr Sparks' grin seemed to grow across his face. 'Oh
yes,' he said. 'He's young, Otto, but he's smart. He's using
the old grey matter.' Mr Schilling lifted one of the dummy's

22

hands to clunk it against the side of his head, making a hollow sound. 'Well, if that's your thinking, let me tell you that I am actually two hundred and fourteen years old. But not looking bad on it, I reckon!' He giggled. 'You know, I *like* you, Owie Boy. I think we could be on to something here.' He swivelled his head to look up at Mr Schilling. 'I really think he could be the one.'

Owen wondered what Charlie was getting at. What *one*?

Mr Schilling looked wary and Owen thought a little scared. 'I don't think he's suitable at all,' he said. 'You need to find somebody more—'

'More *what*? Smarter? Older? Taller? Fatter? I keep suggesting people but you keep ruling them out. Let me remind you, Otto, we don't have that much time . . . the sands are running out, my old friend, in more ways than one. You need to start giving some serious thought to what happens next. You're not well!'

Mr Schilling sighed. 'You're tiring me out, Charlie,' he said. 'You'll have to go back in your trunk.'

Mr Sparks reacted dramatically to this, his eyes rolling in his head, his mouth opening and closing. 'Oh no, don't put me back in the box! Please! I've only been out for five minutes.'

'I told you. I'm tired. I need to rest.'

'Otto, wait! I was only making a suggestion!'

But now Mr Schilling was getting up from the chair and carrying Mr Sparks the short distance across the room to the trunk and it looked to Owen as though the dummy was actually wriggling in Mr Schilling's hands.

'Hold still, damn you!' roared Mr Schilling. 'You *will* go back.' Now he was pushing Mr Sparks down inside the cramped drawer space.

'No, please, just five more minutes. Five more minutes! I'll be good, I promise. Owie! Tell him not to do it!' The drawer slid shut and the voice was magically diminished. 'Otto! Otto, let me out. LET ME OUT! Please . . .'

'I warned you, Charlie. You've got to stop spreading rumours about me. It's not fair!'

'Let me out, Otto. PLEASE! I'll be good, I promise.'

Just at that moment, Aunt Gwen's voice came echoing up the stairs.

'Owen? What have you been doing up there all this time? I've got a hundred jobs waiting for you down here.'

Owen sighed. He left the old man and his dummy to it, wondering as he did so what it took to make a man continue in such a fashion, even when he wasn't on stage. Perhaps, he thought, Mr Schilling was a little crazy. A brilliant ventriloquist though. He went to the door and stepped outside, closing it behind him. But he lingered for a moment, listening, as the two voices continued to rage at each other, one at full volume, one muted by layers of cardboard and leather.

'Otto, listen to me. You can't just pretend this isn't happening. We have to find somebody soon!'

'Charlie, I'm tired. Let me sleep!'

Owen let out a long breath. 'Crazy,' he muttered. But then he thought of his mother, all alone in that horrible place in Denbigh and he felt guilty for even having thought the word. He sighed and went downstairs to find Aunt Gwen.

3

The Deal

There was no sign of Mr Schilling all the rest of that day and Owen didn't have much time to spare. Following Aunt Gwen's barked commands, he filled the hours by fetching and carrying, scrubbing and cleaning and as far as he knew, the old man didn't emerge from his room once.

In between giving out orders, Aunt Gwen fretted about this.

'What kind of a man sits in his room all day and doesn't even order a glass of water?' she asked Owen as he stood at the sink, peeling potatoes for dinner. The chef, Mr Cadwallader, a big, heavy-gutted man with a stubby beard, was at the other end of the large kitchen doing something complicated with a leg of mutton.

'I think he was tired,' said Owen; and thought, I know how he feels.

'What kind of a man *is* he?' continued Aunt Gwen.

'He's an entertainer,' said Owen, not daring to look up from his work. 'One of those ventriloquist people.'

'A what?'

'You know, they have a dummy and they make it speak, without moving their lips. He has this one called Mr Sparks. He put on a little show while I was up there. Er . . . just while I was getting the trunk set up and everything. He was very good.'

'Hmph! No wonder you took so long up there. I ought to take it out of your wages.'

'You don't *pay* me any wages,' Owen reminded her.

'No, but I give you a roof over your head, don't I? A decent bed to sleep in. And a square meal in your belly. That's more than your mother can do for you.'

Owen's hand tightened on the potato knife. He hated it when Aunt Gwen got on to the subject of her sister. The two had never got along with each other and since Ma's dramatic change in fortunes, Gwen seemed to take every opportunity to gloat. She started now on a familiar topic. 'I told Meg, I said to her, "Don't you be getting all high and mighty with me, just because you've met some man. Life has a way of taking you down a peg or two," I said. And sure enough, that's exactly what happened.'

Owen felt like telling Aunt Gwen what he really thought of her, but knew that he couldn't do that. He'd learned by now that the only way to get her to go along with anything you wanted was to appeal to her better nature. And surely even *she* must have one hidden away deep down inside.

'I was wondering . . .' he said.

Aunt Gwen sniffed. 'Wondering what?' she asked him, suspiciously.

'I was thinking that it's been ages since we visited Ma. You did say we could go again, after the summer season. And . . . well, it *is* October.'

Aunt Gwen scowled. 'It's such a job getting there,' she said. 'Those dirty smelly trains. And besides, I don't really see the point. I mean, it's not as if she even *knows* we're there, is it? She just sits in that chair staring out of the window.' She did a mock shudder. 'Fair gives me the creeps, it does.'

'I think she *did* know we were there, last time,' said Owen. 'She squeezed my hand.'

'Yes, well you want to be thankful it wasn't your throat she was squeezing. I tell you, there's nothing much left of the Meg I used to know. I'd be afraid to be left alone with her.'

Just then, the door opened and Effie, one of the younger maids, popped her head in.

'Please, miss, we've had a request for a cheese sandwich and a glass of milk. The gentleman in room seven.'

'Thank you, Effie,' said Aunt Gwen and watched as she closed the door again. She rolled her eyes. 'The last of the big spenders,' she said. 'A cheese sandwich and a glass of milk. I ask you! Mr Cadwallader?'

'I heard, marm,' said the chef patiently. He stopped what he was doing and waddled over to the sink to wash his bloody hands. Then he went to the cold box to get cheese.

'You can take it up to him,' Aunt Gwen told Owen. 'Since you were getting along *so* famously.'

'Umm . . . all right. And . . . about Ma?'

Aunt Gwen shrugged her shoulders. 'We'll see,' she said. Which Owen knew from bitter experience actually meant, 'No chance.' He watched as she strode out of the kitchen, looking for somebody else to order around and not for the first time, he thought wistfully about running away from here and leaving the Sea View far behind.

Owen carried the tray carefully up the stairs and tapped on the door of room seven.

'Come in,' said a weak voice. He turned the handle and pushed open the door. Mr Schilling was lying in bed, the covers pulled up to his chest. His pale features were propped up by a mound of pillows, his grey hair in disarray. He didn't look well at all, Owen thought, even worse than when he'd first arrived.

Owen stood for a moment, unsure of what to do, but the old man beckoned him closer with a skeletal arm. 'Bring it over here,' he said, gesturing at the bedside cabinet.

'Are you all right?' Owen asked him, as he set the tray down. 'I could call for a doctor, if you like.'

Mr Schilling gave him a strained smile. 'It's nothing that any doctor can fix,' he assured Owen. 'It's called old age. You have it all to look forward to, my boy, but it's a long way down the line for you.' He gave a dry chuckle that somehow mutated into a hacking cough. He was obliged to pull a handkerchief from under the covers and hold it to his mouth. When he took it away again, Owen couldn't help noticing some crimson spots on the white fabric.

'You're really not well,' said Owen. 'Perhaps I could . . .'

Mr Schilling waved him to silence. He reached out and picked up the glass of milk with a shaking hand, then lifted it to his lips and drank.

'Hey, what about me?' said a muffled voice from the direction of the trunk and, once again, Owen marvelled at the old man's skill. He'd seen the trick done by other ventriloquists, but never so well. 'Have I been forgiven yet?'

Mr Schilling lowered the glass and set it down on the tray. He looked at Owen. 'Will you oblige me?' he asked, pointing in the direction of the trunk.

'Oh . . . yes, of course.' Owen walked across the room to the trunk and as he did so, he experienced a strange kind of anticipation. He stooped, took hold of the handle of the central drawer and pulled. It slid smoothly out and Mr Sparks' pink features gazed up at him. 'You certainly took your time,' he said.

Owen couldn't help it. He jumped back, startled, because the dummy's mouth had moved along to the words. But how was that possible when Mr Schilling was lying in bed on the other side of the room?

'Are you going to stand there gawping like a goldfish or are you going to pick me up?' demanded Mr Sparks.

'Er . . . yes . . . sure.' Owen looked at Mr Schilling, who was lying there staring blankly up at the ceiling, not taking any interest in the proceedings. Owen reached in and picked

31

up Mr Sparks, handling him with exaggerated care, as though he was a baby. He was amazed to discover that he was surprisingly heavy and that he actually felt warm through his clothes. A low vibration seemed to emanate from him, almost like an electric current. Owen carried the dummy across to the bed and not sure of what to do, laid him alongside his owner. Now two heads stared up at Owen from the pillows – one pale, drawn and anxious, the other round, pink and grinning gleefully.

'That's better,' said Mr Sparks. 'And how is Owie Bowie?'

'I'm well, thank you. How . . . how are you?' A thought flashed through his mind. *You're talking to a wooden puppet, you idiot!* But he couldn't help himself. There was something so compelling about Mr Sparks, something that seemed . . . *real*. But that couldn't be the case. So how was it done? As far as he could see, Mr Schilling wasn't even touching the dummy. His hands were lying by his sides on top of the bed covers.

'Oh, I'm just fine and dandy. Thank you for asking.' Mr Sparks turned his head to one side. 'Nice polite boy,' he observed.

'Yes,' agreed Mr Schilling. 'Very polite.'

'Manners are so important. My old mum used to say—'

'Your mother?' interrupted Mr Schilling. 'Why bring her up?'

'I'm just making conversation! I had a lovely mum, I did. Handsome woman. Lovely flowing red hair all down her back. None on her head, mind you.'

'That's an old one!' laughed Owen.

Mr Sparks looked up at him reproachfully. 'Of *course* it's an old one. But it was brand new two hundred years ago, when I first heard it. Why is everyone a critic these days? It's *so* easy to criticise . . .' His eyes seemed to narrow. 'Tell you what, if you're so good, Owie Bowie, why don't *you* tell *me* a joke?'

'Oh, I couldn't . . .'

'No, come on, big mouth. Let's hear it. Give me your best shot.'

'Umm . . . all right then.' Owen thought for a moment and then remembered a silly little joke he'd heard from one of the boys in school. 'Why is a dog like a tree?' he asked.

Mr Sparks rolled his eyes. 'They both lose their bark when they die.'

'Oh, you've heard it before.'

'Heard it? I *wrote* it! Give me another one.'

'Er . . . well, I . . .'

'Come on, come on, that was useless. Try again!'

'Umm . . . all right. Why did the dentist seem sad?'

'Because he always looked down in the mouth! Oh, for goodness' sake, you can do better than that, surely?'

'Well, I don't know if—'

'Tell you what. Tell me one I *don't* know the answer to and I'll give you threepence. How would that be?'

'That would be great, only—'

'Come on, come on, stop making excuses. Hit me with it!'

'All right.' Owen considered for several moments and then thought he had the answer. 'What's green with wheels?' he asked.

Mr Sparks looked stumped by that one. 'Er . . . a green motor car?' he suggested. Owen shook his head. 'A train? A trolley bus. A . . . pram?' Owen just kept shaking his head. 'I don't know,' muttered Mr Sparks, after a long silence. He sounded quite annoyed about it. 'What *is* green with wheels?'

'Grass,' said Owen. He paused for effect. 'I lied about the wheels.'

Mr Sparks eyes bulged and for a moment, he looked absolutely furious. 'You . . . you cheated!' he complained.

'No he didn't,' said Mr Schilling. 'He just got the better of you, Charlie. There's not many people who can do that.'

'You stay out of this!' Mr Sparks studied Owen for a few moments in silence. Then his wide mouth relaxed into a grin. 'All right,' he said. 'Otto, give him threepence.'

'But *you* made the bet!' protested Mr Schilling.

'I know that. But I can't give it to him, can I? Come on, stump up!' Mr Schilling frowned but he reached out to a pile of change on the bedside cabinet, extracted a coin and handed it to Owen. Owen smiled at it before slipping it into his pocket. 'Thank you,' he said.

'I've just made my mind up about this lad,' announced Mr Sparks. 'Otto, I wouldn't mind having a little chat with him on my own. I think you'd feel much better if you had a nap.'

'I don't *want* a nap,' said Mr Schilling.

'Who said I'm giving you a choice?'

'Look, I want to know what you—'

'Cyan, magenta, ultramarine,' said Mr Sparks in a mono-tone. 'Falling . . . very . . . slowly.'

An incredible thing happened. Mr Schilling's eyes closed and, quite suddenly, he was fast asleep. His bony chest rose and fell silently. Mr Sparks gazed at him for a moment and then turned his gaze back to Owen. 'That's got rid of the old fool,' he said. 'Now, let's talk turkey.'

Owen took a step back from the bed, his heart thumping in his chest. It had been weird enough before, when Mr Schilling was awake and not actually *touching* the dummy. Now . . .

'Who . . . who's operating you?' cried Owen.

Mr Sparks moved his eyebrows up and down. 'Take a wild guess,' he said. 'I told you before, *I* do all the work here.'

'But . . . that's . . . that's not . . . possible.'

'Think not?' Mr Sparks grinned delightedly. 'Then what do you call this, sunshine? An optical illusion?' His brows furrowed. 'Oh come on, step over here, I'm not going to *bite* you!'

Owen took a cautious step closer to the bed. He reached out a finger and prodded Mr Schilling's shoulder. The old man stirred a little but didn't wake.

'Forget it,' said Mr Sparks. 'Mesmerised. A little trick I picked up in Paris when we were touring there in the forties.'

'The forties?' Owen was puzzled. 'But . . . it's only 1919.'

'The *eighteen* forties, you idiot! I learned it from this

Swiss chap, Charles La Fontaine. Very good, he was. Comes in handy from time to time.'

'I don't really understand how . . .'

'Never mind about that! Come on, sit down for a minute, I need to have a serious talk with you.'

Owen lowered himself carefully onto the side of the bed. He felt as though he was dreaming this and part of him stayed tense, ready to jump up and make a run for it if he needed to.

'Relax,' Mr Sparks told him. 'Now, listen carefully. I need your help.' His blue eyes seemed to concentrate their gaze. 'We don't have much time. Old Otto here, anyone can see he's on his last legs. Been good to me over the years, I'll say that for him, but I've put gold in his pocket and food in his belly, so I'd say he's done well out of the arrangement. But he's slowing down. And if there's one thing I've learned in this world, it's that you have to stay on the move. That's where *you* come in.'

'Look, I don't really—'

'Shut your cake hole and listen! There are some people after me. *Bad* people. I won't say too much about them, but you wouldn't want to mess with 'em. They've been after me for a while now. Me and Mr S, we've been keeping one step ahead of them, see? But we used to be *six* steps ahead. And it's poor old Otto, slowing us down. Chances are, they'll come looking for me before very much longer and if I continue to hang around in this dump of a hotel, they'll catch me.'

'Who are these people?' asked Owen. 'What do they want?'

'It doesn't matter,' Mr Sparks assured him. 'That's too complicated to explain right now. All you need to know about them is that they are villains. Now, you know barely anything about me, we've only just met, but let me ask you a serious question. Do you want something bad to happen to me?' He moved his eyebrows up and down. 'Well, do you?'

'Er . . . no, of course not.'

'Well then, here's what's going to happen. Tomorrow morning, early . . . and I mean *really* early, you are going to come to this room and collect me – and then we'll leave this place together and we'll get as far away from here as possible.'

Owen laughed. 'I don't think so,' he said.

'I *know* so,' Mr Sparks assured him. 'I know it so deeply it *hurts*. Let me ask you this, Owie, do you like it here?'

'Well, I . . .'

'Tell the truth!'

'Umm . . . no. No I don't like it, not really. But that's not the—'

'And we already know how you feel about dear old Auntie Gwen.'

Owen sighed. 'That doesn't mean I can just . . . run away.'

'Of course it does! It's your free pass to do exactly that. And don't worry, Owie, I'll make it worth your while. Stick with me, sunshine, and you'll never be hungry again. You'll never want for anything.'

'But . . . what about Mr Schilling?'

Mr Sparks twisted his head around to look up into the old man's slumbering face. 'He's had his day,' he said. 'Aww, look at him. Poor old devil. Fair breaks my heart it does, to do this to him, but . . . now it's a question of survival. He's done his best by me but his best is no longer good enough. It's time for fresh blood.' He turned his head back to look at Owen. 'I knew, the moment I heard your voice, Owie, that fresh blood was you.'

'Oh . . . I see. But look, even if I wanted to leave, I can't just . . .'

'I understand only too well how these things work. It can't all be one way, can it? I have to do something for *you*. So, let me ask you this, what is it you want more than anything?'

'Want?'

'Yes, what is it that rotten old Auntie Gwen won't let you have?'

Owen thought for a moment. 'Well . . .'

'Go on,' Mr Sparks urged him. 'Spill the beans.'

'I keep asking her if we can go and visit my ma. But she just keeps putting it off. Like she doesn't want to.'

Mr Sparks' eyes opened as wide as they could possibly go. Then he sniggered. 'Aww, he wants to see his mummy!' he jeered.

Owen started to get up from the bed. 'If you're going to make a joke of it . . .'

'No, wait!' Mr Sparks' arm shot out and one hand grabbed Owen's wrist with a power that shocked him. He stared down at the hand in dismay.

'You . . . you *can* move,' he said.

'A bit,' admitted Mr Sparks. 'Not that well, though. Lack of practice, I suppose.' Mr Sparks' glossy lips peeled back revealing his shockingly white teeth. 'Sorry about the sarcasm, couldn't help myself. It's like a reflex action with me. Of *course* we can go and see your mum. Provided she's not somewhere impossible.'

'She's in the . . . the . . .'

'Nut house?' offered Mr Sparks, helpfully. 'The booby hatch, the funny farm, the . . .'

'The North Wales Asylum,' said Owen frostily. 'In Denbigh.'

Mr Sparks nodded. 'Well, that's easy enough. It's barely spitting distance. We'll go there first and once you've seen your mum, we'll go where *I* want to go.'

'Which is where?'

'All in good time, young man, all in good time. Now. Do we have a deal?' He lifted the hand from Owen's wrist and held it out as if to shake.

'I don't know,' said Owen. 'If Aunt Gwen catches me, she'll cane the britches off me.'

'Hmm. And she treats you *so* nicely now, doesn't she?'

Owen scowled. 'She treats me like a servant,' he said. 'She works me every spare minute that God sends. And she's beaten me already. Three times.'

Mr Sparks waggled his eyebrows. 'Oh, well I can see why you wouldn't want to leave all that,' he said. 'Very enticing.'

'But we . . . we would come back again, wouldn't we?'

Mr Sparks looked back at him. 'Why exactly would you *want* to?' he asked.

Owen had to admit that he couldn't think of an answer to that one. He looked doubtfully at Mr Schilling, who was still fast asleep, his chest rising and falling. 'And . . . what about him?' he asked.

'What about him?'

'Well, don't you think he'd miss you?'

'I reckon he'd be grateful. He's been saying for ages that all he wants is a nice rest. So why not let him have one? Now, Owen, look at me for a moment.' The blue eyes focused on Owen and seemed to concentrate their gaze. 'Not a lot of people know this, but when I was made, they got my eyes slightly wrong. One of them is a tiny bit bigger than the other. Can you see which one?' Owen stared into Mr Sparks' eyes. He could feel his resistance slipping away like water draining through a colander. A strange red mist seemed to flow through his mind. When Mr Sparks spoke next, his voice had acquired a strange, monotonous tone and Owen felt as if every word was being chiselled into the inside of his skull. 'You know what to do, Owie,' murmured Mr Sparks. 'Be here tomorrow at first light. Four a.m. Be here . . .

or spend your entire life regretting that you didn't come.' He turned his head to look at Mr Schilling. 'Ultramarine, magenta, cyan,' he said. 'Rising . . . very . . . quickly.'

And the old man opened his eyes. He blinked a couple of times and then looked from Mr Sparks to Owen. 'Sorry,' he said. 'Must have nodded off for a moment. Did I . . . miss anything?'

'No,' said Mr Sparks. 'Owie was just telling some more of his jokes. To tell you the truth, I was jealous of you.'

'Jealous?' muttered Mr Schilling.

'Yes. I kept wishing *I* was asleep.' He sniggered. 'Anyway, he was just leaving, weren't you, Owie?'

Owen nodded. He got up from the bed but he still felt dazed and slightly nauseous. I'm not coming back here at four in the morning, he told himself. No way. But even as he thought it, the words somehow lacked conviction. 'I'll see you both later,' he said and headed for the door. He paused for a moment as he turned the door handle and looked back at them, lying side by side on the bed.

'Now, Otto,' Mr Sparks was saying, in that soft persuasive tone. 'Why don't you eat your sandwich like a good boy? You need to keep your strength up.'

Owen went out, closing the door behind him.

4

Moonlight Flit

Owen woke abruptly from a very bad dream. He lay on his back in his narrow bed trying to recall what it had been about, but for the life of him, he couldn't remember any details. Had it been something about . . . travelling through a forest? For a moment, some wisps of the dream came fleetingly back to him, but when he tried to seize on them, they burst apart like confetti and drifted beyond his reach. He always hated it when that happened.

He wondered what time it was. Turning his head to the side, he peered at the cheap alarm clock on his bedside cabinet. A quarter to four in the morning. What could possibly have awoken him so early, tired as he was from a day of hard work? Then he remembered. Mr Sparks was expecting him. He'd told him to be there at four. Well, blow that, Owen told himself. If that stupid dummy thought that Owen was going to get out of a nice warm bed at this unearthly hour and go running off to God-knows-where, he had another think coming. Owen turned on to his side and closed his eyes, attempted to find a way back into the world of dreams – but he couldn't do it. He kept experiencing a mental image of Mr Sparks' shiny pink face, looking at him pleadingly.

I'm not getting up, Owen told himself. I'm too tired. But even as he thought it, he found that he was pushing aside the bedcovers, as though his arms had a mind of their own. He swung his legs over the edge of the bed, sat up and reached out to strike a match and light the candle on the bedside table. He looked around at the bleak little box room that had been his sleeping quarters for the past ten months. Tucked away up on the third floor, it was a bare cheerless place with peeling wallpaper and a badly stained ceiling. There were a few cheap sticks of furniture – a wardrobe, a chest of drawers and a bentwood chair – and that was all that Owen had to call his own.

I'm not getting dressed, he decided. And found himself rising from the bed and doing exactly that. Now he was pulling the battered leather suitcase from the top of the wardrobe, where it had lain undisturbed ever since he arrived here, the action causing clouds of dust to swirl down around him. And now he was actually rooting in the wardrobe and throwing items of clothing into the suit-case, so it was clear that he was planning to do *something*. This is stupid, he thought. Because whatever happens, I'm not going downstairs.

The next thing he knew he was putting on his overcoat and cap. Then he picked up the suitcase and pushed open the door of his bedroom. He stood in the gloom listening intently. A deep silence reigned, apart from the ticking of the big grandfather clock down in the hotel foyer. He thought about using the lift but decided that would be too noisy – so he crept down the staircase, placing each foot with great care, wincing at every creak of wood beneath his tread.

The clock was softly striking four when he finally came to the door of Mr Schilling's room. He lifted his hand to knock but then thought better of it, imagining the sound reverberating through the hotel. So he tried the handle instead and the door opened easily, silently. He peered into the room. The bedside lamp was on and he could see the two figures, still lying side by side on the bed, the way he had left them. Mr Sparks was clearly wide awake, his eyes studying Owen as he closed the door gently behind him and moved closer. Mr Schilling was lying on his side, his face turned away.

'Bang on time,' whispered Mr Sparks. 'Good lad.'

'I don't know why I came,' said Owen sullenly. 'I didn't want to, but somehow I couldn't stop myself. This is stupid.'

'No it's not,' Mr Sparks assured him. 'This is the cleverest thing you've ever done.' He glanced quickly at Mr Schilling. 'And keep your voice down,' he hissed. 'You don't want to wake the old man, do you?'

Owen frowned. 'Aren't you going to say goodbye to him?' he murmured.

'No. What's the point? He needs his rest.' He moved his eyebrows up and down, making that soft creaking sound. 'Well, come on, what are you waiting for? Pick me up.'

Owen set down the case and did as he was told. As he reached across Mr Schilling's sleeping form, he noted that the old man wasn't making a sound.

'Is he all right?' he asked.

'Yes, yes, right as rain. Come along, we're wasting time!'

Owen lifted the dummy from the bed, once again marvelling at the weight and the warmth of him. He popped him against his shoulder, like a mother with a baby. 'Is that what you've brought to carry me in?' asked Mr Sparks doubtfully, peering over Owen's shoulder.

Owen looked down and realised that he was referring

47

to the suitcase. 'No, they're my clothes,' he said. 'Aren't we going to take the trunk?'

Mr Sparks shook his head, making a rattling sound. 'Oh yes, good idea! We'll make great progress dragging that blooming thing around with us! I've been on at Otto for years about dumping it, but would he listen to me?'

'But—' Owen turned to look at the open trunk with its colourful posters and handbills. 'It's got so many lovely things in it.'

'It's dead weight,' said Mr Sparks bluntly. 'Stuff like that drags you down. From here on we're going to be lighter, faster. It'll help to keep us more than just one step ahead.'

Owen wasn't convinced. 'But this case is full of my clothes,' he protested.

'Then we'll have to dump some, won't we?' said Mr Sparks. He grinned. 'Don't worry, I'll buy you more, once we're settled somewhere. Nice ones. *New* ones. You'll be the best-dressed lad in Britain. Come on, less talk, more action!'

Owen sighed. He set Mr Sparks down on the carpet and flipping the case onto its back, he unlatched it and looked at the jumble of clothes inside. 'I don't know what to throw out,' he said. 'One of these jumpers?'

'No, leave 'em. They'll be nice and soft to snuggle into.

Chuck those trousers, though . . . and those tatty old shirts. What are the stripy things?'

'Pyjamas, I'll need those.'

'Hmm. What's in the blue bag?'

'My toothbrush, a hairbrush . . .'

'Yeah, get rid of that stuff. We can always buy new ones, if you need 'em.'

'Really?' Owen reached out and removed the wash bag.

'Yes, really. Right, now there should be just about enough room . . .'

Owen lifted Mr Sparks and placed him gently into the case, arranging the remaining clothes around him. 'How's that?' he asked.

'Well, it's not the Ritz, but it'll have to do.' He sniffed and made a face. 'I'm not being funny but when did you last wash these vests?' He registered Owen's look of outrage. 'All right, all right, keep your hair on. Only kidding.'

Owen went to close the lid but Mr Sparks wasn't quite finished with him. 'Hang on a minute,' he said. 'There's something else, before we leave. I need you to go to the trunk.'

Owen stood up and walked over to it. 'What now?' he asked.

49

'There's a drawer there with a golden sun painted on it. Can you see that?'

'Yes.' Owen reached out and gave the handle a pull. 'It's locked,' he said.

Mr Sparks gave a snort of annoyance. 'The key will be in Otto's waistcoat pocket. Go to the wardrobe and find that.'

'But shouldn't I . . . ?'

'Go on, boy, get a move on!'

Owen turned aside and walked to the wardrobe. He opened the door and found Mr Schilling's clothes hanging neatly within. In one of the pockets of the old man's waistcoat, he found a little brass key. 'This?' he asked, holding it up.

'The very thing. Now, go and unlock the drawer and take out what's inside.' Owen did as he was told, but he was starting to think that Mr Sparks was every bit as bossy as Aunt Gwen. He hoped he wasn't jumping out of the frying pan into the fire. He slotted the key into the lock, turned it and the drawer slid open. Inside was what looked like a soft leather belt with a rectangular pouch on it. 'What *is* it?' asked Owen, pulling it out.

'It's a money belt,' said Mr Sparks. 'Open it.'

Owen unclipped the pouch and drew in a sharp breath

when he saw the contents. It was stuffed with money, paper notes to the value of five, ten and even twenty pounds. 'What's all this?' he asked, confused. He had never seen so much money in one place before.

'That's our insurance,' said Mr Sparks. 'Put the belt on, Owie. Lift up your shirt and strap it around your middle, so nobody can see it.'

'But—' Owen looked towards the bed. 'Doesn't this belong to Mr Schilling? We can't just take it.'

'Course we can. It's a gift. He told me last night, he said, "Charlie, I want you to have this. It'll help give you a new start."'

Owen considered this, but something about it didn't feel right. He began to walk over to the bed. 'I can't just take his money without asking if it's all right,' he said. 'I'm going to check with him.'

'No, don't do that, I told you not to wake him!'

Owen put a hand on Mr Schilling's shoulder – then recoiled as he registered that the old man felt as cold as a slab of mutton. Owen lifted his other hand to his mouth to stop himself from shouting. 'Is he . . . dead?' he whispered.

Mr Sparks sighed. 'I wasn't going to tell you,' he said. 'Didn't want to upset you. He slipped away late last night.

Just after he said that to me about the money. See, he knew he didn't have long. And he wanted to give us the best chance possible.'

'But you . . . you told me not to *wake* him!'

'I was trying to spare your feelings,' said Mr Sparks. 'I thought you might be a bit upset.'

'Upset? Of course I'm upset!' Owen turned away from the bed. He was shaking. He'd never seen a dead person before, not even his father. There'd been a ceremony at the church to mark his passing, but no body to bury. Owen couldn't get over the fact that he'd been talking to Mr Schilling only hours earlier. Yes, of course the old man had been ill, Owen had seen those spots of blood on his hand-kerchief, but he hadn't realised how close to the end he was. To just . . . slip away like that, it was . . . terrifying.

'Breathe, Owie,' whispered Mr Sparks. 'You'll be all right.'

'How can it be all right?' hissed Owen. 'He's *dead*. We can't pretend that hasn't happened.'

'Keep your voice down! People die every day, and you should know that better than anyone, what with your dad and everything. Now, strap that money belt on and let's get out of here.'

Owen did as he was told, securing the belt with trembling hands. He felt numb, shocked to his very core. He looked towards the bed again. 'We can't just leave him like that,' he said.

'We have to. We can't go making a big fuss about this.'

'But—'

'Owie, listen to me! This is what he wanted. He said to me, just before he passed, he said, "Charlie, my one hope now is that you and the boy can make a clean getaway. No matter what happens, don't let anything hold you back." That's what he said to me, minutes before the light went from his eyes. You don't want to let him down, do you?'

Owen's eyes were wet. He shook his head. 'I . . . I suppose not,' he said.

'Right, then. Come on, close up this case and let's get moving.'

Owen got down on his knees and shut the lid of the case. The last thing he saw was Mr Sparks' luminous eyes gazing steadfastly up at him. He secured the latches, and carried the case as quietly as he could to the door before peeping out onto the dark landing. Everywhere seemed deserted. He stepped cautiously out, pulled the door shut behind him and walked along the landing until he was able to peer over the bannisters, down to the foyer. Sitting in a chair at the front desk, he saw the hulking shape of Mr Pugh, the night porter, and for a moment, he thought he was going to have big problems. But then it became clear that Pugh's head was bowed. He was breathing heavily, fast asleep where he sat.

Owen snatched in a deep breath and began to descend the stairs, placing each foot with great care, trying to avoid the steps that he knew from experience would creak beneath his tread. It seemed to take a long time to get to the foot of the stairs and then he was creeping across the woodblock floor towards the main doors. He was almost there when it occurred to him that the doors would be locked; and glancing back, he could see the length of gold chain that hung from Pugh's waistcoat pocket, where he knew the key must be.

But he wasn't about to retrace his steps to try and get it. He thought for a moment and then angled sharp right, into the small library, where he knew there was a ground-floor window. He went to it and tried the handle, but it hadn't been opened in years and had been painted over several times. Owen put down the case and applied both hands to the job, pushing down on the handle with all his strength. Suddenly, it gave, with a loud crack that seemed to echo throughout the house. There was a corresponding grunt from the foyer, the sure sign that the noise had disturbed Mr Pugh. Owen didn't wait to see if the man was coming to investigate. He pulled open the window and flung the case through the opening. He was aware of a muffled grunt from inside it as it hit the grass, but he was already scrambling after it. He dropped to the ground, turned back and pushed the window closed – then crouched as he sensed, rather than saw, somebody come into the room. He hugged the brick wall as a candle light came towards the window and a few moments later, he was aware of Pugh's big silhouette standing there, staring out into the first light of dawn. Owen held his breath. There was a scraping noise as the window catch was secured. Then the light moved away again and Owen remembered to breathe.

'What's going on?' hissed a muffled voice from inside the case.

'Bit of a close call,' muttered Owen. 'But I think we're all right now.' He grabbed the handle of the suitcase and got cautiously to his feet, half afraid that Pugh would still be at the window, glaring accusingly out at him. But there was nobody in sight. Owen walked the short distance to the pavement, then turned sharp left and hurried along the promenade.

There was a sickly grey light, the sun still struggling to rise and Owen could see only halfway along the pier before it disappeared into a thick haze. He could hear the waves rushing fitfully onto the beach, stirring the shingle, and away to his right, the Great Orme was nothing more than a brown smudge.

'Right,' said the muffled voice. 'First of all we—'

'My mother,' hissed Owen.

'What?'

'My ma. You promised we could visit her first.'

'Oh, yes,' said the voice. 'I did say that, didn't I?' Mr Sparks didn't sound too enthusiastic. 'Where did you say she was?'

'Denbigh,' said Owen. 'The asylum.'

'That's right. The nut house. A lovely place to visit . . . but probably not somewhere you'd want to stay for too long.'

Owen nodded. 'We'll need to go to the railway station,' he said, and started walking.

5

Strangers

'The little devil!' snarled Aunt Gwen. She was walking down the hotel's main staircase, her features arranged into a furious expression.

She was having a bad morning. It had started to go bad at seven o'clock, when she'd gone up to give Owen his customary morning call, only to find his room was empty. At first, she'd thought he must be somewhere else in the hotel, making an earlier start than usual, but a swift search had yielded no results and none of the staff admitted to having seen him. She returned to his room for a second look and that was when she noticed the suitcase was gone from the top of the wardrobe. When she looked inside the wardrobe, she saw to her intense displeasure that most of the boy's clothes were also missing.

Finally, the inevitable answer dawned on her. He'd run off. The little swine had packed his things and done a moonlight flit! She seethed inwardly at the very idea of it. She couldn't believe the ingratitude. Hadn't she housed him and fed him all this time, given him a thorough grounding in the ways of the hotel trade? And was this how the little wretch had repaid her? By running off in the early hours like some vagrant? Well, she told herself, she'd teach him a lesson he'd never forget. She'd get straight on to the police and send them after him. They'd drag him back here, by force if necessary and, when she had him all to herself, by golly she'd teach him better manners.

She was on her way down to the foyer to use the telephone when two men strode urgently through the entrance doors, looking as though they were here on an important matter. The first man was perhaps in his mid-thirties, she thought, tall and thin, dressed in a long black coat that came down almost to his ankles. He had a mane of glossy black curls that hung to his shoulders, and his long, clean-shaven face was dominated by a prominent nose and a pair of intense black eyes. They examined Aunt Gwen with apparent interest as she reached the bottom of the stairs. The second man was a good ten years older than his companion and seemed to have been designed as the exact opposite of him. He was short and fat and scruffily bearded.

He wore a thick tweed suit and a small bowler hat was perched precariously on his rather large head.

'Are you the owner of this establishment?' asked the first man – an Englishman, judging by his accent.

'Yes, but if you'll excuse me, I have some urgent business to attend to,' said Aunt Gwen, pointing to the phone on the counter. 'I was just about to phone the police.'

'Ah! Then we have arrived just in time to save you the trouble,' said the thin man. 'Madam, we too are here on a matter of some urgency. We have come to apprehend a dangerous criminal.' He made a strange, theatrical flourish with one hand and she noticed that he wore a pair of black leather gloves. The older, heavier man was pacing around behind his companion, staring impatiently around the place as though expecting to see somebody hiding in the shadows. An odd-looking pair of coppers, thought Aunt Gwen, and not uniformed men, but plainclothes officers, so it must be something important to bring them out here so early on a Sunday morning.

'Well, how extraordinary,' she said. 'So this is about Owen, is it?'

'Owen?' The thin man looked puzzled. 'Madam, I haven't the faintest idea what you're on about. Do you by any chance have a guest staying here by the name of Otto Schilling?'

The second man leaned forward. 'A foreigner,' he said, in an accent that could only have originated in the East End of London. 'A European. An elderly gentleman.'

'I *knew* it,' said Aunt Gwen. 'He's a *German*, isn't he? He told me he was from Belgium, but I wasn't fooled for a moment.'

The two men briefly exchanged looks before the thin one returned his gaze to Aunt Gwen, his dark eyes smouldering. 'Mr Schilling *is* a native of Belgium,' he assured her. 'That much, at least, we are sure of.' He lowered his voice to a whisper. 'Am I to take it that he's . . . still here?'

Aunt Gwen frowned. 'Yes, in room seven. Best room in the hotel, I gave him. Got a view of the pier and everything. He checked in yesterday morning. But, if you don't mind me saying, his behaviour has been most suspicious. He hasn't come out of his room since he arrived. *And* he's eaten next to nothing. A cheese sandwich and a glass of milk! I mean, how suspicious is that?'

Now the two strangers glanced at each other with evident delight.

'He's still here, Wilkins!' said the thin man excitedly.

He seemed to make an effort to calm himself and turned back to Aunt Gwen. 'Take us to him,' he said. 'I suppose you must have a master key?'

'Yes, of course I have, this *is* a reputable establishment. But . . . just a moment, please. Who *are* you, exactly?'

The thin man smiled apologetically. 'Forgive me, madam, in all the excitement I've quite forgotten my manners. You see, we've been on the trail of Mr Schilling for quite some time.'

'Nearly two years,' said the fat man, moving his bushy eyebrows up and down. 'We've followed him halfway around the world and back. A very slippery customer is Mr Schilling.'

The thin man smiled. 'I'm Quinn,' he said. He indicated his friend. 'And this is my associate, Wilkins.'

Wilkins removed his bowler hat and bowed politely, revealing that despite the clumps of mousy hair that stuck out from under the hat, he was quite bald on top.

'I'm Gwen Morgan,' she said. 'The proprietor of the Sea View.'

'Charmed, I'm sure,' said Quinn.

'Delighted,' added Wilkins.

'Well, Mr Quinn . . . Mr Wilkins, of course I'll take you

up to Mr Schilling's room in good time, but if you're not here about my nephew, then first I will have to report his—'

'Madam, I'm afraid I must insist,' said Quinn forcefully.

'Every minute we waste standing here talking could put you and your guests in danger,' added Wilkins. 'Terrible danger.'

'I see.' There was a silence while Aunt Gwen considered this. Then she shrugged her shoulders. The phone call, she decided, would have to wait for a while. 'Very well,' she said. 'If it's as important as you suggest, who am I to refuse?' She went behind the reception desk and found the correct bunch of keys. 'If you gentlemen would care to follow me?' She came out from behind the desk and started towards the lift, but the thin man shook his head.

'If it's all the same to you, madam, you and I shall take the stairs. Mr Wilkins can go in the lift, just to ensure that we do not miss Mr Schilling coming down the stairs as we ride up.'

Aunt Gwen scowled. 'Very well,' she said. 'You're clearly not taking any chances.' Wilkins headed off to the lift and she led Quinn towards the staircase. She glanced back at him as she climbed. 'Would you like to tell me what Mr Schilling has done to demand all this attention? I'm hoping it won't be anything that reflects badly on the reputation of the Sea View. We *are*, after all, Llandudno's premier hotel.'

Quinn frowned. 'I'm afraid, madam, that I am not at liberty to divulge that information. Suffice it to say that Mr Schilling is a very dangerous fellow. Some might say, a criminal mastermind.'

'My goodness. How exciting! He seemed such a frail old man. Doesn't look at all well, if you ask me.' They reached the first-floor landing just as the lift's concertina cage doors creaked open and Wilkins stepped out. The three of them walked along until they came to room seven. Aunt Gwen raised her hand to knock but Quinn intercepted her.

'We . . . er . . . don't want to warn him,' he whispered. He gestured to the lock. 'If you would oblige us?'

She frowned, nodding. She slotted the key into the lock and turned it gently. Then Quinn pushed the door slightly open and peered cautiously inside. Aunt Gwen caught a glimpse of the old man, lying in his bed, mostly covered by blankets. He appeared to be asleep. Quinn and Wilkins glanced at each other and grinned triumphantly. Then they dashed into the room. Quinn seized the old man by his shoulders and pinned him down. 'Finally,' he roared. 'Finally we—'

He broke off and took a step back from the bed. He stood for a moment, staring down open-mouthed at the old man's still figure. He removed a glove and held two fingers against Mr Schilling's throat. Then he groaned and turned away, his expression one of profound disappointment. Wilkins stared at him for a moment, not comprehending. He stepped past Quinn and took a closer look at the prostrate form. 'No,' he hissed. 'He *can't* be.'

'But he is,' said Quinn quietly. 'He got away from us, after all.'

'But not like *this*,' complained Wilkins. 'That's not fair.'

Quinn sneered. 'Fair? It's not a game, Wilkins. It never has been.' He was looking now at the open trunk, with particular attention to an empty drawer in the very centre of it. 'And if I'm not very much mistaken . . .' He went to the trunk, crouched down and examined the drawer. Then he tried all the other compartments, pulling each of them open and dragging out the contents. 'They've *both* gone,' he said finally.

Wilkins turned away from the bed. 'But 'ow is that possible?' he asked.

'I don't know.'

'What do you mean, *both*?' asked Aunt Gwen, who had

watched the entire routine from the doorway. 'There was only Mr Schilling *in* the room.'

Quinn lifted his head and looked at Aunt Gwen. 'I think not,' he said. 'Mr Schilling had a companion. The two of them were . . . inseparable.'

'But he checked in alone, I saw to it myself. And . . . are you saying that Mr Schilling is . . . dead?' asked Aunt Gwen, mouthing the last word with some reluctance. 'In my hotel?'

Quinn looked annoyed at this. 'Miss Morgan, I can assure you he's dead wherever he happens to be.' He got back to his feet and walked to the centre of the room where a scatter of discarded clothing and a blue fabric bag were lying on the carpet. He poked at the latter with the toe of one shoe.

'What's this?' he wondered.

'That's odd,' said Aunt Gwen.

'Odd?' echoed Wilkins, walking over to her.

'Those clothes. They look like . . . well, they look like Owen's things.' Aunt Gwen came forward. She stooped, picked up the wash bag, unbuttoned it and peered inside. 'Yes,' she said. 'These are most definitely his.'

'Owen?' echoed Quinn. 'You mentioned him earlier . . .'

'My nephew! That's why I thought you were here in the

first place. He's gone missing, you see. I went to wake him up this morning and he wasn't in his room. No sign of him anywhere.'

Quinn regarded the scattered clothes thoughtfully. 'Right. And . . . how old is . . . Owen?' he asked.

'He's twelve, nearly thirteen.' Aunt Gwen buttoned the wash bag. 'Now I think of it, he did seem to be spending a lot of time up here with . . .' She waved a hand in the direction of the bed. '*Him.* And you have to ask yourself . . . what are the boy's things doing in here? I noticed the suitcase had gone from his room, this morning, but—'

'A suitcase?' growled Wilkins. 'How big?'

Aunt Gwen scowled and held her hands out three feet apart to indicate a size. 'About so big, I suppose. Why does that matter?' The two men exchanged looks. This seemed to mean something to them.

Quinn moved closer. 'Do you have any idea where the boy might have gone?' he asked.

'None whatsoever.'

'Oh, come along, madam, he's your nephew. You must have *some* idea what goes on in his head. Where are his parents?'

'His father's dead. His mother – my sister – she's . . .'

'She's what?' asked Wilkins impatiently.

'Well, if you really must know, she's in an asylum. The North Wales Lunatic Asylum in Denbigh.' She thought for a moment. 'Come to think of it, Owen was only pestering me about her yesterday.'

'Pestering you?'

'Yes. Saying he wanted to go and visit her. But I told him, it's not really convenient just now. Here, you don't think . . . ?'

Again, the two men looked at each other. 'We really must be going,' said Quinn. He and Wilkins started towards the door.

'Just a minute!' protested Aunt Gwen. 'You can't leave.' She pointed with evident reluctance towards the bed. 'What about him?'

'What *about* him?' asked Quinn.

'Well, what should I do?'

'If I were you, I'd call the police,' he said.

'The . . . but . . . I thought you two were . . .'

'Police?' murmured Wilkins. 'Can't imagine what gave you that idea.'

'Because you . . . you said . . . you were after a criminal. You gave me the impression that you were . . . *official*.'

'Sorry about that, I'm sure,' said Wilkins.

'And . . . what am I supposed to tell the police? That some old fellow has died of a heart attack?'

Quinn looked at her, his expression grave. 'You may tell them whatever you wish,' he said. 'As to the cause of death, that will be for them to decide.' There was a brief silence. Then he smiled and said, 'Lovely meeting you.' And he and Wilkins went out of the room and down the stairs to the exit. They were about halfway down, when Aunt Gwen strode out onto the landing, her hands on her hips. She stared indignantly after them.

'Another thing,' she said. 'Who's going to pay for the room?'

Quinn and Wilkins walked a short distance along the promenade until they got to the place where they'd parked the car. It was a black Daimler Phaeton, custom made, and Wilkins' pride and joy, even though the vehicle actually belonged to Quinn. Wilkins took great pleasure in driving it though. Some people he'd met had expressed their disapproval that he should agree to drive a German car so soon after the Great War, but he took no notice of them. As far as he was concerned, there wasn't another automobile to match it anywhere in the world. He unlocked the door and climbed in behind the steering wheel, while Quinn settled himself in to the passenger seat. They sat for a moment in silence.

'I really thought we 'ad him for a moment,' murmured Wilkins.

'Yes, But we're still close. I can feel it. They can't be more than a few hours ahead of us.'

Wilkins frowned. 'You think that's where they've gone? The asylum?'

'It seems to make sense. You know how Sparks operates. He latches on to the vulnerable ones, finds out what it is they want, then offers it to them. You scratch my back and I'll scratch yours. If the boy wanted to see his mother, of course the creature would use that.' Quinn reached into his pocket and took out a revolver.

Wilkins glared at it. 'I really wish you hadn't brought that along,' he said. 'You know I don't like guns. And besides, I really don't see the need.'

Quinn sneered. 'You're hardly in a position to lay down any demands,' he said. But he opened the glove box and dropped the gun into it. 'The gun was for the old man,' he explained. 'Just in case he had some kind of weapon, hidden away. I hardly think we'll need it for a twelve-year-old boy.' He closed the glove box and looked at Wilkins. 'You know how to get to Denbigh?'

'I'll find it,' Wilkins assured him. He seemed to think for a moment and then laughed quietly.

'What's so funny?' asked Quinn.

'That woman.' Wilkins jerked a thumb over his shoulder in the general direction of the hotel. 'Thought I was still with the police.' He laughed again and this time, Quinn laughed with him, but only for a few moments. Then his gaze hardened and his mouth rearranged itself into a tight, unforgiving line.

'Denbigh,' he said.

Wilkins started the engine, put the car into gear and drove away.

6

Debut

The train trundled rhythmically through the Welsh country-side and Owen sat gazing thoughtfully out of the window, as a seemingly endless parade of green fields and hedges slipped past him. After a long and boring wait at the station, he had managed to secure a seat on the first train of the day, which turned out to be surprisingly busy for so early on a Sunday morning. He'd felt rather strange handing over the money for his fare at the ticket booth, strange and horribly guilty, knowing that the money he proffered for payment had belonged to poor Mr Schilling, who lay dead in his bed back at the Sea View hotel.

Owen wondered if Auntie Gwen had discovered the body yet. He knew that she'd already be aware of her nephew's absence, that she'd have realised the moment she came up to his room to give him his usual early morning shout at seven o'clock. He trembled to think what she might be

71

saying about him now or what she would be doing to ensure that he was brought right back to her. Auntie Gwen was not the sort to let go of something she wanted and she *did* want Owen, even if it was only as an unpaid worker.

He glanced warily up at the luggage rack above his head, where he had stored the suitcase. For the time being at least, Mr Sparks was keeping quiet, which was a good thing, since Owen wasn't the only traveller in this compartment. The seat opposite him was occupied by a stout mother and her two young children, a boy and a girl of around seven or eight years old, who for reasons best known to themselves, were staring at Owen as though he had a black smudge on his nose. Each of the children had a large bag of sticky sweets and they kept popping one after another into their mouths and sucking noisily. On the seat beside Owen, sat a middle-aged businessman dressed in a sober black suit. He had stern, ruddy features and a drooping black moustache. He was absorbed in a Welsh language newspaper and seemed to take no interest at all in his fellow travellers.

Owen found himself reviewing the events of the last day with a faint air of disbelief. Not for the first time, he thought about leaving the train at the next station and abandoning

Mr Sparks to his fate. Nobody would have blamed him for doing such a thing. And yet, even though the impulse was there, he somehow felt completely incapable of acting upon it. It was as though he somehow felt responsible for Mr Sparks – as though the dummy was his son or his brother or some other family member. Which was ridiculous when you thought about it. After all, he was no more than a lump of cleverly carved wood. Though, if that *was* the case . . . how was he able to talk? And think? And even move around a little, all without the help of a human operator? None of it made any sense.

'Tickets, please!' Owen looked up to see a uniformed conductor entering the compartment, a burly fellow with a handlebar moustache. Owen fumbled in his pocket for the ticket he'd purchased back at Llandudno station. As he held it out for inspection, he felt horribly nervous, imagining that the guard would somehow recognise him and say that the ticket had been purchased with a dead man's money. But the conductor just gave Owen a jovial smile and used a metal punch to stamp the ticket.

'Denbigh,' he observed. 'What takes you there, lad?'

'This flipping train, obviously!' said a voice from above Owen's head and the conductor looked up in surprise, before glancing around at the other passengers. 'Who said that?' he asked the occupants of the compartment, but received nothing more than baffled looks for his trouble. He returned his gaze to Owen and his eyes narrowed suspiciously. 'Was that *you*?' he asked sternly.

'No, sir,' Owen assured him.

'It was *me*,' said a high-pitched voice and now everyone turned to look, open-mouthed up at the luggage rack. 'And I tell you what, I'm nearly suffocating in here! Owie, lift me down for a moment, I need some air.'

'I . . . I can't,' protested Owen, aware of his face reddening.

'Of course you can.'

Now the conductor looked outraged. 'Whoever's up there, I hope you have a ticket,' he said. 'It's an offence to ride on a train without one,'

'I don't need a ticket!' said the voice. 'Owie, get me down from here!'

Owen looked around the compartment with a sinking feeling. Now everyone was staring at him as though he'd done something terrible and he remembered how *he'd* felt when he'd first heard Mr Sparks' voice coming from inside the trunk. His face burning, he stood up, pulled down the suitcase and unlatched it. He took Mr Sparks out from his nest of clothing and sat him on his knee, dumping the empty case by his feet.

The reaction from the other passengers was dramatic. The conductor looked relieved, the businessman astonished and the mother and her two children quite simply delighted. The children were so surprised they'd even stopped eating sweets for a moment.

'Well, you certainly had *me* fooled,' the conductor told Owen.

'That wasn't difficult,' observed Mr Sparks shrewdly. 'You look like you'd need help to tie your shoelaces.'

There was a moment of deep silence, while the conductor looked offended. Then he seemed to relax a little and he smiled. 'Very clever,' he told Owen. 'But . . . aren't you a bit young to be doing an act like this?'

'Erm . . . no, not really,' said Owen. 'I . . . I've been doing it for a while now.'

'That's right,' said Mr Sparks. 'He isn't as young as he looks.'

'How old is he?' asked the little boy.

'Older than you and younger than me,' Mr Sparks assured him. 'Mind you, don't believe a word he tells you.' He snapped into one of his little ditties. 'Owen Dyer, Owen Dyer, he's a rotten little liar. He says he's just as old as me, but we all know he's ninety-three!' He cackled delightedly and his small audience laughed along with him. 'I lied about the age,' he added. 'He's really seventy-four but it didn't rhyme!'

'You're a funny-looking fellow,' observed the woman.

'True,' agreed Mr Sparks. 'But then, *I'm* made of wood. What's your excuse?'

The lady gasped in mock outrage. 'How dare you?' she shrieked but Owen could see that, deep down inside, she was actually delighted by his impudence.

'I dare, madam, because being made of wood means that I can get away with all sorts of things that you lot would *never* say.'

'For instance?' asked the woman.

'Like for instance, that rouge you're wearing on your cheeks . . .'

'What about it?' asked the woman, mystified.

'It's a bit overdone, isn't it? Did you apply it with a trowel? Was it a bet to see how much you could apply in one sitting?'

The woman gasped and for a moment, seemed speechless. 'Well, *really*!' she said at last, clearly not as delighted as she had been before.

'Oh yes,' agreed Mr Sparks. 'Really. As in *really* not the kind of thing that suits a woman of your age!'

'Mummy, I don't think he's very nice,' said the woman's daughter.

'And I suspect you're a little brat,' said Mr Sparks, 'but because you have blue eyes and blonde hair, you'll probably get away with it all your life.'

Now Owen was aware that the woman was looking at him accusingly and felt prompted to try and referee the conversation.

'N . . . now then Charlie,' he said. 'That's . . . a bit unfair. There's no need to be rude to people.'

'Oh my goodness, it actually *talks*!' exclaimed Mr Sparks. 'For a moment there, I wasn't sure which one of us was the dummy.' He turned and waggled his eyebrows at Owen and suddenly, the boy thought he knew exactly how Mr Schilling must have felt, being blamed for all the awful things that Mr Sparks came out with.

'Charlie, please don't—'

'I thought we spoke about this earlier,' interrupted Mr Sparks. 'Only my *friends* get to call me Charlie. I haven't quite made my mind up about you. What *are* you, Owen Dyer? I wonder . . . Are you friend or are you foe? Will

you stay or will you go? Are you stupid? I don't know!'
He made a little bow to the other passengers. 'People,
welcome to my show!'

Owen didn't know what to say to that.

'That's quite a good technique you've got,' said the man
in the suit, speaking for the first time.

Owen turned to look at him. 'Thank you,' he said.

'But if you don't mind me saying, your lips are a bit of
a giveaway.'

'I . . . beg your pardon?'

'Your lips. They move a bit when the dummy's talking.'

'Oh, I don't think so,' said Owen.

'Oh yes, undoubtedly.' The man was staring at him challengingly. 'I mean, don't get me wrong. You're very good
for your age. But I'd say you still have a lot to learn.'

Owen felt a sudden rush of annoyance. Why would
anybody say something like that when it clearly wasn't
true? 'Well,' he began, 'I don't think—'

'Who *are* you?' interrupted Mr Sparks, staring at the
man.

'Me?' The man shrugged. 'I'm . . . just a travelling salesman.'

'And what do you sell, exactly? Apart from free advice
for ventriloquists?'

'Er . . . I . . . sell furniture, if you must know.'

'I see. And what's your name, Mr Travelling Salesman?'

'It's Harold. Harold Stables.'

Mr Sparks turned back to look at the woman and children opposite. 'This is the tale of Harold Stables, who manufactured chairs and tables. He thought himself a clever chap, but kept on talking loads of—'

'Charlie, no!' interrupted Owen. He looked at Mr Stables and laughed nervously. 'I'm terribly sorry, he says these things and I can't seem to stop him.'

'Yes, very amusing,' said Mr Stables, though he didn't look in the least bit amused. 'As I said, you're quite good, but—'

'Fancy yourself as a bit of an expert, do you?' asked Mr Sparks.

'Er . . . no, not at all. I'm merely saying that I can see the lips moving, so—'

'Sounds like a challenge to me! We clearly need to make things more difficult.' He looked at the two children for a moment. 'Tell you what, why don't you two greedy little pigs stop stuffing your faces and feed Owie some of those sweeties? Go on, as many as you like. Then we'll see how he does.'

The children looked at their mother as though seeking permission, and when she reluctantly nodded, they jumped off their seats and started pushing sweets into Owen's mouth, until they could get no more in. Owen tried to protest but to no avail. He sat there, embarrassed, his cheeks distended. Now the children moved back to their places and watched expectantly.

Mr Sparks waggled his eyebrows and began. 'Mrrrffff!' he said. 'Glubble flurp snarggle glott.'

The businessman smiled triumphantly. 'See? Not so easy is it?'

'Only kidding!' roared Mr Sparks. 'Let me see now, what would be a fair test? Oh yes!' He began to chant as loudly as he could. 'Round the rugged rocks, the ragged rascals ran! She sells seashells by the seashore! The Leith police dismisseth us! The Leith police dismisseth us! The Leith police—'

'All right,' growled the businessman. 'You've made your point.' He scowled at Owen and then reached grudgingly into his pocket and pulled out a shilling. 'There,' he said, handing it over. 'Just to show there's no hard feelings.'

Owen looked at the coin in his hand, unable to say anything because his mouth was still crammed full of sticky sweets. Mr Sparks spoke for him. 'Very decent of you, sir. Thanks for being such a good sport.' He looked up at Owen and fluttered his eyelashes. 'Remember that shilling, Owie,' he said. 'That's just the first of many coins we'll earn together.'

Owen sat there in uncomfortable silence as the train rocked and clattered along the metal rails.

Wilkins pressed the horn once again but the Daimler was still surrounded by a seemingly endless flock of sheep, which had spilled through an open gateway onto the road. There was no sign of a shepherd in attendance and even when he tried edging the car forward, the stupid creatures just stood their ground, baaing like idiots. He wound down the window and bellowed at them. 'Get out of it!' he roared. 'Go on, shift yer carcasses!' His shouts had no effect whatsoever.

Quinn sighed. 'There's no point in getting excited,' he said. 'It will take as long as it takes.'

Wilkins looked at Quinn incredulously. He'd worked for him for more than two years now and never ceased to be amazed by how relaxed the thin man could be, even under times of great duress.

'But we're so *close*,' snarled Wilkins. 'Closer than we've ever been. Don't that bother you?'

Quinn shrugged. 'I believe in fate,' he said. 'I believe that I'm destined to capture that abomination eventually and whether it takes me a day, a month or a year is of no consequence. I *shall* capture him, of that I have no doubt. This . . .' He waved a gloved hand towards the windscreen. 'This is just a minor distraction.'

Wilkins sighed and turned his attention to what he could see through the windscreen – namely a sea of woolly white rumps, clogging up the road ahead of him. It occurred him, not for the first time, that working for Quinn had to be the strangest job he'd ever had. After all this time, he felt that he still knew very little about the man. Oh, he knew he was fabulously rich, he'd seen the palatial mansion in Buckinghamshire where he lived, but he didn't know how Quinn had come by his wealth or even what drew him to spend his life chasing after oddities like Mr Sparks.

'You realise,' murmured Wilkins, 'that he'll probably be looking for a new identity now? It's what he's always done.'

Quinn nodded, but said nothing.

'Bit of a turn up for the books, though,' continued

Wilkins. 'A twelve-year-old kid! I mean, young and impressionable is one thing, but that's ridiculous.'

'Perhaps he saw something in the boy,' said Quinn. 'Something he thought he could work with.'

Wilkins frowned. He was aware how foolish it sounded. They were, after all, discussing a wooden puppet. For a long time, Wilkins hadn't believed any of it was possible, but over the past year, as the search continued, he'd gradually come around to changing his point of view. He reached into his pocket and pulled out a folded sheet of paper. He carefully unfolded it, until he had it open on his lap. It was an ancient theatrical poster, its edges frayed and yellow.

'Why are you always looking at that?' muttered Quinn.

'Just reminding myself, ' said Wilkins. 'Sometimes, it's 'ard to believe.'

'Believe it,' said Quinn.

It was a black-and-white poster for the Variété Théâtre, Paris dated 1782, an act which featured a magician called Lucien Lacombe and his hilarious assistant, 'Charles'. In the picture, Lucien was depicted sitting on an ornate throne. He was a slim man with an immaculately trimmed beard. He wore a richly embroidered robe and a turban. On his lap sat what was clearly a ventriloquist's dummy. The dummy's clothes were different from the ones that he wore now. In the eighteenth century he'd sported a jester's outfit complete with a three-pronged hat. But the face was exactly the same. The huge eyes seemed to stare knowingly at Wilkins across an interval of more than two hundred years.

'Do you think the boy has any idea?' murmured Wilkins. 'Of the danger he's in?'

Quinn shrugged. His face showed not a shred of sympathy. 'People should be more careful about the company they keep,' he said.

A loud shout made them look up. A burly Welsh shepherd in a crumpled hat had just emerged from the field. He was waving a stick and cursing the stupidity of his flock. A couple of border collies raced through its midst and started to harry the sheep back towards the field. The farmer gave the occupants of the car an apologetic wave.

Wilkins folded the poster and placed it carefully back in his pocket.

'How far now?' asked Quinn.

'Just a couple of miles,' said Wilkins.

Then, as the last of the flock trotted in through the gates, he gunned the engine and drove away.

7

Asylum

The taxi cab motored slowly in through the gates of the asylum. Owen sat in the back with the case balanced across his knees, feeling like a member of the royal family. He had never ridden in a taxi before. Aunt Gwen wouldn't have considered paying for such a luxury, no matter how important the situation, but the single cab had been parked in front of Denbigh station when they'd emerged from the exit and, when he'd told Mr Sparks it was there, the dummy had instructed him to get into it and go straight to the asylum, never mind how much it cost. 'We've got to get you to your mother,' he'd whispered from inside the case. 'That's all that matters right now. A promise is a promise so we'll spare no expense.'

The driver brought the cab to a halt and Owen climbed out. He stared down the wide straight approach of the drive at the forbidding grey building ahead of him. Rows of blank windows seemed to stare at him unwelcomingly and above him a central tower reared its square head towards the angry grey sky. It looked, Owen thought, more like a prison than anything else, which he supposed was pretty much what it was. He swallowed, then turned back to the driver's open window. 'Will you wait for us, please?' he said. 'We won't be long.'

The driver, a portly man wearing a cloth cap, raised his eyebrows. 'We?' he echoed.

'I mean, "me",' said Owen hastily. 'There is only me. Obviously.' He could feel his cheeks burning so he picked up the suitcase, turned, and began to walk slowly towards the entrance of the asylum.

'Careful,' hissed a voice from inside the case. 'Or they'll be locking you up along with your mother.'

Owen paused for a moment and spoke in a low voice. 'Pipe down,' he said.

'You what?'

'If anybody hears you, who knows what might happen? You'll have to stay quiet.'

'All right, all right, keep your hair on.'

Mr Sparks fell uncharacteristically silent, but Owen stood where he was for a moment, wanting to be sure the dummy had really got the message. When he finally felt reassured, he went forward again and climbed the stone steps to the big front doors. He pushed them silently open and walked in to the massive reception area, a place of gleaming white tiles and polished brass rails, a million miles away from the horrible starkness of the wards and cells that Owen knew from experience lay at the heart of the building. He took a deep breath and approached the reception desk, where a white-uniformed, shrew-faced woman sat, scribbling on a sheet of paper. She didn't seem to be aware of the new arrival, so after a few moments, Owen coughed politely and she looked up, regarding him sullenly over the top of her spectacles.

'Can I help you?' she asked him disapprovingly.

'Yes, please. I've come to visit my ma.'

The woman scowled, as though she didn't much like that either. 'Name?' she asked him.

'Owen.'

She rolled her eyes upwards. 'Your *mother's* name?' she said.

'Oh . . . sorry. Megan. Megan Dyer.'

She glanced at a book in front of her. 'You don't appear to have made an appointment,' she said, as though it was the worst sin in the world.

87

'Er . . . no. Not exactly. But . . . it's always been a Sunday when I've visited her before. I haven't been for quite a while.'

'Is there somebody else with you?' asked the woman.

Owen glanced down at the suitcase in alarm. Was it that obvious?

'There isn't . . . I mean, it's not—'

'An *adult*?' the woman prompted him.

'Oh. Oh, I see.' Owen relaxed a little. 'No, I . . . I usually come with my aunt Gwen, but she was . . . very busy.' Owen tried an apologetic smile, but it had little effect. 'I've come a long way,' he added. 'All the way from Llandudno.'

'It's very irregular,' said the woman. 'But take a seat over there and I'll see what I can do.' She gestured to a row of upholstered benches and he did as she'd suggested, sliding the case onto his knees as he settled himself down. He watched as she picked up a telephone and spoke into it.

'Hatchet-faced old cow,' muttered Mr Sparks.

'You couldn't even *see* her,' Owen whispered back.

'No, but I could picture her.'

'Shhh!' Owen glanced around, terrified of being overheard, but nobody seemed to be taking any notice of him. There were only a few people sitting in reception, the men in their

Sunday suits, the women in elaborate dresses and bonnets. Everybody liked to dress smartly when they were obliged to visit this place. They all sat in silence with glum expressions, because nobody was particularly happy about being here.

'I wish I could see out of this thing,' complained Mr Sparks. 'I'm going to get you to make a little hole in the leather, so I can peep out and—'

'Quiet!' Owen warned him. He could see that a man had just stepped out from a doorway and was coming towards him, a big, heavyset fellow wearing the white jacket of an orderly. He had curly blond hair and a ruddy face and he was smiling pleasantly. 'You've come to see your mother, is that right?'

Owen nodded. 'Yes, sir.'

'Well, I don't suppose a brief visit will do any harm. She seems quite calm today.' He looked thoughtfully at the case on Owen's lap. 'Looks like you've come to stay,' he observed. 'Is that some things you've brought for your mother?'

'Er . . . yes . . . sort of.'

'No food in there, is there? Most of our lot are on special diets. We don't want them gorging themselves on sweets and biscuits.'

'Oh no,' Owen assured him. 'No food.'

'So what then?'

'Just . . . stuff.'

The man seemed amused. 'We have to be careful what people bring in, see? Just in case there's anything . . . unsuitable. Things patients might use to . . . you know, harm themselves. Tell you what, why don't you pop it open and we'll have a quick look?'

Owen tried not to panic. 'Oh, do I . . . really have to?' he asked.

'Yes, please,' said the man, firmly. He was still smiling but now it looked a little forced. 'In your own time.'

Owen swallowed hard. He unlatched the case and lifted the lid. Mr Sparks lay in his nest of clothing, gazing blankly up at the ceiling.

The man gave a grunt of what sounded like disgust. 'What have you brought that thing for?' he asked.

'I thought it . . . might cheer Ma up,' said Owen.

'Cheer her up? Give her a fright, more like. I've never seen such an ugly specimen!'

Owen cringed, waiting for the inevitable comeback from Mr Sparks but it didn't happen. He just lay there, stock-still, the smile plastered to his face.

'Ma was always fond of Charlie,' said Owen. 'Said he was like . . . like one of the family.'

'Really?' The man poked around in the case, a doubtful expression on his face and Owen told himself he must be wondering what the *rest* of the family looked like. 'Takes all kinds, I suppose,' he muttered. He sighed. 'Yes, all right then, I don't suppose it'll do any harm.' He gestured to Owen to close up the case and as he did so, an instant before the lid closed, Mr Sparks slipped him a sly wink. Owen latched the case, grabbed the handle and followed the orderly out of the reception area.

The sleek black car raced on along the narrow road. It passed a wooden signpost that announced DENBIGH 3 MILES. Wilkins glanced at Quinn, but he was slumped in his seat, seemingly lost in his own thoughts. Not for the first time, Wilkins found himself wondering how he had ever ended up working for a man like Quinn. And as he often did at such moments, he thought about the very first time he'd met him.

It was a few days after Wilkins had been thrown out of the police force. It had come at him out of the blue. Like most of his associates, Wilkins had never been slow in

91

accepting the occasional bribe. It had always been seen as the done thing around Seven Dials, where he worked as an inspector and where he'd started as a young constable many years earlier. But a new police superintendent had come to work at the station, a zealous campaigner for truth and justice and a man with a spotless reputation. The police department at Seven Dials was known to be a hotbed of corruption and it soon became clear that an example would have to be made. Wilkins had been taking bigger bribes than his associates, so he was first in the firing line.

On the day he'd met Quinn, Wilkins had been at home with his wife, Ruby, moodily reading the newspaper, which had devoted most of its front page to the story of Wilkins' dismissal.

'It's a nice likeness of you, Alfred,' said Ruby, trying to be helpful. The two of them had been married for nearly fourteen years. Ruby was sweet and accommodating but, it had to be said, not the brightest firework in the box.

'A nice likeness?' cried Wilkins. 'Oh well, at least there's some good news in all this!' He looked at Ruby helplessly. 'What are we going to do?' he asked her. 'We're ruined.'

'Well, surely they'll give you your job back when all this

blows over,' said Ruby. 'I mean, I understand that they're a bit annoyed at you, but—'

'They're more than a bit annoyed!' snapped Wilkins. 'You don't seem to understand. I've been sacked! That means no wages, no pension . . . nobody's going to give me a job after this little lot!' He slapped the newspaper with the flat of one hand. 'They've painted me as an absolute villain. They 'aven't even got their facts straight.' He neglected to tell Ruby the main thing they'd got wrong was the size of the bribes he'd accepted, which were actually much bigger than was stated in the newspaper.

'You'll just have to retrain for something else,' she suggested.

'But what?' He shook his head. 'I've been a copper all me life, I don't know how to *do* anything else.'

'Love, there's a War on. There's sure to be *something* you can do. I'll have a word with Bert, I'm sure he'll find you a position.' Bert was Ruby's brother, a painter and decorator. He'd escaped being called up because of a minor disability.

'I'm not painting houses!' protested Wilkins. 'I'm a copper. I need something that's suited to my skills.'

Just then, the doorbell rang. Ruby looked at Wilkins questioningly. 'Who can that be?' she asked him.

'How would I know? If it's another reporter, tell them to get lost.'

'Very well, my dear.' Ruby went out of the room in a swish of satin skirts, leaving Wilkins to reread the newspaper's lurid account of his exploits. He noted that apart from the size of the bribes, the rest of it was annoyingly accurate.

Just then the door swung open and Quinn strode into the room. He stood there, smiling at Wilkins in a most disagreeable manner. The former chief inspector's gaze swept expertly over the newcomer, noting the man's intense dark eyes, his unusually long hair and one puzzling detail: a tiny silver badge attached to the lapel of his coat, which featured what looked like two armoured soldiers mounted on just one horse. What was that supposed to signify? Ruby appeared in the doorway behind the newcomer, looking apologetic. 'I'm sorry, dear,' she said. 'He was most insistent.'

'Was he?' Wilkins glared challengingly at Quinn. 'Whatever paper it is you write for, I'm not interested,' he said.

'I can assure you, I'm not from a newspaper,' said Quinn. He looked pointedly at Ruby, until she took the hint and went out, closing the door behind her. 'But on the other hand, I do *read* them. And I've been reading all about your exploits, Mr Wilkins. Very entertaining reading it makes, if I may say so. Which is why I'm here to offer you a job.'

'A . . . job?' Wilkins stared at him. 'Is this some kind of a joke?'

'Not at all.' Quinn moved closer and indicated the newspaper. 'Quite a piece they've done on you,' he observed. 'They've painted you as a ruthless, conniving cheat who wouldn't think twice about selling his own grandmother, if he thought he could make a few bob out of it.' He paused and studied Wilkins for a moment. 'Of course, villains are everywhere. But you're a *special* kind of villain, aren't you? One with all the contacts and experience of a veteran police officer. That's a rare combination of talents.'

'You . . . you shouldn't believe everything they print in this rag,' protested Wilkins, shaking the newspaper.

'Oh, I agree. That's why I read three other papers, before I made up my mind about you. I'm glad to report that they all speak with one accord. Chief Inspector Alfred Wilkins, they announce, is a low-down, two-faced crook of the lowest order. And luckily for you, I can use a man like that.'

Wilkins felt his face growing hot. 'How . . . how dare you!' he snarled.

Quinn ignored him. 'Spare me the indignation,' he said. 'Let's put it simply. You're out of a job. And I'm prepared to pay you twice the wages you received as a police officer.'

Wilkins gulped. 'You . . . you what?' he cried.

'Don't decide yet,' Quinn told him. He reached into his waistcoat pocket and pulled out a card, which he pressed into Wilkins' hand. 'Come and see me when you're ready,' he suggested. 'And I'll tell you what I have in mind.'

With that, he'd turned on his heel and let himself out of the room. Wilkins stood there, staring stupidly at the card. Ruby reappeared in the doorway.

'What was all that about?' she asked.

Wilkins was still staring at the card, noting Quinn's address in Buckinghamshire, a place that Wilkins had driven past a few times in the course of his duties. It was a handsome pile that was little short of a stately home. He shook his head. 'I'm not sure,' he admitted, 'but I'll tell you something, Ruby. I've a feeling my luck's about to change.'

8

Visiting Time

Ma still had a small room of her own, though the word 'cell' might have described it better. It was bare and cheerless, nothing but white-tiled surfaces and a single metal-framed bed. Peering through the grille on the steel door, Owen could see that she was sitting in her familiar spot in front of the barred window, gazing out at the hospital grounds. She was turned away from him and, for the moment, he couldn't see her face. The orderly produced a large bunch of keys on a length of chain and proceeded to unlock the door. 'Not too long now,' he warned Owen. 'She tires easily.'

Owen nodded. When the door swung open, he stepped into the room, but she didn't turn to look at him.

'I'll be outside if you need me,' added the orderly. 'Just give me a shout.' He looked at Owen intently. 'You all right?' he asked. Owen nodded. The orderly stepped back into the corridor, closing the door gently behind him.

Owen stood there. Now that he was here, he wasn't exactly sure what to do. When he'd visited before with Aunt Gwen, she'd always set the tone, prattling on about the hotel and the various problems she'd had to deal with, but Owen had never been much good at small talk. He set down the case on the tiled floor and moved nearer to her chair.

'Ma,' he said. 'Ma, it's me.' Now she *did* glance up, her pale blue eyes flickering over him for a moment, but they registered no sign of recognition. She looked so thin, he thought, thin and pale and anxious, the eyes somehow too big in her ravaged face. She seemed to have aged several years since he last saw her. She wore a shapeless white hospital gown, from which her arms and legs protruded like white-painted sticks. 'It's Owen,' he added, as though it might make some difference. He nearly said, 'Your son,' but stopped himself.

She nodded, sighed, as though his presence had somehow filled her with a terrible sadness. She turned her gaze back to the window. 'He's late,' she said.

Owen fetched another chair from the far side of the room and set it down alongside hers. 'Who's late?' he asked her, though he already knew the answer. This was a familiar refrain.

'Gareth,' she said. Owen's father. 'He said he'd be back for dinner but he's terribly late.' She shook her head. 'It'll be ruined.' She seemed to consider for a moment. 'Shall I give you yours now, or would you rather wait till he gets here?'

Owen didn't know what to say to that. He reached out and enclosed one of her hands in both of his.

She looked down at the hands as though trying to figure them out, as if they were a puzzle that needed deciphering. 'He promised me he'd be back for dinner,' she repeated.

'Ma, Da's gone,' said Owen. He didn't know what else to say.

'Gone?' She turned her head and looked at him, a puzzled expression on her face. 'Gone where?' she asked him.

There was a long silence while he considered some possible answers to her question. Gone away to war. Gone to be a soldier. Gone to hell and damnation. Gone to silent dirt of an unmarked grave in France. But even if he'd known which one of these answers was correct, he couldn't have brought himself to say any of them, so he simply told her, 'I'm not really sure.'

She smiled. 'Such a silly man,' she said. 'I told him, you should wear a scarf, it's cold out there, you could catch a chill. But did he listen to me?' She shook her head. 'He never listens.' She returned her gaze to the window. 'So we'll just sit here and wait for him, shall we?'

There was a long silence. Owen racked his brains trying to think of something else to say to her, but try as he might, he couldn't think of anything. What was he supposed to do? Discuss the weather? Tell her about the horrible life he had suffered at Auntie Gwen's hotel? Mention the recent Spanish 'flu epidemic that was in all the papers? Or, perhaps, let slip the fact that he was on the run with a ventriloquist's dummy? Well, he had to try something so he opted for what seemed the easiest option.

'The . . . the weather's not bad for the time of year,' he said.

Another long silence. It seemed she had no opinion on this.

'They . . . they say we could be in for a bad winter, though.'

Again, silence.

Then to his absolute horror, he heard another voice, a high-pitched, muffled voice, coming from the suitcase on the other side of the room. 'Oh, come on, Owie, is that the best you can do?'

Owen threw a furious glare in the direction of the suitcase. 'Be quiet!' he hissed. 'This is nothing to do with you.'

'I appreciate that. But I thought you came her to *talk* to her.'

'I did, but—'

'Well, you're doing a terrible job of it, if you don't mind me saying so. The weather? Surely you can do better than that?'

'It . . . it's none of your business!'

Now Ma had become aware of the new voice. She turned to look down at the case, clearly intrigued, a puzzled smile on her face. 'Gareth?' she murmured. 'Is that you?'

'No it is not!' said Owen, a little more forcefully than he'd intended. She looked offended. 'Ma, it's just a . . . a friend,' he said, not really knowing what else to say. 'Just . . . somebody I met.'

'A friend,' echoed Ma. 'In your suitcase?'

'It's hard to explain,' said Owen. 'You see, I—'

'Pleased to make your acquaintance, Mrs Dyer!' said Mr Sparks, with exaggerated glee. 'Owen's told me *so* much about you.'

'Has he really?' Ma seemed delighted and, for the first time in ages, lucid. 'Only good things. I hope.'

'Oh yes, he speaks very highly of you, Mrs D. In fact,

if I could get out of this ruddy case, I'd like to shake you by the hand. Any friend of Owen's is a friend of mine and, after everything I've heard about you, it would be nice to actually clap eyes on you. I understand that Owen gets his good looks from your side of the family.'

'Shut up!' snapped Owen. 'Stay out of this! I told you, it's not your business.'

'Owen!' Ma looked appalled. 'Don't speak to your friend like that. Where are your manners?' She smiled apologetically down at the case. 'I'm sorry, Mr . . . I'm afraid I didn't catch your name.'

'It's Sparks, madam. Charlie Sparks. At your service.'

'Mr Sparks. Delighted to meet you.' She looked at Owen. 'Well, don't just sit there, Owen, get your friend out of that thing. He must be very hot.'

'Yes, Owie, take me out for a moment, there's a good fellow.'

Owen looked imploringly at his mother. 'You really don't want to meet him,' he said.

'Well, of course I do!' she corrected him. 'I like to meet all your friends.' She gestured to the case, her expression cross. Owen sighed. He might have known the dummy would be incapable of keeping his mouth shut for more than ten minutes. There was nothing for it but to do as Ma asked. He got up from his chair and walked slowly over to the suitcase. He had a bad feeling about this. He kneeled down, unlatched the case and lifted the lid, scowling in at Mr Sparks' pink, smiling face.

'I'm warning you,' he whispered. 'Be on your best behaviour.'

'Don't worry,' Mr Sparks assured him. 'I'll just be my charming self.'

'Don't you *dare*,' Owen warned him.

He reached in and lifted the dummy into his arms. Then he stood up and started to walk back towards his mother.

Her reaction was dramatic. Her eyes widened as she registered what Owen was carrying. Then she recoiled, so violently she almost seemed to shrink back into herself. Her features rearranged themselves into an expression of pure terror. 'What's . . . *that*?' she hissed.

'Steady on,' said Mr Sparks. 'You could hurt a fellow's feelings!'

'It's all right,' Owen assured her, settling into the empty seat. 'It's just a . . . silly old wooden dummy.'

'Oh, please,' said Mr Sparks, 'talk about me as though I'm not here!'

But Ma was shaking her head from side to side, her eyes wide with panic. 'No,' she said. 'No, no, no, get rid of it, Owen. Drown it! Burn it! It's bad. Can't you see? It's evil!'

'Ma!' Owen was shocked by the sudden turn she'd taken. 'Really, he's absolutely harmless. There's no need to—'

'Can't you *see*?' shrieked Ma. 'Can't you see what it is?'

'Now, now, calm down, madam,' reasoned Mr Sparks. 'We've come a long way to see you, Owie and me. He said to me, "Charlie, I want to see my dear old mum" and I said to him—'

'Get it away from me!' Ma lashed out suddenly with one arm, catching Mr Sparks a blow across the side of his head and knocking him clean out of Owen's arms. He tumbled to the floor, his skull hitting the tiles with a loud clunk.

'Oww!' shrieked Mr Sparks. 'You've hurt me, you silly cow!'

Owen started to get up from his chair but Ma grabbed the lapels of his coat and pulled him back down again, displaying a power that both shocked and scared him. 'Owen,' she shrieked. 'Owen. Get rid of that thing. Get rid of it!'

'But Ma, I—'

'It's bad! It's evil!'

Just then the door opened and the orderly hurried back into the room, his former charming grin replaced by a stern, no-nonsense look. 'What's going in in here?' he cried. 'What did you *say* to her?'

'I didn't . . . I just—'

Ma was raving now, shrieking and shouting something about the Devil hiding behind a grin and the orderly had to restrain her, had to forcibly push her back down into her chair.

Owen stared at her for a moment, feeling terrible. 'Mum, I don't understand what you—'

'Get away!' shrieked Ma, and her eyes seemed to have doubled in size. 'Get away from here and take that devil with you!' Owen turned and saw that Mr Sparks was splayed on the floor, staring resentfully up at Owen. There was a big, jagged crack running down one side of his head from temple to cheek. Owen walked over to him and picked him up.

'I don't know what happened,' murmured Owen. 'She just—'

'Never mind that!' hissed Mr Sparks. 'Get me away from her before she kills me.'

'But she—'

'Can't you see I'm injured?' Owen looked closer at Mr

Sparks' head. He saw to his surprise that something was leaking out of the crack. Something grey.

'What's that?' he asked.

'Just get me out of here,' whispered Mr Sparks. 'Owie, *please*!' Owen saw something on the dummy's face that he'd never seen there before. A look of fear. As he picked the dummy up, he realised that the little body was shaking. He carried Mr Sparks over to the case, kneeled down and set him carefully inside, before closing the lid. He stood up and turned back to look at his mother. She was struggling in the orderly's grip, her back arched, her mouth open. Her thin body was shaking convulsively.

'Devil!' she growled. 'Little devil! Little *monster*!'

The orderly turned his head to look at Owen. 'Better get out, lad,' he advised him. 'Wait for me in the reception and I'll come and have a word with you.'

'Yes sir.' Owen turned away and walked out of the door. But as he stepped into the corridor, Mr Sparks voice piped up, harsh and urgent. 'We're not staying. Get me out of this madhouse. Now!'

9

On The Run

Owen headed back towards the reception, moving along anonymous grey corridors, his footsteps echoing on the tiled floor.

'We can't just leave,' he reasoned, ignoring the questioning looks he was receiving from other people passing by. 'The man said we were to—'

'I don't care what he said!' came the muffled reply. 'I'm hurt. I need to get help as soon as possible. Take me to the taxi, NOW!'

The urgency in the dummy's voice invited no compromise. So Owen continued back the way he had come, following the signs that led to the reception area. He pushed through the entrance and stood for a moment, gazing around. Then he headed for the front door.

'Just a moment!' called the woman at the desk, but Owen ignored her. 'I say, you boy. Come back here!' He pushed out into the open air, went down the steps and strode across the forecourt towards the taxi, which was waiting, as arranged, a short distance away. Just as he was approaching it, another motorcar came racing up the drive from the direction of the road, going flat out. It shot past the taxi for some distance, before the driver slammed on the brakes and it slewed to a halt, scattering gravel in all directions.

'What was that?' asked Mr Sparks' voice, sounding fearful.

'Another car,' said Owen. 'A big fancy one. Two men are getting out of it—'

'Quick! Into the taxi!'

Owen did as he was told, throwing the case onto the leather seat and settling in beside it. He looked over his shoulder to see the two men running towards him, one tall and thin, a long black coat flapping behind him, the other short and tubby, one meaty hand clamping a bowler hat onto his head.

'Where to?' asked the driver casually.

'Er . . .' said Owen.

'Back to the station!' hissed Mr Sparks. 'Hurry.'

'Yes, er . . . back to the station, fast as you can!'

'Very well . . .' Now the cab driver was looking into his

rear-view mirror. 'Hello!' he muttered. 'Who are those two?'

'Drive!' bellowed Owen, and the cab driver instinctively put his foot down. The vehicle shot forward, wheels spinning on gravel, before they found purchase and the cab headed towards the exit. The two men pursued it for a short distance, waving their arms and shouting something but then realising they were outpaced, they broke off and hurried back towards their own vehicle.

'What's going on?' demanded the cab driver. 'Who are those men?'

Owen panicked. 'They . . . they . . .'

'Here, they're not policemen, are they?' The cab driver began to slow down, as though having second thoughts. 'Look, I don't want any trouble.'

'No, they're . . . bad men!' shouted Owen, desperately trying to think of something that would convince the driver. 'They're . . . Germans.'

'Germans?' cried the cab driver incredulously.

'Yes. German spies!'

'Get away.' The man sounded doubtful, but he did speed up again.

'Yes, they . . . I found out about them and they're after me! They want to shut me up.'

'I see.' The cab driver licked his lips nervously. 'So . . . wouldn't I be better taking you to the police station?'

'No. No, I have to get out of Denbigh. I need to catch a train to . . . to London.'

The taxi driver looked doubtful. 'Why London?' he asked.

'Because the . . . the Foreign Office is there, isn't it? I need to warn them. About the spies.'

The cab driver still didn't look convinced. 'How do you know they're spies?' he asked.

'They were staying at my aunt's hotel in Llandudno. I took them up a sandwich and I overheard them talking . . . in German.'

'You speak German?'

'Er . . . no. But I thought it was funny, you know? So I stood by the door and listened. Then they started speaking on the phone to somebody in English. And they were plotting to . . . to blow up a building. I came here to tell my mother about it . . . she works here, you see and . . . and she told me to get to London, straight away. She said, "Go to the Foreign Office and tell them everything you heard." So . . . so, we've got to get back to the station, as quick as we can.'

The cab driver looked in his rear-view mirror. 'They're following us,' he announced grimly.

Owen glanced over his shoulder. The big shiny black car was coming in pursuit, swerving dangerously around the bends on the narrow country road.

'You've got to speed up,' demanded Owen.

'That's a Daimler, they're driving,' said the cab driver. 'It can outrun this old bucket in a heartbeat.' He thought for a moment. 'Come to think of it, isn't that a German car? You'd think they'd at least try to keep a low profile.'

'You can't let them catch us,' Owen warned him. 'If they do, they'll . . . they'll kill both of us.'

'Surely not?' whispered the cab driver.

'I'm telling you. They're armed and dangerous. I heard them say they've already shot somebody else who found out about them.'

'Oh my goodness.' The cab driver stared at him desperately for a moment. 'But what can *I* do?' he asked. 'I wouldn't have a chance of outrunning them.'

'Offer him money,' whispered a muffled voice. Owen nodded. He lifted his shirt and groped around in the money belt. 'I'll give you a pound,' he said.

'More!' hissed Mr Sparks.

111

'Er . . . I mean, five pounds!'

'Offer him ten, you idiot!'

The cab driver was peering frantically around the back of the cab. 'Where's that ruddy voice coming from?' he cried, before returning his gaze to the road ahead.

'What voice?' asked Owen.

'I thought I heard somebody . . . in the case?'

'Don't be daft. How could anybody fit into a suitcase?'

'Yes, but I could have sworn . . .'

Owen reached into the money belt and pulled out one of the big white ten-pound notes. He waved it enticingly. 'Do we have a deal?' he asked.

The cab driver's eyes widened for a moment. He was clearly tempted. Then he hunched down over the wheel. 'I know a few short cuts,' he said.

Owen looked back. The Daimler was dangerously close now, so close that he could see the grim expressions of the two men travelling in it. Neither of them looked friendly.

'They're getting very—' Owen broke off as the cab turned suddenly sharp left into a narrow, winding lane. The manoeuvre threw him sideways onto his seat and he landed heavily on top of the suitcase.

'Careful!' snapped Mr Sparks.

'Quiet!' hissed Owen. He looked back. He saw that the big black car had failed to make the turn and was racing on past.

'That'll buy us a bit of time,' said the taxi driver. 'There's a few more like that between here and the station.' He studied Owen in the mirror of a moment. 'So tell me about this plot,' he said.

'Plot?'

'To blow up the building. Which one was it?'

'Oh, I . . . I think they said something about the . . . the Houses of Parliament.'

'Of course! That makes perfect sense. Another reason why you have to get to London?'

'Er . . . yes.'

The driver looked puzzled. 'But . . . if they're planning to do *that*, what were they doing in Llandudno?'

'I think they . . . wanted somewhere out of the way,' said Owen desperately. 'Where they could draw up their plans without being disturbed.'

'Well, they'd certainly get that in Llandudno,' admitted the cab driver.

Owen sensed rather than saw movement behind him.

He looked back and the Daimler had reappeared, catching up by the second.

'They're coming!' he shouted.

'I thought it would slow them up more than that,' muttered the cab driver. Now the other vehicle was trying to edge around the side of the cab, but the road was too narrow to allow it and the sides of the Daimler ripped chunks of greenery out of the hedgerow. The car's horn blared indignantly as though demanding that the taxi cab slow down.

'Oh, pipe down, Fritz,' muttered the cab driver. 'Now, somewhere round 'ere, there ought to be . . . ah!'

He wrenched the steering wheel hard to the right and the cab shot through the open gates of a field and went juddering and bouncing across the uneven ground. Once again, the Daimler raced on by, but the sound of its squealing brakes told Owen that it wouldn't be long in correcting the mistake. He tried to ask the cab driver where they were going, but the vehicle was bouncing so violently, he couldn't actually form words. Several rude ones, however, came out of the suitcase as it was flung up and down on the seat. Owen slapped a hand on it. The cab descended a steep hill, then levelled out as it slid through a patch of mud and plunged headlong through a narrow gap in a hedge. There was a violent bump as it went over a rough kerb, then angled sharp left and with a manic screeching of tyres, raced on along an even narrower lane than before. On either side of them hedges clattered and banged against the bodywork.

'This is playing hell with my paintwork,' complained the cab driver. 'Who's going to pay for it? That's what I'd like to know.'

Owen reached into the money belt and pulled out another tenner. He waved the two of them at the driver. 'How far now?' he demanded, remembering to breathe.

'Just up the road a bit. You should see the . . . ah!' He broke off in an obscure Welsh curse as a familiar-looking radiator grille appeared in the mirror behind him. 'Don't those Huns ever give up?'

The cab swung sharp left again onto a wider road and now Owen saw ahead of him the imposing grey stone entrance of the station. The cab driver brought the taxi to a squealing, shuddering halt. Owen pushed the two ten-pound notes at him, grabbed the suitcase and jumped out of the cab. As he did so, he was horribly aware of the Daimler, pulling into the forecourt a short distance behind him. He didn't hesitate but ran through the open doors of the entrance and straight past the ticket booth, ignoring the indignant shouts of the moustachioed man behind the glass. He caught sight of a sign that read TRAINS TO CHESTER and ran onto the platform, aware as he did so that a train was already there and beginning to move away.

'We're too late!' yelled Owen, but the voice that answered him from the suitcase was in no mood for compromise.

'We've got to catch that train, Owie!'

Owen took a deep breath, put his head down and went in pursuit of the train, stretching his legs out and pumping his free arm like a marathon runner. He came up alongside the rear carriage, but the train was already accelerating, the engine pumping out great clouds of steam. Behind him, Owen heard a wild yell and when he glanced briefly back, he saw that the thinner of the two men was gaining ground on him, his long legs eating up the distance between him and his quarry. The second man trailed some distance behind.

Owen looked to his right again and fixed his gaze on a particular door – the last door of the last carriage, the only one he had any chance of reaching. He saw that the window of that door had been left slightly open, so he put everything he had into one final push, hoping against hope that he could make the leap. And then, suddenly, just as he was steeling himself to do exactly that, a man appeared at the door. He opened it and leaned out, one hand hanging onto the door frame, the other extended, offering his help. Owen weighed up the distance, snatched a quick breath and leaped, throwing himself across the space. He seemed to hang in the air for a long, silent moment and then the toes of his feet thudded onto the small wooden step that jutted out from under the door and his left hand found the welcome grasp that was being offered to him. His right hand, stretched out behind him, still held the suitcase and Owen realised, even as he hung there, that the thin man was reaching out his own arms to make a grab for it. The man lunged, just as Owen snatched the case out of his reach and allowed his saviour to pull him into the carriage. The door slammed shut behind him with a loud thud. Owen collapsed onto the floor and sat there, gasping for breath, hugging the case against him. Then he realised that several pairs of eyes were looking down at him. He glanced up to see that he was in a compartment with three other travellers, two women and the man who had pulled him to safety, a big wiry-looking fellow with dark hair and a thick moustache.

'Well that was close,' he said and his companions laughed, more from relief than anything else. 'Pity the other chap didn't make it. Your father, was it?'

Owen shook his head. 'Never saw him before in my life,' he said and allowed himself a smile. He got to his feet, turned back to the door and stuck his head out of the window. Back on the platform, already dwarfed by distance, the bowler-hatted man was helping his lanky colleague to his feet. Owen felt reckless enough to give them a little wave. Then, picking up the suitcase, he stowed it on the luggage rack and settled himself into a spare seat beside his saviours with a long sigh of relief.

'Are you all right?' asked Wilkins, helping Quinn up. Wilkins was breathing so heavily from the run, he could hardly speak.

'Do I *look* all right?' hissed Quinn, scowling. He brushed the dust off his trousers with a gloved hand. 'That little— I almost had the case, Wilkins! It was *inches* away.'

Wilkins nodded, understanding his employer's frustration and noting, not without a certain satisfaction, that Quinn's world-famous composure was finally beginning to crack. 'Well,' he gasped, 'we know where . . . where the train's 'eaded.' He pointed to a sign on the station building. 'There'll be a phone in the . . . office here. All we need to do is get the . . . Chester police to arrest the boy when he steps off the train. Then we'll . . . drive up there and . . .'

'What if they get off *before* Chester?' asked Quinn.

Wilkins frowned. 'Well all right, we'll . . . we'll phone the police at *every* stop along the way. I'll call in a few favours. And then we—' He broke off. Five men were approaching them along the platform. Four of them were dressed in railway uniforms and they were accompanied by the man who had been driving the taxi cab. They all had grim expressions on their faces. Wilkins decided to take the lead. He stepped forward, smiling jovially. 'Ah, gentlemen, I'm . . . so glad you're 'ere. Perhaps you can be of assistance? We're police officers and—'

'We *know* who you are,' said the first uniformed man, a grey-haired fellow who Wilkins took to be the station-master. 'This gentleman . . .' He nodded to the cab driver. '. . . has told us all about your wicked plans.'

'Our . . . what?' cried Quinn.

'You have to hand it to them,' said the cabbie. 'They've disguised their voices well enough.'

Quinn laughed. 'What are you talking about?' he cried.

'We take a dim view of you people coming over here to try and disrupt this country,' said the stationmaster. 'So you two can just wait with us until the police arrive and then you can have a nice long talk with them.'

'We *are* the police!' snapped Wilkins.

'Yes, and I'm Kaiser Wilhelm,' said the cabbie.

'Have you gone mad?' snapped Quinn. 'Now look, we need to go to your office and use your telephone.'

'Oh, I bet you do,' said the stationmaster. 'You'd love that, wouldn't you? Then you'd be able to phone your associates and leave them a coded message!'

'You . . .' Quinn and Wilkins exchanged baffled looks. 'Look,' said Quinn, pointing at the cab driver. 'I don't know what this imbecile has told you, but we've no intention of waiting for the police. We have urgent business to attend to. Now kindly step aside and let us pass.'

One of the uniformed men, a big, brawny fellow with a black moustache, took a step closer. 'Yes, go on, Fritz, *please* try and get by me. That'd make my day that would! My older brother died in the trenches.'

'Fritz?' Quinn thought about it for a moment and then the penny dropped. Despite the awfulness of the situation, he couldn't help but laugh.

'What's going on?' asked Wilkins, still mystified.

'They think we're Germans,' said Quinn.

'We don't think, we *know*,' said the cab driver. 'And we've no intention of letting you anywhere near the Houses of Parliament. So you boyos aren't going nowhere. And just to make doubly sure, I've punctured every tyre on that fancy German car of yours! So stick that in your pipe and smoke it!'

10

Portsmouth

Owen hurried along the quayside, clutching the paper bag of supplies tightly to his chest. Darkness was falling and the weather had turned cold and stormy, the sky a roiling fury of bruise-black clouds. Powerful gusts of wind stirred the restless grey waves into violent motion against the quay, throwing up explosions of white foam. Owen was tired and hungry and he didn't even want to think about the last couple of days, days which had dissolved into an exhausting blur of train and motorcar travel as he and Mr Sparks had made their way steadily southward to the coast.

Owen spotted the feeble light above the door of the filthy little guesthouse in which they were lodging and stepped gratefully in off the street. They'd arrived in Portsmouth only a couple of hours earlier and Mr Sparks had instructed Owen to bring him straight to the Alhambra. Owen got the impression that Charlie had stayed here before, but it was hard to see any appeal. It certainly had none of the charm and cleanliness of Aunt Gwen's hotel and he couldn't imagine why the dummy had chosen it, but he'd already learned that it didn't pay to put up any argument. Mr Sparks did as Mr Sparks wanted and there was no other option but to go along with him. The desk clerk had raised an eyebrow when a twelve-year-old boy asked for a room for the night, but the fact that Owen had offered to pay up front in cash had soon smoothed over any misgivings.

Owen walked across the badly lit foyer, which smelled strongly of paraffin fumes. In a tiny cubicle in one corner, a desk clerk, a thin, furtive-looking fellow, was sitting reading a newspaper. He didn't even glance up as Owen walked past and made his way straight up the narrow staircase to the first floor.

He tapped gently on the door of room nine and then went in. Mr Sparks was sitting on the scruffy single bed, where Owen had left him, propped up against a couple of pillows. He looked vaguely comical with one of Owen's vests wrapped tightly round his head, but there was nothing comical about his mood, which had grown steadily darker as they'd journeyed south.

'Did you get the stuff?' he growled.

'Yes. Sorry it took so long but it wasn't easy to find the—'

'Never mind that. Get over here and have a look at my head.'

Owen bit his lip, thinking that the odd 'please' and 'thank you' wouldn't go amiss, but he didn't say anything. He walked over to the bed, sat down beside Mr Sparks and began to unpack the contents of the paper bag: a roll of bandage, a tin of sticking plasters, a pair of scissors, a can of putty and a loaf of bread. Mr Sparks looked down at the latter in bemusement. 'What did you get *that* for?' he asked.

'I was hungry,' protested Owen. 'I haven't eaten anything since breakfast. It's all right for you, you've no idea what it feels like to have an empty belly.'

'Yes, yes. Well, you can eat just as soon as you've taken care of my poor noggin.' He glared at Owen. 'I can't believe I let you talk me into seeing that mad mother of yours!'

'I didn't *talk* you into anything!' protested Owen. 'I didn't even want you to see her. I told you to stay in the case.'

'Well, I wish you'd managed to convince me. I was only trying to help, and look where it got me.'

'You *scared* her,' said Owen. 'I'm still not sure why she took such a fright.'

'Because she's barmy,' snapped Mr Sparks. 'Someone like that should be locked up, where they can't harm others.'

'She *is* locked up,' Owen reminded him.

'Yes, well she needs to be restrained. She could have killed me.'

'It was just a bit of a bump.'

'A bit of a bump? Is that what you call it? I wouldn't be surprised if there's permanent damage. Even as I sit here, I can feel my mind . . . going.'

Owen looked doubtfully at his purchases and frowned. 'Are you sure that putty is the right thing?' he asked. 'I mean, it can't be very—'

'It's a temporary measure,' Mr Sparks assured him. 'Just until I can get the job done properly.'

'Well, I suppose you know best.' Owen reached up and began to unknot the vest from around the dummy's head. 'This might hurt a bit,' he said. It was hard to believe that a lump of wood could actually feel pain, but Mr Sparks had complained of it all the way here and sure enough, as

Owen pulled the fabric away from the wound, the dummy's face registered an expression of pure agony. 'Aargh, be careful!' he snarled.

'Sorry.' Owen examined the temporary bandage, which was badly stained with dark grey fluid. 'What *is* this stuff?' he muttered.

'It's my teapot,' said Mr Sparks.

'Your *what*?' cried Owen.

'Er . . . my . . . my . . .' Mr Sparks grunted as though unable to find the right words. 'My thoughts. My . . . mind. All right, now, take the tin of putty and lift off the bicycle . . .'

'The what?'

'The . . . the lid! Use the scissors to prise it up. There, good. Now, get some of the putty out and knead it until it's nice and soft. Yes, that's the way. Work it between your fingers. Now, my boy, take some of the putty and gently . . . gently, I say! Work it into the . . . the . . .'

'Crack in your head?' suggested Owen.

'Precisely. Be careful though, because . . . aargh! That's so sore!'

'Sorry.' Owen tried to be as gentle as he could but he'd never had to do anything like this before and he didn't have the least idea if he was going about it the right way. After a few minutes of pushing and prodding, which elicited a whole string of grunts and curses from Mr Sparks, he'd managed to fill in the entire length of the 'injury' with a seam of khaki-coloured sludge. He sat back and surveyed his handiwork. 'I think that's it,' he said.

'You're sure? There's nowhere left where anything can . . . leak out?'

'No, I think I got it all.'

'Good. Right, take a bandage and wind it tight . . . I mean, *really* tight around my onion . . . my head! Yes, that's right. Now I . . . owww! Owie, I'm not being funny, but don't ever consider taking up a career in medicine. You haven't got the hands for it.'

'Sorry, I'm sure,' said Owen. He wound the bandage several times around Mr Sparks' head and secured it in position with a strip of adhesive plaster. 'There,' he said. 'All done.'

Mr Sparks gave a sigh and slumped back against the pillow. His pink face seemed paler than usual and Owen was amazed to see drops of moisture on his forehead as though he was sweating. His eyelashes fluttered for a moment and Owen thought that he might be about to drift off to sleep, but then he seemed to remember something, and the eyes opened again. 'Did you do the other thing?' he asked. 'The errand?'

Owen nodded, reaching for the bread as he did so. 'The very first thing, just like you said. I called to the address you gave me, but Mr Nail wasn't there. An old woman in a wheelchair . . . I think it must have been his mother, she didn't say . . . she said he was out on a job at the docks, so I left her our address and asked him to call here.'

'Did you impress upon the woman how urgent it was?'

'Yes, I told her we had to see him *tonight*.' Owen broke off a crust of bread and began to tear at it wolfishly, swallowing down large chunks without bothering to chew it.

Mr Sparks watched him disapprovingly. 'You wouldn't win any prizes for good manners,' he observed.

'I'm starving!' protested Owen. 'If you'd let me stop for a proper meal on the way here, I wouldn't be eating like this.'

Mr Sparks seemed to soften a little. 'Owie, I'm sorry about this, I really am. The way it's worked out and everything. You know, once we're clear of those people, I'll make it up to you. I'll buy you those clothes I promised you. And we'll make sure you get some decent grub. It's just, with everything happening so quickly, there was no time to think. And I was afraid I was going to lose my cabbage . . . er . . . my envelope . . . er . . . my *mind*!'

'I don't really understand,' said Owen, making an attempt to eat at a more leisurely pace. 'I mean, if you're just made of wood, what's all that stuff leaking out of your head?'

'It's . . . complicated,' Mr Sparks assured him. 'You're just a kid. I wouldn't expect you to understand.'

Owen shrugged his shoulders. 'Well, you could try me,' he said. He thought for a moment. 'What you told me when I first met you . . . about how you were a real boy? Is that what this is all about?'

'Umm . . . sort of . . .' Mr Sparks seemed uncomfortable. 'Listen,' he said, 'when Nail gets here, leave the talking to me. And don't worry about pretending that it's *you* that's really talking. Nail knows about me. He's one of the few people who does.'

'Who is he?'

'Just somebody I've used before. A trawlerman. He has his own boat, you see. He's got me and Otto out of a couple of scrapes before now.'

'And he's always known about you?'

'Not always. The first time we met, we kept up the

pretence. I did the talking and Otto just chipped in with the odd comment, as though it was some kind of act. But we soon stopped doing that.'

'Why?'

'Because the man isn't as stupid as he looks. I could tell that he knew how it really was. So pretty soon, we stopped pretending. Everything was fine after that. He was very fond of Otto. The two of them got along well. I'm not sure how he'll take the news that he's gone.'

Owen scowled. He didn't like talking about Mr Schilling. It made him think about the old man lying dead back at the Sea View hotel. Not that he'd still be there, of course. Surely somebody must have taken his body away by now. Which reminded him of something else.

'Those men who are chasing us . . .' Owen raised the subject for perhaps the sixth time since they'd set off. 'You promise they're not the police?'

'I've already told you, Owie. They are *bad* men. Men who cannot be trusted. If they were to get their hands on me, I don't know where I'd end up. Murdered, most probably. Experimented on like some animal. But of course, the police *will* be looking out for us too, make no mistake about that!'

'But why? We haven't done anything wrong, have we?'

'Well, technically, yes. We left poor old Otto lying dead in that hotel, didn't we? The police don't take kindly to that kind of thing.'

'But I didn't want to leave him! You said we had to go. You said—'

'It doesn't matter now. What's done is done, so there's no use crying about it. But trust me, the coppers will be looking for us. Why do you think we're staying in this rat hole? It's not because it's so luxurious or anything. We're just keeping a po lofile . . . I mean a low profile!'

'If Aunt Gwen ever gets her hands on me, my life won't be worth living,' said Owen glumly. He found he'd suddenly lost his appetite, so he pushed the rest of the loaf back into the paper bag.

'We'll be fine,' Mr Sparks assured him. 'Once we're across the channel . . .'

'That's another thing. I've never been abroad before. And . . . well, I can't speak any French.'

'You surprise me! I'd have thought you'd be *au fait* with *le français*.'

'Eh?'

'Never mind. I'll do the talking for both of us. I speak the lingo.'

'But . . . I don't understand why we have to go all the way to France. Surely there must be somebody in England who can repair you?'

'No, Owie, let me assure you there isn't. I've been damaged. Badly damaged. And there's only one person who I can trust to put me right. He happens to live in France.'

'Well, all right, but what about—' Owen broke off as a fist pounded on the door. He looked at Mr Sparks in alarm. 'Who's that?' he asked, apprehensively.

'Sparks, are you in there?' boomed a deep voice.

The dummy's eyes flickered in recognition. 'It's Nail,' he whispered. 'Remember. Leave the talking to me.' He raised his voice. 'Enter!' he said.

The door opened and a man stepped into the room, a stocky little fellow, wearing a thick reefer jacket and a cloth cap. His face was heavily bearded and a pair of beady black eyes peered into the room from beneath wild, overgrown brows. The room immediately filled up with a powerful odour – the unmistakable stink of raw fish. It was evident that he must have come straight from his work at the docks. He noticed Mr Sparks and smiled. Then his gaze moved across to Owen and the smile faded.

'Where's Otto?' he asked.

'Ah, of course, you won't have heard,' said Mr Sparks. 'A terrible thing. I'm afraid poor Otto isn't with us any more.'

'Not with us?' Mr Nail looked puzzled. 'How do you mean exactly?'

'I mean he's shuffled off this mortal coil. He's . . . not to put too fine a point on it . . . snuffed it. It was very sudden. His heart, you see. Fragile as a paper bag. It just gave out on him.'

Nail looked genuinely upset. 'Oh dear, what a pity. I always liked Mr Schilling. One of life's gentlemen, he was.' The beady eyes focused on the bandage. 'And what's happened to you?' he asked, pointing. 'You look like you've been in the wars.'

'Just a bit of a bump,' Mr Sparks assured him. 'Nothing to worry about.'

The man's gaze flicked back to Owen. 'And who's this?' he asked.

Owen was about to answer but Mr Sparks got there first. 'This is my new partner, Owen Dyer.'

Mr Nail sneered. 'Him? He's just a kid.'

'I appreciate that, but he's good. Trained by Otto he was, for just such an eventuality. Weren't you, Owen?'

Owen nodded and Mr Sparks continued. 'Otto knew he

133

didn't have long, you see. And he knew he had to pass the baguette on . . .'

Nail looked puzzled. 'The baguette?' he echoed.

'Er . . . the *baton*! Owen was his protégé.'

'I see.' Mr Nail frowned. 'So, what was so urgent you needed to see me straight away? My old mum was in a fair old tizz about it. Said some kid had turned up at the 'ouse, giving 'er orders.'

'Oh, I didn't do that,' protested Owen. 'I was polite.'

Mr Sparks ignored him. 'It's the usual thing, Lemuel,' he said. 'We need to get across the channel. No questions asked.'

Mr Nail lifted a hand to rub at his beard. 'I don't think you'll be going anywhere for a while. Have you seen what it's like out there? Blowing a fair old gale, it is. You'll need to hold your horses for at least twenty-four hours.'

But Mr Sparks was shaking his head, an action that seemed to cause him considerable pain, judging by the gasps for breath that Owen heard escaping from him. 'You . . . don't understand. We need to go *tonight*.'

'What's the big hurry?' Mr Nail studied the two of them with interest. 'What have you been up to this time, Charlie? Robbed the flipping crown jewels, have you?'

'Of course not!' Mr Sparks gave an unconvincing laugh. 'No, we . . . we have to get over there for . . . an appearance. At a theatre in Paris. Very prestigious show, it is. They're depending on us.'

'Hmm. Well, it's going to take quite a lot of convincing to get me to put my boat out on *that* sea,' said Mr Nail, pointing towards the room's single window. 'Very dicey out there, it is.'

Mr Sparks lowered his eyelashes. 'I thought the usual fee?' he murmured. 'Ten pounds. In cash.'

Mr Nail looked shifty. 'I don't think that's enough,' he said. 'That's what you pay me when it's nice and calm.'

Mr Sparks smiled. 'A fair point,' he admitted. 'How about . . . fifteen?'

'Twenty-five sounds better,' said Mr Nail. 'Danger money.' Then his eyes narrowed. 'Take it or leave it.'

The grin stayed on Mr Sparks' shiny face but his eyes flashed with malevolence. 'You . . . drive a hard bargain, Lemuel,' he observed. 'But I'm in no position to quibble. Twenty-five pounds it is.'

Mr Nail grinned, his teeth startlingly white against the black of his beard. 'A pleasure, as always,' he said. 'Meet me on the dock at midnight. The usual mooring.' And with that, he went out of the room, closing the door behind him.

'He seemed nice,' said Owen.

'Nice? He's a ruddy thief, that's what he is! He knew I was desperate. Twenty-five pounds.' He growled and turned his head to look at Owen. 'How are our finances?' he asked.

Owen frowned. 'Not that great,' he said. 'Once I've taken out the twenty-five . . .'

'Yes?'

'We'll have twenty-eight pounds, two shillings and four pence.'

Mr Sparks raised his eyebrows. 'That's very accurate,' he observed.

'I'm good at mental arithmetic,' Owen assured him.

'Hmm. Well, it could be worse, I suppose. It could be no pounds, no shillings and four pence. We'll just have to be carpet, won't we?'

'Carpet?'

'Careful! I mean, careful.'

'I suppose so.' They fell silent for a moment, but outside, the wind was making a terrible commotion. 'What we were talking about before,' said Owen. 'About that stuff that's coming out of your head and whether you're real or not . . .'

'I can't get into that now,' said Mr Sparks. 'I'm proper worn out. I'm going to grab forty winks, while I've got the chance.'

'But . . . what about me?' asked Owen.

'You? I'm counting on you to give me a call at half past eleven, so we can head down to the quayside.'

'But . . . what if *I* fall asleep?'

'Please don't.' Once again, Charlie seemed to soften, his expression pleading. 'Please, Owen, you've got to try and stay awake. You're the only person I can count on now. The only one I can trust. And I promise, once we're out of danger . . . once we're across the water, I'll make it up to you. Deal?'

Owen frowned. 'Deal,' he said.

'Thanks, kid. I knew I could rely on you. You know, you're my only friend now. There's nobody else I can trust.'

And with that, Mr Sparks closed his eyes and slumped back against the pillow, fast asleep.

11

All At Sea

Owen had never felt so sick in his entire life. He and Mr Sparks lay side by side on a grubby little bed in a grubby little cabin, where Mr Nail, once he'd pocketed his fee, had commanded them to keep themselves hidden for the entire trip. The place stank of a mixture of petrol fumes and raw fish and the world seemed to be rising and falling around them in a juddering, shuddering rhythm, the waves seemingly intent on smashing the tiny fishing boat to pieces. There was a single porthole, which offered nothing more than a view of great plumes of water crashing against it.

'I'm going to be sick,' announced Owen.

'No you're not,' insisted Mr Sparks. 'It smells bad enough in here already.'

'I can't help it! My stomach . . .'

'Just try and put your mind on something else.'

'How am I supposed to do that?'

The boat gave a particularly violent lurch and Owen was aware of his meagre dry bread dinner rising up within him. He groaned and clamped a hand over his mouth.

'Owen, listen to me! You're *not* going to be sick.' In the gloom of the cabin, Mr Sparks' eyes seemed to glow with an eerie light. 'Look, I'm going to tell you a story,' he said. 'Something to take your mind off this.'

'But I can't . . .'

'Quiet! Are you listening?'

Owen nodded, though moving his head seemed to make him feel even worse. 'I'm listening,' he croaked.

'Good. Then I'll begin.' Mr Sparks took a deep breath. His head was very close to Owen's, so close that the boy could feel the dummy's warm breath gusting onto his face, breath that smelled like the mothballs that Auntie used to put at the back of the linen cupboard. 'Once upon a time,' said Mr Sparks, 'there was a little French boy called Charles Lacombe . . .'

Owen nodded, trying to ignore the frantic lurching in his belly.

'Charles lived with his mother and father on the edge of this big forest . . .'

That struck a chord with Owen. Hadn't he dreamed of

a forest, the morning that he'd run away from Auntie Gwen's hotel? He remembered now how he'd been walking through shady green depths, the trees towering above him, the birds singing up in the canopy . . .

'It was called Paimpont Forest and a lot of people believed it was the Brocéliande, the forest of King Arthur – you know, the sword in the stone and all that malarkey?'

'But . . . I thought he was Welsh?' muttered Owen.

'Oh, he's every nationality if you believe what people tell you. They all want a bit of King Arthur, don't they? But never mind about that! Charles' father was called Lucien and he was a toymaker, a bit of a big cheese around the area where he lived on account of how skilled he was at his craft. He made dolls and puppets and little wooden carriages, stuff like that, and because many of his customers were members of the local aristocracy – you know, barons and earls, real toffs – he was able to make a very comfortable living out of it. Charles' mother was called Marianne. She doesn't figure much in this story but she was decent enough to Charles and all that. Used to sit him on her knee when he was a toddler and sing him songs of the day. *Sur le Pont d'Avignon . . .*'

'*Frère Jacques?*' suggested Owen.

'Yeah. That sort of thing. French stuff. Anyway, when

Charles was old enough to walk, Lucien used to take him into the forest to show him this ancient tree. Big old thing, it was, branches thick as your waist, been there for *thousands* of years. Lucien told him about a local legend that said this was the tree in which Merlin had been imprisoned by Vivianne, the sorceress, who was the Lady of the Lake, you know, the one that brought Arthur his special sword . . . can't remember what it was called . . .'

'Excalibur?'

'Yeah, whatever, don't interrupt! Where was I? Oh yeah, one day, when Charles and Lucien were visiting the tree, Lucien noticed that a big brick . . . er . . . a big branch had fallen off, so he picked it up and carried it back to the shop, saying that when the wood was properly seasoned, he'd carve something out of it. He was full of these strange ideas. He put the branch in the corner of his workshop and forgot all about it.

'Now, when Charles was ten years old, him and some of the local lads used to go into the forest in the summer time, to this lake, where they liked to swim.'

'Wasn't there a proper swimming baths?'

'No, you nit, this was in the olden days! I thought I told you that.'

'No, you didn't!'

'Well, it *was*, this was like the seventeen hundreds or something, proper olden times. Anyway, this lake they went to had a high rock sticking out over the top of it and some of the bigger boys used to dare each other to climb up there and dive off into the lake, showing off and all that. But none of them would ever do it because it looked, you know, really dangerous and people always said that anyone who *had* tried it always came a cropper. Now, Charles wasn't what you'd call a really good swimmer . . . he was a bit puny to tell you the truth, so he used to make excuses not to go up there. But this one particular day, some girls had come along to watch and there was one girl in particular that Charles really liked. Fabienne, her name was, pretty little thing with blonde hair and blue eyes, cute as a button!'

'It sounds like you've actually *met* her!'

'Will you stop interrupting? So . . . er . . . ? Oh yes, Charles, he wanted to, you know, impress Fabienne, like young lads do, so against his better judgement, he climbed up onto the high rock, intending to dive in. Well, he got all the way up there and looked down and realised it was a lot higher than he'd thought, but Fabienne was watching him, and he would have felt a right chump if he'd backed down, so he sort of steeled himself and dived in.

'Before you say anything, yes, it *was* stupid of him. He should have known better and the other boys ought to have warned him off, because there were deep bits and shallow bits and nobody really knew where was the safest place to go in. But boys being boys, they didn't bother to do that, so . . . well, not to put too fine a point on it, Charles went down like a rock, smacked his head on the bottom of the lake and broke his flipping neck. Dead, instantly, he was.'

'Oh no, that's terrible!'

'Bit of an understatement. Fabienne *was* impressed, mind you, but in the worst possible way. And the lads . . . well, they had the tricky task of fishing Charles' body out of the lake and carrying it back through the woods to his house. His parents were . . . as you might imagine . . . devastated about what had happened to their only son. Marianne had . . . well, I suppose they'd call it a nervous breakdown these days . . .'

'Like my ma,' murmured Owen.

'Yeah, like your ma. Lucien wasn't much better off. He couldn't work, he couldn't sleep, it was as though his life was over and done with. Anyway, they buried poor Charles in the garden right by the cottage . . .'

'Are you allowed to do that?'

'You were *then*! They didn't have all the silly rules we've got now. You could plant somebody in your window box if you felt like it! Anyway, life went on but the Lacombes were barely getting by. Marianne spent all her time in her room, crying. Lucien tried to get her out of there, but she was wasting away poor thing, barely eating more than a crust of bread a day and it began to look as though she wouldn't last much longer than her poor son. Lucien didn't know what to do for the best.

'And then . . . it must have been a couple of weeks later . . . there were a lot of bad storms. The area's known for them. Lucien was sitting in his workshop one night and for some reason, his eyes fell on the old branch in the corner, you know, the one from the so-called "enchanted" tree and he had this sort of mad brainwave. He went and fetched the branch over to his workbench and he started going at it, carving something new.'

'What was it?'

'I'm coming to that! My word, you're impatient! Lucien didn't eat nor sleep for five days and nights, so obsessed he was with the thing he was making. Now, I'm not sure entirely what the plan entailed, but it had something to do with galvanism. You ever heard of that?'

'No.'

'Well, see, this scientist called Luigi Galvani, an Italian feller, as you might guess from his name, he'd done some experiments with frogs' legs . . .'

'Frogs' legs?'

'Yes, frogs' legs, you heard me right!'

'Are you being funny?'

'No, straight up! History, that is. You look it up, sunshine. Now, it's all a bit complicated but apparently, this Galvani fellow started pumping electricity into these frogs' legs . . . this is *after* they'd been chopped off the rest of the frog, you understand . . . and by all accounts, the legs started dancing a jig all by 'emselves!'

'Oh, now come on, that's a bit far-fetched!'

'No, it's absolutely genuine, Owie, I promise you! Lucien must have read about this stuff somewhere and he was desperate enough to believe that there could be something in it, because the next thing you know, he's only gone and shoved a long metal pole through the roof of his workshop! People round about the place started to say that he'd gone

145

pure loopy and poor old Marianne had to keep turning away all these customers who'd ordered fancy toys for their kids, so there was no money coming in and things was beginning to look pretty grim for the Lacombe family.

'Well, one night, there was a big storm, a real humdinger – rain, wind, thunder, lightning, the works! At one point, somebody living nearby claims they saw Lucien out in the garden in the pouring rain and he was digging furiously as though his very life depended on it. Later on that same night, somebody else reported that a lightning flash had hit the metal pole sticking up out of the roof and a great puff of smoke flew up into the sky. That same person swears they heard Lucien let out a yell but whether it was a cry of pain or a shout of joy, he wasn't sure and by this time, people were so afraid of Lucien, nobody wanted to go and check that he was all right.

'Somehow, Marianne managed to sleep through the whole thing. The next morning when she dragged her sorry carcass out of bed, she found the door of the workshop open and she could hear voices coming from inside. When she went in, she got a terrible shock. Charles' dead body was stretched out on a workbench, all covered in mud and slime. It had these wires and things attached to it and it looked sort of . . . burnt. Not a pretty sight. But that wasn't the half of it! Lucien was sitting beside the bench, looking all thin and bedraggled and perched on his knee was this dummy he'd made. And Lucien was talking to it! When Marianne asked what the blinking flip he thought he was doing, the dummy looked up at her and said, in Charles' voice, "Hello Mother, I'm back," whereupon she just fainted away on the spot.'

'Charlie? I mean, Mr Sparks . . . is this . . . is this *your* story?'

'It's *a* story. Something to take your mind off being ill.'

'Yes, but it sounds as though you—'

'Make of it what you like! But let me finish, all right? Oh yes . . . Lucien took no notice of Marianne. When she eventually came round, he was still talking to the dummy and it was talking right back at him, and it really *did* sound like Charles' voice. Well, Marianne decided that Lucien had gone insane. She'd had enough, hadn't she? Packed a bag and cleared out of there, went to live with her mother in the neighbouring village, saying she wanted nothing to do with this 'devil-doll' that Lucien had made. As for Lucien, he abandoned his business and forgot about all the orders that were still outstanding.

'Luckily for him, that was when his younger brother, Michel, moved back from Paris where he'd been working in the theatres making props and so forth. He was quite a skilled toymaker himself, so he took over that side of things. He applied himself to the business and got stuff going again. Lucien, meanwhile, was just obsessed with his new toy. He spent hours sitting there, talking to it, listening to it. Michel was convinced his brother had lost his mind, even thought about having him committed to an asylum. Oh, no offence, Owie! But how could he do such a thing to his own brother? Then, one morning, Lucien announced that he had come up with a bright new future for himself and his . . . son. He told Michel that he was bound for Paris and he asked his brother to furnish him with introductions to all the theatre people that he'd worked with over the years. He told his brother that he'd return when he'd made his fortune. Everyone thought he'd lost his mind and nobody – not even Marianne – could account for the fact that he seemed to have become a gifted ventriloquist overnight. He'd never shown any skill at that before.

'You've got to remember, Owie, these were very superstitious times and a lot of the locals started muttering about the Devil and so forth. There were some people who wanted

Lucien tried as a witch! So when he finally set off for Paris, everyone breathed a big sigh of relief and waited for things to return to normal.

'What nobody could have expected was that Lucien Lacombe and the "Incredible Charles" would prove to be the hit of the century. But they did! The first variety theatre they auditioned for gave them a spot in their latest show and the audience reaction was incredible. Within a matter of weeks, the act was topping the bill and in a couple of months, it was the toast of Paris.

'When Lucien and Charles finally found time to return to the shop, Lucien had enough money to pay off all the debts and even to buy the premises outright. Using the shop as a base and leaving Michel to take care of the business, the act set out to tour the world . . . they went to Italy, Spain, Belgium, you name it! And that was just the start of— Owie? Owie? Are you listening to me?'

But Owen was asleep and dreaming and this time, the dream was not of a deep, dark forest but of a huge music hall packed with people in strange costumes, the men wearing frock coats and powdered wigs, the women dressed in elaborate satin dresses in a multitude of vibrant colours. Everyone's gaze was fixed on the brightly lit stage where a tall thin man, dressed in a richly embroidered gown and wearing an orange turban, sat on an elaborate golden throne. And on his knee, dressed in a multi-coloured jester's outfit sat Mr Sparks, or at least an earlier version of him, grinning maniacally and chattering away in a language that Owen didn't understand. Whatever he was saying must have been funny because the crowd around Owen threw back their heads and roared with laughter. They clapped their hands and stamped their feet and chanted his name over and over, 'Charles! Charles! Charles!' And the chanting rolled like the roar of an angry ocean and the music hall swayed back and forth, up and down, in a turbulent restless rhythm, as the tiny fishing boat lurched on across the water to an unknown destination.

12

Brittany

The forest. He was back in the forest again, tall, slender trees towering over him for as far as he could see, bathing him in their green dappled light. He was walking along a narrow twisting track and there in front of him, emerging from the undergrowth as though it was somehow part of the vegetation, was a cottage. It was like something from a fairy tale, small, white-painted, the roof thatched, a thin column of smoke billowing from the chimney and rising into the blue sky . . .

'Owie, Owie, wake up! I think we're there!'

Owen opened his eyes and came slowly, painfully back to reality. He lifted his head and peered around the filthy cabin. Sunlight was pouring in through the porthole, the sea had calmed itself and as far as he could tell, he'd managed to avoid throwing up in the night, which was something to be very thankful for. He felt pretty awful though, his stomach an empty aching void, his mouth dry as a bone, his head throbbing with a dull ache.

'Take me up on deck,' urged Mr Sparks. 'Come on, stir yourself!'

Owen rolled around into a sitting position and scratched his head. Mr Sparks was glaring at him impatiently. He still had the bandage wrapped around his head and Owen couldn't help but notice that a large grey stain had seeped through the fabric at the side of the dummy's head. 'Where are we?' he muttered.

'France, of course! Where did you think we were, Mars? Come on, shake a tail feather!'

Owen blinked himself back to wakefulness. He picked the dummy up, swung his legs over the side of the narrow bunk and got unsteadily to his feet, then stumbled towards the short flight of wooden steps that led to the deck. 'The suitcase!' Mr Sparks reminded him, and Owen obediently picked it up. He climbed the steps, unlatched the door and pushed it open. The world came at him in a rush of salty air, wind and sunshine. Squinting, he stepped out onto the lurching deck and saw that the boat was puttering slowly towards a little wooden jetty set into a rocky shoreline. As far as Owen could see there was not another soul in sight. He carried Mr

Sparks along the deck to the wheelhouse where Mr Nail stood at the tiller, guiding the boat expertly into shore. He glanced over his shoulder as he heard footsteps approaching.

'That's a trip I wouldn't like to have to repeat,' he roared. 'At one point I thought we was headed straight to the bottom of the sea.' He glanced quickly around. 'It's settling down nicely now, though.' He nodded towards the jetty. 'The usual place,' he said. 'Just as you asked.'

'I appreciate it,' Mr Sparks told him. 'You've saved the day once again.'

Mr Nail grinned, showing those jagged white teeth. 'And this concert that you were so keen to get to . . . where exactly is it taking place?'

'Why? Thinking of booking a seat, were you?' asked Mr Sparks.

'Oh, no time for that, I'm afraid. I'll be heading straight back. Got work waiting for me back in Portsmouth.' He winked. 'No rest for the wicked,' he observed. He studied Mr Sparks intently, no doubt noticing the stained bandage. 'Are you feeling all right?' he asked.

'Never better,' Mr Sparks assured him.

Mr Nail lifted a hand to stroke his beard. He seemed unconvinced. He tilted back his head and looked at the

sky. 'I dare say the return trip will be a lot easier for me.'
He shot a challenging stare at Owen. 'Think you can handle
it from here?' he asked.

Owen was about to reply but Mr Sparks got there first.
'He'll be fine, Lemuel. He's not as stupid as he looks.' He
twisted his head to gaze up at Owen. 'Get me into the
case,' he suggested.

Owen sighed. He was beginning to think that he'd have
been better off staying with Auntie Gwen. At least he
understood how she *worked*. He set the case down flat on
the deck and unlatched it, then lowered Mr Sparks carefully into his nest of crumpled clothing. He was about to
close the lid but the dummy seemed to have an idea. 'Hold
on a moment,' he said. 'Lemuel, have you got a knife we
can borrow for a moment?'

Mr Nail grunted and reached into his pocket. He pulled
something out and threw it across to Owen. It was a clasp
knife with several blades and other implements folded into
the handle. Owen examined it for a moment. 'What's this
for?' he asked.

'I want you to punch a decent-sized hole in this case,'
Mr Sparks told him. 'Here, in the middle of the short side,
so I can peep out and see what's going on.'

Owen frowned. 'My ma and da gave me this,' he muttered.

'Oh, it doesn't matter! It's a battered old thing, anyway. Go on, Owie, do it for me. I'll get you a new one, once I'm all sorted out. Maybe even a big trunk, like Otto had. You liked that, didn't you?'

Owen scowled. It seemed to him that Mr Sparks had done nothing but make promises ever since they'd run off together, but so far there was very little to show for it. The only reason he'd managed to eat anything in the last twenty-four hours was because he'd taken the initiative and purchased a loaf of bread.

Mr Sparks seemed to realise what was on Owen's mind. 'Listen,' he said, 'the heat's off now. Once we step out onto that jetty, it's just a short walk to this little village I know called Erquy. There's a lovely inn there. I'll get them to rustle you up a proper cooked breakfast. Fried eggs, bacon, sausages . . . you name it.'

Owen's stomach gurgled at the mention of food. 'Full English?' he asked hopefully.

'Well, full *French*, anyway,' said Mr Sparks. 'And the Frenchies *are* the finest chefs in Europe. Cross my heart and hope to die. You'll see, it'll all be much better from here on in.'

'All right, then.' Owen examined the knife for a moment. He found a round metal implement with a spike at the end of it, the kind of thing that Aunt Gwen had once told him was for removing stones from horses' hooves. He pulled it out with a click. Then he looked for the right spot on the inside of the case. 'Here?' he suggested, pointing.

'A bit higher,' said Mr Sparks. 'Yeah, that should be about right.' Owen put the tip of the metal spike to the inside of the case and applied steady pressure, grunting with the effort. After a few moments, the tip emerged on the far side and Owen twisted it around a few times, to make the opening bigger. Then he pulled the spike out again. 'How's that?' he asked.

'Perfect!' said Mr Sparks. 'Oh, I'll be able to see everything now.'

The boat was moving alongside the jetty now. Owen folded the knife shut and threw it back to Mr Nail, who caught it expertly and returned it to his own pocket. Owen closed the lid of the case and secured the clasps. He stood up, grabbed the handle of the case and moved across to the side of the boat. As it slid past the jetty, he jumped nimbly ashore.

Mr Nail didn't even bother to moor the boat, but turned

the wheel and headed straight back out to sea. He glanced over his shoulder and gave Owen a fleeting grin. 'Take care, lad,' he roared. 'Send me a postcard!'

Then the boat was moving away, heading for deeper waters. Owen stared after it for a moment and experienced a sudden, curious sensation. For an instant, he wanted to throw the case aside, leap into the water and swim after the boat, shouting for Mr Nail to take him back to Portsmouth, so he could start the long journey back to Llandudno. Once there, he would face the wrath of Auntie Gwen and take whatever punishment was coming to him. In that instant, he actually saw himself doing all that. But the moment passed and he could see that the boat was already too far away for him to swim after it. He heard Mr Sparks' muffled voice coming from inside the case.

'What are we waiting for?'

'Nothing,' muttered Owen. 'I was just . . . waving Mr Nail goodbye.'

'Good riddance, I say. I won't be using him again in a hurry. Twenty-five quid! At least Dick Turpin wore a mask! Come on, let's get going.'

Owen turned and began to walk, his footsteps clumping on the weathered boards of the jetty. After a short distance, a narrow stony path led onwards along the rocky coast and he took the path, walking briskly. When he glanced back again, Mr Nail's boat was no more than a dark brown smudge on the blue horizon. 'How far is it?' he asked. 'To this village?'

'Not so very far. Ten or fifteen minutes' walk.'

'And is that where *he* is?'

'He?'

'The man who can fix you?'

'Oh, no, there's a way to go yet before we reach Paimpont.'

'Is . . . isn't that the place you were talking about last night? The . . . forest?' Memories of the dream came back to him, the deep, unfathomable trees and that strange fairy-tale cottage . . .

'You wait till you taste breakfast at the inn, Owie. You'll think you've died and gone to heaven. But listen . . .'

'Yes?'

'Obviously, you'll need to leave all the talking to me. Er . . . I don't suppose you speak any French at all?'

'*Bonjour*,' said Owen. '*Au revoir*. That's about it.'

'All right. That'll have to do. We'll do it like it's all part of the act. Like you can only talk through me. If anyone asks you something just pull a funny face and I'll answer for you. They'll love it! Hopefully there'll be a decent-sized crowd in. That way we can earn the price of your breakfast and maybe a bit more besides. We need to start building up our fighting fund.'

'And how will we get to this Pam . . . Per . . . ?'

'Paimpont. Oh, you leave that to me, kid. I'll take care of *everything*.'

13

Meanwhile . . .

Wilkins guided the Daimler in through the ornate gates of Quinn's country home and cruised up the driveway towards the front entrance, the huge three-storey house with its high walls looking more like a medieval castle than somewhere a person might actually live. He motored past the immaculately tended tennis courts and the extensive stables, where a groom dressed in jodhpurs and boots was brushing out the mane of a magnificent Arab stallion. One day, Wilkins promised himself, he'd have a place like this . . . in his dreams.

On a more modest note, he was at least glad to have the car back on the road again. It had been quite a bother getting hold of four brand-new tyres for a German vehicle and a pretty penny they had cost too, but Quinn had signed the cheque without raising an eyebrow and had instructed Wilkins to get straight back out there to do some sniffing around. He didn't intend to let the trail go cold.

For a day or so, there'd been absolutely nothing of any use, but now from out of the blue, Wilkins had been given a hot lead. He pulled the vehicle to a halt outside the main doors, got out of the car and crunched his way across the gravel towards the flight of marble steps that led up to the front door.

He paused on the top step for a moment and surveyed Quinn's kingdom, wondering for perhaps the hundredth time how the man had ever managed to acquire such wealth. Probably born into it, Wilkins thought, the lucky blighter. Wilkins had never used his contacts to find out more information about his employer. It would have been easy enough to do so and there would surely have been little chance of being discovered and yet . . . and yet, he was too wary of Quinn to ever take such a chance. The man scared him in a way that he could never fully explain, even to himself. Quinn was tenacious, fanatical . . . and deep down, Wilkins thought, very, very dangerous. In the end, perhaps some things were better left unknown.

He turned back to the massive oak doors and pulled the cord that rang a bell somewhere deep in the bowels of the building. After a short wait, the door swung silently open and there stood Quinn's elderly manservant, Ainsworth, a thin, ravaged-looking fellow with a hawklike nose and tiny, red-rimmed eyes. 'Good morning, Mr Wilkins,' he said, bowing his balding head.

'Morning, Ainsworth. Mr Quinn at home?'

'Indeed he is, sir. He's down in the vaults, working on the Collection.'

Where else? thought Wilkins. Ainsworth went to lead the way but Wilkins dismissed him, knowing it would take much longer if he allowed the decrepit old man to lead the way. 'I know where it is,' he said.

'Very well, sir.' Ainsworth bowed again and turned back to secure the door. Wilkins walked along the central hallway with its ancient oil paintings, tapestries, heraldic shields and suits of armour. As always at such times, he noticed one prominently placed portrait at the top of the staircase, which depicted a man dressed in a suit of silvery armour. He was holding a flag in one hand, which displayed the image of a two-headed eagle and in the other, a broadsword with a similar design etched into the blade. The face of the warrior that stared proudly down at Wilkins across the centuries looked remarkably like Quinn. An ancestor? Almost certainly. And did it also have anything to do with the little badge that Quinn wore on his lapel, the one featuring two armoured knights on horseback?

Wilkins made a beeline for a plain wooden door tucked away beneath the overhang of the marble staircase. He pushed it open and headed down the stone steps beyond which led him to what had once been the vaults of the building, but which now housed the Collection – Quinn's souvenirs of a lifetime devoted to uncovering the secrets of the paranormal.

As Wilkins walked into the main room, his gaze swept this way and that over the random assortment of ancient relics housed in glass cases and beneath transparent domes – the ancient bones of supposed saints, various voodoo dolls and alleged cursed items, assorted weapons, figurines, statues, toys and goodness knew what else, every one of which came with some bizarre story attached. This statue, for instance, was said to have wept tears of blood at various times over the years. That spear was said to have been the instrument that wounded Jesus of Nazareth when he hung on the cross and, over there in the corner was an allegedly cursed piano that on certain summer evenings was said to be capable of playing a tune all by itself.

Wilkins took a pretty dim view of all of it and he could

hardly credit that a grown man would devote so much time and energy to such nonsense, but Quinn had kept him in gainful employment over the past two years while they had hunted Charlie Sparks, so Wilkins made sure to stay silent about such opinions. And besides, the ventriloquist's dummy was something else, something that Wilkins, despite a lifetime's disbelief in all things supernatural, could not readily explain. There was something there that simply defied all understanding.

He turned a corner at the top end of the vault and saw Quinn, dressed in a white lab coat, standing in front of a wooden bench, studying something intently. As Wilkins drew closer he could see more clearly what it was. On the bench stood a large glass tank filled with water, the top covered. In the water, a sleek white creature was twisting and turning, thrashing its legs wildly as it struggled to stay alive. A rat. Wilkins noticed a heavy lead weight attached to its tail that prevented it from rising to the surface. Quinn was watching the creature impassively, a stopwatch held in one gloved hand.

'Well?' Quinn said. He hadn't looked up and for a moment, Wilkins didn't realise that the remark was addressed to him. He sighed. 'Are you going to stand there like a great silent fool or do you have something to say to me?' he asked.

'Oh, sorry.' Wilkins felt flustered in his employer's presence. He always did. 'Er . . . how did you know it was me?' he wondered.

'The smell,' said Quinn, matter-of-factly. 'A mingling of stale cigar smoke, brandy and sweat with just the faintest hint of cheap cologne.'

The rat stopped twisting around in the water. Its back legs gave a final convulsion and then it was still. Quinn punched the stopwatch to stop the hands and set it down on the bench. He noted the time in an exercise book, writing in small neat letters. He removed the lid of the tank, picked up a pair of tongs and fished the dead rat out, then dropped it onto a heap of other bedraggled shapes lying in an open container to his left. Over to his right, more rats waited in an open-topped cage, each of them with a heavy lead weight attached to its tail. It was probably Wilkins' imagination, but he thought the creatures all looked distinctly apprehensive.

'Er . . . right.' Wilkins watched as Quinn reached into the cage, selected another victim and lifted it out. He dropped it into the tank of water, replaced the lid and hit the button on the stopwatch.

'Well?' he repeated, making no attempt to mask his irritation.

'Oh . . . er . . . I just received a telegram from one of my informants,' said Wilkins. 'One of my best lads. He's based in Portsmouth.'

'Lucky old him,' sneered Quinn, but he never took his eyes off the twisting, thrashing shape in the water. 'And how are things in . . . Portsmouth?'

'Umm . . . interesting, actually. At least, I think you'll be interested. My contact said that a boy matching young Owen's description was seen on the docks a couple of nights ago. Carrying a suitcase.'

'Was he now?' Quinn was moved enough to turn and glance at Wilkins. 'But why Portsmouth, of all places?'

'Well, the boy was spotted getting aboard a boat. Late last night. A fishing boat belonging to a certain Lemuel Nail, a trawlerman. My contact told me that this Nail is a bit of a rum fellow. Always got something going on the side, if you know what I mean. I thought I should come straight over and tell you the news.'

'Good.' Quinn's thin lips twisted into the ghost of a smile. 'Well, for once Wilkins, you've done the right thing.' He seemed to think for a moment. Then he set down the stopwatch and began to unbutton his lab coat. 'We'd better get straight down there,' he said.

'To Portsmouth?' muttered Wilkins.

Quinn directed a scalding look at him. 'No, to Felixstowe, the cockles are nicer there!'

'Felixstowe? But—'

Quinn grimaced. 'Of course to Portsmouth! We'll have ourselves a little chat with this Mr Nail, I think. Find out what he knows.' He glanced at Wilkins. 'I trust you're all packed and ready to go?'

Wilkins nodded. 'Always,' he said. 'But er . . .' He waved at the tank, the wriggling, writhing creature in the water. 'Don't you . . . don't you want to finish the experiment first?'

'Experiment?' Quinn glanced at the tank and then draped his lab coat over the back of a chair. 'What experiment? I was bored. I was just passing the time.' He thought for a moment, then sniggered. 'Experiment,' he muttered. 'That's a good one.' He turned and led the way towards the exit. 'Come on,' he said. 'Time and tide wait for no man.'

Wilkins hesitated for a moment and studied the poor, pathetic creature that was still struggling in the deadly embrace of the water. For a moment, he thought about rescuing it and returning it to his companions in the cage, but he didn't want to risk incurring Quinn's wrath. He leaned a little closer to the tank.

'I know how you feel,' he muttered. He reached out a hand and stilled the stopwatch. Then he followed his employer out of the room.

2

THE BROCÉLIANDE

14

Arrival and Departure

The horse and carriage moved slowly along the remote country road, the elderly driver hunched and silent at the reins. Owen rode beside him on the hard wooden seat, his suitcase balanced across his knees. For the time being at least, Mr Sparks was keeping quiet. Owen got the impression that he might be sleeping. He'd been doing a lot of that today.

The two of them had picked up the ride at an *auberge* back in a place Owen didn't even know the name of. He and Mr Sparks had been dropped off there by a lorry driver who had brought them all the way down from a bustling little town called Lamballe and the old man had been sitting alone in the country inn, enjoying a quiet glass of anise, when Owen had arrived, tired and hungry. Mr Sparks, peeping out from his hiding place had seen the old man and had urged Owen to get him out of the case, so he could go to work.

Owen was past caring. Since arriving at the inn in Erquy, the last couple of days had been like this, arriving somewhere and sitting like a great dumb idiot, with Mr Sparks perched on his knee, chattering away in fluent French, eliciting laughs, comments and even occasional coins from those he encountered. Owen had no idea what he was saying . . . making fun of his stupid operator, no doubt. In the *auberge*, it had been an audience of only one. What the old man thought of Mr Sparks' act, he didn't say, but he must have been impressed when Owen managed to devour a huge cheese sandwich and drink a cup of coffee, while Mr Sparks prattled on regardless. As it happened, things turned out well. The old man was taking the road to Paimpont and said that he would be able to drop them at the top of a track where Owen could easily walk into the forêt de Brocéliande. Now Owen and his wooden companion were finally drawing close to their destination.

And sure enough, there was the forest, looming on the horizon away to their left, but it was not as Owen had visualised it in his dreams. There it had been cloaked in tones of deep green, but in reality it featured all the vibrant shades of autumn – rich russets, burnished copper and dazzling gold. The trees swayed and quivered restlessly in the wind and from the branches rained a seemingly endless cascade of leaves that caught the sunlight as they drifted slowly down. As the carriage drew steadily closer, it was evident that this was an ancient place, something that had remained untouched by mankind for thousands of years. The old man saw Owen staring at it and chuckled.

'*C'est bon, n'est-ce pas?*' he murmured. He reminded Owen a little of Mr Schilling, tall and thin with a shock of white hair, though his lined face suggested that he'd had a much harder life.

'Er . . . I only speak English . . . or Welsh,' Owen told him and the old man gave him a puzzled look. He must have been wondering exactly who had done all the talking back at the *auberge*. But he shrugged his narrow shoulders and rephrased his comment in halting *anglais*. 'Er . . . it is . . . nice, the *forêt, oui?*'

Owen nodded. 'Yes,' he agreed. 'Very nice. Have you . . . er . . . lived here a long time?'

'All my life,' said the old man. 'When I was . . . er . . . how you say, *petit*? A . . . leettle boy? I used to play in there with my . . .' He waved a hand. '*Mes amis?*'

'Your friends? Yes, I understand.' Owen found himself thinking of the story that Mr Sparks had told him, about

173

the lake where boys used to swim. He found himself wondering if it was still there, if boys still dived from the high rock into the dangerous water, but it would have been far too complicated a question to ask the old man, so he just smiled, nodded and returned his attention to the forest which, as they continued on their way, seemed to be drawing closer and closer to the road. Soon, there was only a narrow verge between the two. Owen gazed dreamily into the shaded depths of the trees, the thick trunks rearing up as far as he could see. He was close enough now to hear the foliage rustling in the wind and to notice birds flitting in and out of the lower branches. There was something otherworldly about this place. Somehow, it was easier to believe that Mr Sparks could have originated here, in a world that seemed to defy all notions of time and logic.

After what seemed like hours of travelling, they came to a place where a narrow dirt track veered off from the road and cut through the very heart of the forest. It was here that the old man pulled on the reins and drew the skinny black horse to a halt. '*Voilà*,' he said. He pointed along the track and continued speaking in French, but then seemed to check himself and started again. 'You er . . . must . . .

walk that way,' he said, pointing along the road. 'You will
. . . find the place you seek. Down there.'

Owen nodded. He lifted the case and swung himself
down from the seat, noting as he did so that he had 'pins
and needles' in his backside. He smiled up at the old man.
'Thank you,' he said.

'*Au revoir*,' said the old man. 'I hope you find . . . what
you are looking for.' He lifted a hand briefly then snapped
the reins against the horse's back. The carriage moved
slowly onwards and Owen stood and watched until it had
dwindled into distance. Then he looked down at the case.
'Mr Sparks?' he said. 'We're nearly there. Mr Sparks?'

There was no answer. Owen set the case down on the
grass verge, unlatched the clasps and lifted the lid. Mr
Sparks lay on his back amidst layers of crumpled clothing.
His eyes were closed, his teeth bared. Owen noticed with
a twinge of worry that there were big fat drops of sweat
on his forehead and he was breathing loudly, raggedly. The
grey stain on the bandage was bigger than before. Owen
reached out and prodded the still figure on the shoulder.
'Mr Sparks!' he said, urgently. 'Wake up.'

The eyes flickered open with that dry, rasping sound.
'Wh . . . what? What's happening?' He stared at Owen for

a long moment, as though not recognising him. 'Did we . . . did we get across the carpet?'

'The . . . carpet?' Owen stared at him. 'I don't . . .'

'I don't mean the carpet. I mean the treacle . . . the custard . . . the *sea*!'

Owen frowned. 'Oh yes, three days ago,' he said. 'Don't you remember? Mr Nail brought us. We've been travelling ever since.'

'Travelling. Travelling. My memory's unravelling. What's the point of going places, seeing all those twisted faces? Oops! I forgot to tie my laces!'

'Mr Sparks? We're there. You know, the forest of Brossy-wotsit.'

Mr Sparks head moved from side to side. 'You're lying,' he said. 'Why would you do that? Why would you lie to me? We can't be there, because we only just crossed the custard . . .'

'No, really. The old man brought us. He only just left. He says I can walk from here.'

'Help me up,' gasped Mr Sparks. 'I need to see.'

Owen placed a hand under the dummy's back and lifted him so that he could look out of the case. There was a brief silence, then: 'It's true!' gasped Mr Sparks. 'We really *are* here.' He made a strange croaking sound and his shoulders began to move up and down. Owen was astonished to see tears welling in his glass eyes and trickling down his pale face. Then he twisted his head to stare up at Owen.

'Dying,' he murmured.

'Oh, that's just because it's autumn,' said Owen.

'You don't understand,' whispered Mr Sparks. 'I fear we're too late. I think . . . I think I'm going . . .'

'No,' Owen assured him. 'No, you just have to hang on a bit longer. We're close now, really close.' He eased Mr Sparks back down into the case. 'You rest, I'll get you there.'

'But you don't understand, Owie! There's a . . . maggot . . . in my brain . . . I think . . . it's driving me insane . . . I want to scream, I want to shout! All my thoughts are . . . leaking out!'

'Please hang on!' shouted Owen. He lowered the lid and secured the catches. He stood up, grabbed the handle of the suitcase and stared along the narrow dirt track. There was no sign of life as far as he could see and the track seemed to go on forever. A long low groan came from the suitcase. Owen snatched in a deep breath, knowing that there was not a second to waste. Then he began to run.

* * *

Lemuel Nail strolled along the quayside, feeling rather pleased with himself. He'd finished early for the day and why not? He had twenty-five pounds in paper money hidden safely under his mattress and his plans for the evening were to stroll down to the Mermaid Tavern and drink himself insensible, along with his usual bunch of cronies. Perhaps, for a change, he'd even stand them the odd drink. Just to show what a nice fellow he could be when he put his mind to it. But first, he needed to eat a decent meal, the better to soak up all that beer. He had earlier given his mother some money to buy the ingredients for a special dinner and tonight, for a change, it would be meat, not fish. A nice porterhouse steak was what he fancied and he had every reason to believe that this was what his mother would have waiting for him.

He came to the weathered door of her little quayside house and hesitated as he noticed something unusual. A big shiny black automobile was parked on the road outside the house, a Daimler, he thought, though he was no great expert on motorcars. Whatever it was, it must have cost the owner a pretty penny. He paused for a moment to peer in at the driver's window, telling himself that he'd have to do a lot more illicit trips across the English Channel to earn enough to buy something like that. Still, he shouldn't grumble, he was doing far better than most of his friends, who were still back at the dockside, gutting fish for a living. He turned away, walked to the door and pushed it open.

Mother never locked her door, preferring to allow her few friends to pop in whenever they felt like it.

Mr Nail had expected to be greeted by the aroma of his mother's plain but satisfying cooking, but he was disappointed to smell nothing more than the usual faint odours of paraffin and dirt. The house was also unnaturally quiet.

'Mother?' he asked. There was no answer. He walked along the narrow hallway and pushed open the door to the tiny sitting room. Mother was there, sitting in her wheelchair in her usual place at the table, but she was not alone. Two men were with her. One sat in a wooden chair beside her, a beefy arm around her shoulders, as though he was an old friend, but he didn't seem in the least bit friendly. Mother's face was a frozen mask of pure terror. She was looking at Nail with a pleading expression in her eyes. The other man, a tall thin fellow with long curly hair, sat in an armchair, a short distance away from the others. He was smiling dangerously at Mr Nail, and the fisherman couldn't help notice that in one gloved hand, he was holding a gun.

'Lemuel,' he said, in a voice that was as smooth and calm as warm oil. 'Here you are at last. We were wondering what had happened to you.'

Mr Nail took an urgent step towards his mother, but as he did so the thin man cocked the hammer of the gun with an audible click, so he took a step back and lifted his hands to show that they were empty. 'What's this all about?' he croaked, though he already knew. Of course he did.

'It has come to our attention,' said the thin man, 'that you took a passenger out on the sea a couple of nights ago. Midnight, I believe. A young boy carrying a leather suitcase.'

Mr Nail licked his lips. 'What of it?' he asked.

The thin man's smile deepened. 'It's of interest to me,' he said. 'Particularly, what the boy was carrying *in* the suitcase. I wonder, would you know what that was?'

Mr Nail shrugged. 'Clothes, I expect.'

There was a long silence while the thin man gazed at him in silent accusation. 'Let's be clear on this,' he said at last. 'We've just spent the last hour or so getting acquainted with your charming mother . . .' He paused to direct that venomous smile in her direction. 'If you want something bad to happen to her, Lemuel, please *do* keep on lying to me. If on the other hand, you would prefer to keep her exactly as she is now, then let me explain what you need to do.' He leaned forward in his seat. 'You will tell me everything you know about the boy and the creature that he carries in that case. And I do mean *everything*. Every last little detail, even things that you might think are of no importance. Then you will tell me where you took the boy and his wooden companion and finally, you will take me and my associate to the very same spot where you last saw them. Do you understand?'

'But that . . . that's France. I took them across the channel.'

The two strangers exchanged glances.

'Heading back to where he came from?' suggested the heavyset man, who sounded like a Londoner.

'It would seem so,' said the thin man. 'But of course, that makes perfect sense. When we went back to speak to the orderly at the asylum, he said he thought the dummy had been damaged.' He turned back to glare at Nail. 'Your boat is seaworthy?' he asked.

'Well . . . yes, but . . . that's quite a trip, you know. And there are expenses . . . getting hold of the petrol isn't easy. Costs an arm and a leg.'

'That doesn't matter,' said the thin man. 'I don't expect you to work for nothing. I suppose your last passengers had to pay you for your services. I will of course match the fee they paid.'

'But sir, that was . . . that was thirty-five pounds!' Nail just couldn't help himself. He had to try and improve on his previous trip. It was his instinct to do so and he'd just gone along with it. But instantly he sensed his mistake.

There was another long silence. Then the thin man shook his head. He looked disappointed. He turned and pointed the gun in the direction of Nail's mother, as if taking aim.

'*Twenty*-five!' shouted Nail hastily. 'I'm sorry, I made a mistake. They . . . they paid me twenty-five pounds. Please, sir, don't hurt her!'

The thin man looked doubtful but after a few moments, he lowered the gun. 'Now,' he said, 'I can see you're telling the truth. Don't ever try to lie to me, Lemuel. Because I can read you like a book. Furthermore, I would suggest that you rather overcharged your last passengers, probably because you knew that they were desperate. So, I propose to pay you ten pounds for the trip. How does that sound?'

'Very good, sir, thank you, sir!'

'Excellent. Well, Lemuel, we're going to set off tonight,

once we've laid in a few provisions, but before we do, you are going to tell me everything you know about Mr Sparks and his new companion. And, should you even try and deviate from the absolute truth for one split second, believe me, I will know instantly and my associate, Mr Wilkins, will ensure that you regret doing so for the rest of your life. Do I make myself clear?'

'Absolutely,' said Mr Nail.

'Jolly good. Well, in your own time then?'

Mr Nail nodded. He took a deep breath. And then he began to talk.

15

Home Run

Owen ran frantically along the dirt track, his eyes straining to spot some sign of habitation. As he ran, the golden leaves of autumn fell all around him, as though the entire world was dying. On either side of the narrow track the trees towered above him. They seemed to be crowding in, their jagged, half-naked branches clawing at the sky. When he'd first started running, there'd been the occasional low groan of pain from the suitcase, but now everything was ominously silent. He was just beginning to think that it really was too late, when the track took a long slow curve to the left and, up ahead of him, seemingly looming out of the forest itself, was the cottage. It was exactly as it had looked in his dream – low, white-painted walls, a thatched roof and a stubby chimney, from which a column of grey smoke rose. It was like something out of a fairy tale and Owen knew in an instant that this had to be the place.

He didn't slow down. He was almost out of breath now, his heart thudding like a drum in his chest, but he crossed the space like a champion sprinter and lurched to a halt, gasping for breath, in front of the plain wooden door. Above it, a small elegantly carved sign announced a name. *G. Lacombe.* The surname struck a chord with Owen. The story that Mr Sparks had told him on the trawler, hadn't there been a Lacombe in that? Wasn't it the name of Mr Sparks' original owner? But there was no time to think about that now. A bell pull hung in front of the door, attached to a length of chain and Owen yanked it repeatedly, the sound clamouring in the silence, but nobody came to answer the call. Growing impatient, he tried the handle of the door. It turned easily and swung open on well-oiled hinges. Owen stepped inside and stood looking uncertainly around.

It was clear he had come to the right place. He was standing in what looked like a toyshop, with a simple wooden counter directly in front of him. On the counter and ranged on shelves all around the room, were wooden toys of every description. Puppets, dolls, automobiles, trains, biplanes, Jack-in-the-boxes, tops, hoops, castles, dolls' houses and much, much more, all of them beautifully crafted and painted in a profusion of bright shiny colours that thrilled the soul and dazzled the eye. They were a bit young for Owen, though in different circumstances he would have happily browsed here for hours, admiring the craftsmanship, but he was desperate and knew he had already wasted too much time. 'Hello?' he shouted. 'Is there anybody here?' His voice seemed to echo in the enclosed space.

He listened intently. At first he heard nothing but the slow, steady ticking of an unseen clock. Then he thought he heard the sounds of movement somewhere beyond this room, the slow, measured creaking of footsteps on floor-boards. Owen held his breath. Suddenly, with a harsh click that nearly made him jump out of his skin, a door behind the counter opened and a man stepped into the room. He stared at Owen for a moment, looking vaguely surprised. Then he smiled.

He was a big fellow, probably in his late fifties, Owen thought, but it was hard to be sure. He had a genial, red-cheeked face that was fringed with a scruffy beard, and his straight black hair was long and just as unkempt. He was dressed in khaki overalls, the front of which were liberally stained with streaks of different coloured paint. '*Bonjour*,' he said. '*Excusez-moi, mais je ne—*'

'I'm sorry,' interrupted Owen. 'I'm sorry, but . . . I don't speak French. Do you speak any English?' He stepped quickly up to the counter and swung the case up onto it.

The man nodded. 'Yes, of course, a little.' He regarded the case warily. 'What is this you have brought me?'

For answer, Owen unlatched the lid and flung it open. The man stared down at the contents in amazement. 'Charles,' he whispered.

Mr Sparks stirred slightly as though responding to the voice. His eyes flickered and then creaked open. 'Gerard,' he whispered. 'Long time . . . no see. And it's Charlie now . . . you know that.' He gave a low groan. The eyes closed again and he lay still.

Gerard looked at Owen accusingly. 'But what has happened?' he asked. He pointed a big index finger at the stained bandage around the dummy's head. 'Did you do this?'

'No! No, it was somebody else. It was . . . an accident. He had a fall. Cracked open his head. He said I had to bring him here.'

The man looked dismayed. He seemed to think for a moment, then reached into the case and swung Mr Sparks up into his powerful arms. He turned and headed for the

door through which he had just entered. He didn't invite
Owen to follow him, but the boy walked around the
counter and went after him anyway. Now they were in a
small workshop, a place that smelled of the delicious scent
of freshly carved wood. Shavings crunched like autumn
leaves under Owen's feet and from the walls hung tools
of every description – saws, chisels, hammers, planes.
From the rafters hung a selection of wooden toys in various
stages of construction. Gerard hurried over to a bench
on which rested a half-finished model yacht, a beautiful
thing, but he swept it aside as though it was a piece of
junk and laid Mr Sparks down in its place. He began to
undo the bandage around the dummy's head, his big fingers
working with quick precision. 'When did this happen?'
he asked.

'Umm . . .' Owen found it was difficult to work it out.
So much had happened since then. 'It must have been four
. . . maybe five days ago? We were in Llandudno . . .'

'Where?'

'It's in Wales. Er . . . *Le Pays De Galles*, I think you
call it? Mr Schilling turned up at my aunt's hotel and—'

'Where *is* Otto?'

'He . . . er . . .' Owen realised you were supposed to

break such news gently, but there seemed to be no other way than to put it bluntly. 'He died.'

Gerard stopped for a moment as the words registered with him. 'Oh no,' he said, shaking his head. 'How . . . how did he . . . ?'

'He was old,' said Owen, as though that was explanation enough. 'I'm sorry,' he added.

Gerard shook his head. He clearly wanted to ask more, but must have decided that he had no time to waste. He went back to unwinding the bandage. The last bit came away revealing a dressing that was soaked with grey matter and Gerard muttered something under his breath.

'Is it bad?' whispered Owen.

'Bad enough,' said Gerard. Mr Sparks began to stir under his hands, as though fresh pain had hit him and Gerard leaned forward and whispered a sequence of words into his ear. He immediately settled and his eyes closed again. Owen was reminded of the way Mr Sparks had put Otto to sleep that time. What was it he called it? Mesmerism.

'He'll sleep now,' said Gerard. He looked towards the corner of the workshop, where something lay covered by a grubby tarpaulin. He left Owen where he was and walked over to it, then pulled back the sheet, to reveal some oddly shaped offcuts of gnarled wood. He crouched down and rooted through the pieces as though looking for something in particular. Finally he selected a smallish chunk and carried it back to the workbench.

'Is that the special wood?' asked Owen. 'From Merlin's tree?'

Gerard looked at him in surprise. 'How do you know about the tree?' he asked.

'Charlie told me. On the boat, coming over. He told me a story about Lucien Lacombe and Charles.' He looked at Gerard, remembering the wooden plate over the door of the shop. 'Lacombe,' he said. 'You have the same name.'

Gerard nodded. 'Yes. Lucien's brother, Michel, was my er . . . big, big, big grandpapa.'

'I think you mean . . . great?' Owen corrected him.

'Yes, perhaps.' Gerard placed the piece of wood in a vice at one end of the bench and tightened it. 'I used to speak the English better but now I am somewhat rusted?' He looked again at Mr Sparks and pointed to the strangely coloured crack in his head. 'Putty?' he muttered.

'It was his idea,' insisted Owen. 'I only did what he told me.'

'You probably saved his life,' said Gerard. 'But I am

going to have the demon of a job getting this out without removing . . .' He waved a hand, unsure of how to say what he wanted. He pointed at the grey stain on the bandage. 'We will just have to hope that not too much is lost.'

'He's been saying strange things,' said Owen. 'Getting the wrong words. Forgetting stuff.'

Gerard nodded. 'I guess that makes sense,' he said. He went over to a wall and selected a sharp-bladed plane. He came back to the piece of wood and began to push the blade expertly across it, taking off slices of the rough brown bark to reveal the clean smooth wood beneath. Owen watched, entranced. He saw that Gerard was expertly working the wood into a curve and realised that he was shaping it to match the curve of Mr Sparks' forehead. Gerard paused for a moment and looked at Owen.

'If this . . . bores you . . .' He pointed to another door at the back of the workshop. 'There is a kitchen through there. You can make coffee . . . eat food?'

Owen shook his head. 'If it's all the same to you, sir, I'd rather watch.'

Gerard grunted. 'Suit yourself,' he said. He went on with his work. After a little while, he had a smooth, curved piece of wood. Now he set down the plane and went over to another worktop, where he selected some small metal tools, with different-shaped hooks and points on them. 'Now for the tricky bit,' he said. He selected a hook-shaped tool and, leaning over Mr Sparks, he started working it carefully into the mud-coloured seam of dried putty. When he found purchase, he pulled gently back and eased out a small chunk. He had a clean cloth ready to pat back any grey stuff that threatened to leak out. He worked carefully, methodically, going from top to bottom of the opening, until he'd removed all the filler. Within, Owen could see a wet pulsing grey substance.

'What *is* that?' he whispered.

Gerard shrugged. 'I suppose you would call it his *cerveau*?' He registered Owen's puzzled look and struggled to find the right word. 'His . . . brain.'

'He has a brain?'

'I do not know what else you would call this.' Gerard did a last careful scrape around the edges of the opening and then wiped them clean with the cloth. Now he picked up the piece of wood he'd planed and tried it in position. There was still a little more work to be done. He took a pencil from the bench and drew some faint lines along the edges of the piece, indicating where more wood needed to be removed. He secured the wood in the vice and after choosing a smaller plane, went to work again. 'So, how did you come to be with Charles . . . with Charlie?' he asked.

'Well . . . that's hard to say. He was at the hotel, see, and . . . we just got talking. He told me that Mr Schilling was ill and that it was slowing the two of them down. Then he said that I should call for him the next morning and take him away from there because people were after him. I . . . didn't want to do it but somehow, I sort of couldn't help myself.'

Gerard sighed, shook his head. 'That sounds about right,' he said. He looked at the dummy lying in front of him and waved an admonishing finger. 'Oh Charlie, *tu es très mauvais*.' He continued with his work. 'And Otto?' he asked. 'You said he died?'

Owen nodded.

'And you just . . . left him there?'

'Well, yes. It had only just happened, you see, that same night.'

Gerard stopped working and looked at him. 'And how exactly did he die?' he asked and his expression was grave.

'In his sleep,' said Owen. 'He must have been worse than he looked.'

Gerard frowned. For a moment, he seemed deeply troubled. He muttered something under his breath. Then he shook his head and removed the piece of wood from the vice. He tried it in position, then put it back and shaved a fraction more off one edge. When it was almost exactly right, he went and got a sheet of sandpaper and started gently rubbing the edges of it. 'Maybe you're right,' he said. 'Otto had been with Charlie for many years. He was certainly old.' His hands moved with practised skill, smoothing the edges of the wood. 'So now, Charlie has chosen you?' he asked. 'To be his . . . operator.'

'Is that what I am?' Owen thought for a moment. 'Yes, I suppose he has.' Now that he thought of it, it was the only description that fitted. 'But there have been others? Before Otto, I mean? Charlie told me a story about a boy that drowned and he said that it happened in the seventeen hundreds, but . . . well, that can't be right, can it? That's hundreds of years ago.'

Gerard didn't pause in his work. Now the curved wedge of wood was almost a perfect fit. It needed just a touch more sanding. 'There have been, I think, six others since Lucien, who was the first. People in different countries around the world. Some lasted a long time, others only a month or so. Otto was in his twenties when he began. And this . . .' Gerard waved a hand over the still figure beneath him. 'This is only the third time in my life that I have seen Charles . . . Charlie . . . whatever he calls himself now. He has had many names, but to me, always, he is Charles.' He laughed bitterly. 'He comes here only when he is in trouble.'

'And . . . he really is as old as he says?'

Gerard nodded. 'The first time I saw him, I was in my teens – I had only just begun to work here with my papa. It was a small problem, that time. A broken elbow. We fixed that together, my papa and me. I remember him saying that I would need to learn how to fix Charles, because he would be back again some day. Like the expression you have in your country. The bad penny that always turns up? The next time, I was, I think, forty years old. Again, not a big job. His leg joints were wearing out, they needed replacing.' He pointed into the corner of the room. 'Always, it has to be this wood. But what has happened now . . .' He blew air out from between pursed lips. 'This is serious, I think. Maybe I cannot fix him this time.'

'Oh, but you have to!' said Owen urgently. 'He's . . . he's all I've got now.'

Gerard looked puzzled. 'What about your parents?' he asked.

'My father was killed in the War,' said Owen bleakly. 'And my mother . . . she . . . she's very ill. She hardly knows who I am.'

'So who looks after you? You said something about a hotel?'

'Yes. It belongs to my aunt Gwen. She . . . she's not a nice person. And when Charlie said we should run away from there, I just went along with him.' Owen gazed down at Charlie. 'Now I . . . kind of feel responsible for him,' he said.

Gerard sighed. 'So many people want him to live, don't they?' he observed. 'A lot of people like Charles. Apart from those who hate him, and believe me there are many of those too. He has done bad things, I think. Things you would not forgive any ordinary man. And for all that you care about him, I bet he has not been particularly nice to you, eh? I bet he has made you dance to his tune.'

Owen frowned. 'I suppose he has,' he admitted. 'But for all that . . . I would hate anything bad to happen to him. I feel like he's depending on me now.'

Gerard shrugged his big shoulders. 'Of course, I will try

to save him,' he said. 'It's what I do. But you should be prepared for the worst.'

He slotted the wedge into the opening in Mr Sparks' head and Owen could see that now that with a little pressure applied, it would fit in there perfectly. 'How did you learn to work wood like that?' he asked.

'From my father, of course, who learned from his father before him. It is a role you are born into. Oh, in my youth, I lived in London for a time. It was where I learned to speak your language even though now I am not so good, I think, as I was. I enjoyed my time there, but . . . I somehow knew I would always come back here. That it was waiting for me. When my father was near the end, he sent for me and I took his place. It's what we Lacombes do.' He set the wedge down on the workbench. '*Bien*,' he said. 'Now we need a little *colle* . . . what is the English word? Ah yes. Glue.' He went over to another bench and returned with a pot and a fine brush. He unscrewed the lid of the pot, slipped in the head of the brush and carefully smeared the edges of the wedge with white goo. Once he'd done that, he pushed it back into position, having to use just a little effort to get it properly aligned. 'Now for the difficult bit,' he said. He opened the vice as wide it would go and repositioned

Mr Sparks so that his head was lying between the jaws. Then slowly, as gently as he could, he tightened the vice until a little glue oozed from the cracks in the fit.

'Do you *have* to do that?' asked Owen apprehensively.

'I'm afraid so,' said Gerard. He mopped away the residue with a cloth and smiled encouragingly. 'We have to be sure that it is completely sealed,' he said. '*Voila*.' He stepped back from the bench and studied his handiwork, his hands on his hips. 'Now we can only wait,' he said. 'He needs to rest for a while.' He studied Owen thoughtfully. 'You must be tired and hungry after your long trip,' he said. 'Come, I will get you something to eat.'

Owen nodded. Now that he thought about it, he *was* hungry. He followed Gerard to the door, but paused to look back at the little figure lying on the bench. 'He *will* be all right, won't he?' he murmured.

'We will see,' said Gerard. He lifted a hand to show Owen that he had two fingers crossed. Then he opened the door and led Owen into the kitchen.

16

Supper

Owen sat at the pine table in Gerard's simple kitchen and devoured a bowl of earthy meat stew, served with hunks of wholemeal bread. It was getting dark now and Gerard had lit a couple of hurricane lamps, which gave the small room a warm, cosy feel. Until the food was placed in front of him, Owen hadn't realised exactly how ravenous he was. On the other side of the table, Gerard sat with his own meal, eating more sedately and sipping at a glass of red wine. 'You *were* hungry,' he said.

Owen nodded, his mouth too full for the moment to make a reply. He glanced around the kitchen as he ate, taking in the small black wood-burning stove, the rough-plastered walls, the battered-looking wooden dresser and cupboards. Gerard was clearly a skilled toymaker but it didn't seem to be keeping him in a life of luxury. He seemed to have read Owen's mind, when he said, 'It is not much of a place, but it suits me.'

Owen swallowed down the last of his stew. 'Oh no, it's nice,' he said. 'A bit off the beaten track . . .'

Gerard looked puzzled. 'I do not understand this phrase,' he said. 'Off the . . . track?'

'I mean, you're . . . a long way from a town.'

'Ah, *oui*. Well, this is where the shop has always been. Lucky for me that all those hundreds of years back, Lucien bought the place, so I can live here rent-free. But of course, it gets harder to make the ends meet . . . is this how you say it? Make the ends meet?'

Owen nodded. He pushed a hunk of bread around the bottom of his bowl, to mop up the gravy.

'You would like more *lapin*?' asked Gerard.

'*Lapin*?' Owen wasn't familiar with the word.

Gerard had to think for a moment to remember the English word. 'Rabbit,' he said, pointing to the bowl. 'I caught that rascal in a snare only yesterday.'

'Ah . . .' Owen dreaded to think what Aunt Gwen would say if she heard he was eating rabbit. She had always maintained that it was 'for peasants'. But somehow, defying Aunt Gwen only made it seem more enjoyable.

'Yes, please,' he said. 'It's delicious.'

Gerard took Owen's empty bowl and walked over to a large casserole that stood on the wood burner. He spooned a generous dollop of stew into the bowl and carried it back.

'Thank you,' said Owen. He started on his second helping, eating at a more leisurely pace now that his initial pangs were satisfied. 'So,' he said, between mouthfuls, 'this same shop has been here since . . . the seventeen hundreds?'

'*Oui*. It does sound fantastic when you say it like that. Maybe because it is so remote, nobody takes much notice of us.' He took another gulp of his wine. 'It has been a long time, but I fear it is coming to an end.'

Owen frowned. 'What makes you say that?'

Gerard shrugged. 'There is nobody to take over from me when I am gone. I never married, never had children. I am unique amongst the Lacombes in that respect. I suppose I just never met anybody I could get on with enough to live with them for the rest of my life.'

'But . . . couldn't you find a . . . what do they call it? An apprentice or something?'

Gerard chuckled. 'I fear that wooden toys are also coming to an end. They already belong to another time. I went to a toy fair in Paris a couple of months ago and I saw clock-

201

work metal toys there. You wind them with the key and they do amazing things. They walk, they jump, they dance! I thought to myself, Gerard, that's the future.'

Owen scoffed. 'I think what Mr Sparks can do is more amazing than any clockwork toy!' he said.

'True enough. But, Mr Sparks, as you call him, he is the one in a million. I cannot make another one like him. Lucien Lacombe made him and nobody is really sure how *he* did it. I would be willing to bet that if he came back from the dead, he would not be able to repeat the trick. And I'll be honest with you. It is not something that *should* be repeated.'

'Why not?'

'Because Charles is the product of a man's desperation. Think about it! A dead child, an enchanted tree and a lightning storm. He did not come from happy beginnings. And he does not bring happiness to those who know him. You met Otto Schilling. Did he seem like a happy man to you?'

'Well, no,' admitted Owen. 'He seemed . . . nice though.'

'When you are twelve years old, *everyone* seems nice. But he was a haunted soul. He was still a young man when I first met him and let me tell you . . .' He paused for a moment. 'I'm sorry, I still do not know your name,' he said.

'It's Owen. Owen Dyer.'

'Well, Owen, Otto was a happier man in those days. Please don't think I am criticising but . . . you need to think about what you are getting yourself into.'

This remark puzzled Owen. 'What do you mean?' he asked.

Gerard took another sip of wine. 'I'm saying that when Charlie came into your life, I don't expect he *asked* you if you wanted to join with him, did he? I bet he just told you what was going to happen. You did not have any real choice in this matter.' He thought for a moment. 'Let me ask you this, were you happy where you were?'

'Well, no,' admitted Owen. 'It was a horrible place. My aunt . . . she . . . she treated me like a slave.'

'Well, there you are. That's how it is with Charles. Always, he finds the people who are weak, unhappy, people that he knows he can bend to his will. It was the same with Otto when they first met. As you say, he was a nice enough man, but he had no ambitions. He had been disappointed in a romance, I think, a woman he wanted to marry who turned him down. He didn't know where he

203

was headed. Not until Charlie came along and made up his mind for him.'

Owen frowned. 'Are you saying that Mr Sparks isn't good for me?'

'I'm saying that people need to make their own decisions.' He made a sound of exasperation. 'I don't know why I am telling you this,' he added. 'I'm as bad as any of them. He has us all dancing to his tune, doesn't he? If I can see what is wrong, how is it I'm still here in this lonely place waiting for the odd time when he shows up needing help? You tell me that!'

Owen considered the question for a moment. 'Perhaps because you *care* about him too?' he suggested.

'That may be so, but let me ask you this. Do you think he cares about me? You? About anyone but himself?'

'Well . . .'

'Think about this, Owen! Think how long he has existed. He is a survivor and to survive in the way he has, he must be selfish. He uses people like us, in order to go on surviving, day by day. And when we have outlived our usefulness, what happens to us then, eh?'

'I don't know what you mean.'

'Well, think about it for a moment. Think about Otto.

Did Charles hesitate to leave him and go away with you?'

Owen frowned. 'Well, no,' he said. 'But . . . what else could he do? Otto was dead and . . . and there were people after them, so . . .'

'That is reason enough to abandon somebody?'

'Well, he didn't feel *good* about it. He told me that. And . . . he said that it was what Otto wanted.'

'Oh, really? And Charles didn't think twice about leaving his body in that hotel.'

'He hated to do it. After all, they were *friends*.'

'You think so? Did you not hear the way they spoke to each other?'

'Well, perhaps they did bicker a bit.'

Gerard laughed at that. 'The way I remember it, they were at each other's throats most of the time.'

'All right, but . . . you see, Mr Sparks is so helpless, and . . .'

Gerard laughed at this. 'That is what he would have you believe,' he said. 'But he has made a career of seeming helpless, getting others to do all the hard work for him. Trust me, he's not as feeble as he pretends.'

'You . . . you sound like you . . . *hate* him,' said Owen.

Gerard shook his head. 'It's not that,' he said. 'If I truly hated him, when I had his head in that vice, I'd just have carried on tightening and tightening it until . . .' He stared into the middle distance for a moment as though picturing himself doing it. 'But how could I ever do such a thing to him? After all is said and done, he is family.'

'Family?' Owen questioned the word automatically, but somehow it felt like the only one that made any sense.

'Yes. He was Lucien's son, before he became . . . whatever it is he is now. So, *hate* is the wrong word, Owen. I do not hate him. But I do not much *like* what he does to the people who care for him. People like you and me.'

Owen pushed his empty bowl aside. Now that his stomach was full, a powerful tiredness was creeping steadily up on him. But there was still one more question he needed to ask before he slept. 'Back in Wales,' he said. 'Those people who were chasing us.'

'Oh yes?'

'Two men. I thought they were police but Mr Sparks said they were just . . . bad men. Do you have any idea who they were?'

Gerard shook his head. 'I cannot say. But there have always been people who want to get their hands on Charles. People who want to find out what he is, how he works. People who believe that he is . . . what would you call it? An . . . aberration. Something that goes against nature. Something . . . evil.'

'He's not evil,' protested Owen. 'Just a bit . . . mischievous.'

Gerard smiled despite himself. 'Ah, is that what he is? I always wondered.'

Gerard sighed. He thought for a moment. 'And these men who were chasing you? Where are they now?'

'I think we managed to give them the slip,' said Owen. 'Back in Wales.'

'Let us hope so,' said Gerard. He studied Owen for a moment, no doubt noticing his drooping eyelids. 'You're tired,' he said. He gestured to another doorway off the kitchen. 'Why don't you stretch yourself out on my bunk?' he suggested. 'I will need to keep an eye on our patient through the night.' He got up from his seat and fetched a candle set into a tin holder. 'You'll need this,' he said. He took a box of matches from his pocket and lit the candle, then handed it to Owen. 'Make sure you blow it out before you go to sleep,' Gerard warned him. 'A lighted candle can be dangerous.'

Owen nodded gratefully. 'Thank you,' he said. He got up from the table and started towards the door, but hesitated and looked back as another thought occurred to him. 'What you said before . . . about tightening that vice around Mr Sparks' head. You . . . wouldn't do that, would you?'

Gerard laughed. 'No,' he said. 'It's tempting but I will do my best to resist.' He smiled. 'Tell me Owen, what is it about Charles that makes you want to look after him?'

Owen thought for a moment. 'I suppose because he's like me,' he said.

Gerard frowned. 'Like you?' he murmured. 'How?'

'He's all alone in the world,' said Owen. He doesn't have anybody else to look out for him.'

Gerard nodded. 'Goodnight, Owen,' he said.

'Goodnight.' Owen went through the doorway and found himself in a tiny white-painted room. In one corner, there was a rough-looking single bed and beside it, a small table. He carried the candle across to the table and set it down. Then he sat on the bed, kicked off his shoes and laid himself on top of the blankets. He turned on his side and noticed a low bookcase with a selection of titles ranged on the shelves. Owen reached out and selected a book at random. He examined the cover illustration, which depicted a comical-looking wooden puppet walking along a cobbled street. He wore odd-looking bib-fronted shorts and a shapeless hat with a colourful feather stuck in it. The title was familiar to him from primary school, though he had never actually read the book. *Pinocchio*. Underneath this was a name, which Owen presumed, must be the writer. *Carlo Collodi*. Owen opened the book and glanced at a sample page but it was written in French, so he returned it to the bookcase, blew out the candle and closed his eyes. He lay there, sleep closing steadily on him but even as he began to drift away, a last thought crossed his mind. Gerard had seemed worried about the two men that had chased after them back in Wales. But they could have no idea where Mr Sparks was now . . . could they?

The thought sank like a stone into a calm pool of water and Owen went down with it, without putting up a fight. He slept a deep, dreamless sleep.

The trawler chugged slowly up to the jetty, cutting through the calm moonlit water and this time, Mr Nail took the trouble to grab hold of a mooring rope and loop it around a post. The two men stood on the deck, holding their suitcases, looking far from impressed with their destination.

'You're sure this is the right place, Lemuel?' murmured the thin man, who Mr Nail had already learned to have a healthy respect for. 'This looks like the back end of nowhere.'

'Oh yes, sir,' said Mr Nail. 'Only place I've ever dropped him off.' He pointed to the track at the end of the jetty. 'I've never actually seen it, but Sparks said something about there being a little town at the end of that path. I heard him promising the boy breakfast at some kind of café.'

'Sounds good to me,' said the big man. 'Me belly thinks me throat's been cut.' He stepped clumsily off the boat and onto the pier, using the suitcase for balance, but the thin man hesitated a moment as though there was something he'd forgotten to do. He reached into his pocket and took out a plain white envelope. 'Your fee,' he told Mr Nail and held it out. But as Mr Nail reached for it, he pulled it away again. 'A couple of things before I pay you,' he said. 'You will forget that you brought us here.'

'Er . . . yes, sir, whatever you say, sir.'

'You will speak of it to nobody. And let me assure you that if for any reason you've brought us here on a wild-goose chase, I will come straight back to Portsmouth, by the quickest route possible. I will seek out you and your charming mother and I will ensure that neither of you are ever in a position to speak of it again. Understood?'

Nail nodded grimly and Quinn finally handed him the

envelope. He picked up his suitcase and stepped onto the jetty. Then he turned back. 'One last thing,' he said.

'What's that?' asked Nail.

'When you get home, for pity's sake have a bath. You smell like a barrel of smoked mackerel.' With that he strode off along the path and his companion followed. After a short distance they had vanished into the night.

Mr Nail scowled. 'And goodnight to you,' he growled. He unhitched the rope and headed back to the wheelhouse, but on the way he stopped for a moment and sniffed at his own armpit. Maybe, he decided, the thin man had a point.

He continued on into the wheelhouse, opened up the throttle and headed back out to sea, thinking that humble as his home was, he couldn't wait to be there again.

17

Omens

Owen opened his eyes and lay on his side in the unfamiliar bed, vaguely aware that something had woken him. A noise. A creaking sound. His eyes focused and he saw that the door of his room was slowly opening. Beyond it was a deep, unfathomable blackness.

He waited, hardly daring to breathe. Then a familiar figure loomed out of the darkness and stepped into the room. Aunt Gwen. She came and stood over Owen, frowning down at him with evident displeasure, her lips pursed into a tiny dot of disapproval. He noticed with a jolt of apprehension that she had one arm held behind her back.

'The trouble I've had finding you,' she said. 'You've led me a merry dance, Owen Dyer.'

Owen opened his mouth to make some excuse but found that he had no words in him. His tongue seemed to be momentarily stuck to the roof of his mouth. He could only lie there, staring helplessly up at her.

'I *did* warn you,' said Aunt Gwen. 'I told you what would happen if you disobeyed me again. I said there'd be *consequences*.'

The arm came out from behind her back and he saw that it was clutching the familiar length of bamboo cane.

He was aware of beads of sweat popping on his brow and trickling down his face. 'Please,' he managed to whisper. 'Don't. I . . . promise I'll be good.'

Aunt Gwen was smiling but there was no warmth in it. 'Good?' she sneered. 'You wouldn't know the meaning of the word, boy. I always said you'd turn out just like your mother. Good for nothing.'

Just then, Owen became aware of movement at the open doorway – a small, pink-faced figure with red hair was crouched there, smiling malevolently up at Aunt Gwen, as if appraising her. Owen opened his mouth to say something but at that same moment, Charlie lifted his other hand and raised a finger to his lips. Then he winked.

'Well, come on,' said Aunt Gwen, still looking impatiently at Owen. 'What are you waiting for? Get up and take your punishment.'

'Please,' whispered Owen. 'Please . . . don't . . .'

That was as far as he got because at that moment, Charlie gave a wild shriek and sprang through the open doorway, moving in a lithe, feral way that Owen had thought him incapable of. He seemed as though he had springs in the heels of his shoes, moving upwards and forwards across the space and landing with a thud against Aunt Gwen's back. Owen saw her eyes widen in surprise and then her mouth opened in a scream of agony as Charlie's white-gloved hands closed around her throat. Aunt Gwen dropped the cane and lifted her arms to try and push her assailant away, but he was clinging tightly onto her, cackling dementedly as he did so. She lost her footing and fell forward onto the bed, her features arranged in an expression of pure agony.

'Help me!' she croaked. 'Owen, please help me!'

He couldn't move. He lay there, with Aunt Gwen's dead weight pinning him to the bed. He saw that now Mr Sparks was peeping over her shoulder, grinning insanely. He said in that sly, wheedling voice, 'Isn't this what you wanted, Owie? Isn't this what you've been *praying* for?'

Owen sat up with a gasp to find himself alone in the unfamiliar bedroom. His face and neck were soaked with sweat and he had to look around to reassure himself that there really was nobody else there. His head was filled with a close-up image of Aunt Gwen's face as she'd screamed. It had seemed so real . . .

He sat for a moment, allowing his breathing to settle. He wondered how long he'd been asleep. There was no sign of a clock anywhere in the room, so after a few moments, he swung his legs off the bed, stood up and went to the closed door. He pushed it slightly open and peered into the room beyond, nervous that something horrible might be waiting on the other side of the door, ready to jump at him out of the gloom. But it was just the small kitchen he remembered from before and it was quite empty. He walked across it and tried the next door, the one that led to the workshop. It swung silently open.

Gerard was sitting slumped at the bench, over the still form of Mr Sparks. The room's single window showed the pale grey light of early morning. Owen went in and could see now that the big man was dozing, his bearded chin resting on his chest.

Owen coughed gently and that was enough to startle Gerard awake. He grunted, then gazed at Owen for a moment as though confused. After a few moments, he seemed to remember and nodded a bleary greeting. 'You slept well?'

Owen nodded. He didn't think he'd better mention the dream. He pointed to the sprawled figure on the workbench. 'Charlie?' he whispered.

Gerard frowned. He regarded the figure as though he'd forgotten all about him until now. Then he shrugged his shoulders. 'I suppose we will have to wake him some time,' he said. 'Let us see how he is.' He leaned forward and gently unscrewed the vice from around the dummy's head. Then he whispered the sequence of words into Mr Sparks' ear. For the longest time, there was no reaction whatsoever. Then one of the dummy's eyes creaked momentarily open, before snapping abruptly shut again. Owen moved closer to the bench.

'Mr Sparks?' he murmured. 'Charlie?'

This time, both eyes opened and they surveyed Owen with a flat, disinterested stare. 'Well, whoop-de-doo,' he said.

'Are you . . . are you feeling all right?' asked Owen.

'A . . . a . . . apple strudel,' said Mr Sparks.

Owen and Gerard exchanged worried looks. 'What is that supposed to mean?' asked Gerard.

'It means . . . I . . . you . . . not . . .' Mr Sparks closed his eyes for a moment as though trying to gather his thoughts. Then the eyes sprang open and the mouth assumed a manic grin. 'Apple strudel, what a treat! Get a portion, nice and sweet. Just the thing I like to eat.' The eyes quivered, the grin faded. He stared at Owen forlornly. 'Why did I wash that?' he asked. 'Why did I wash it in . . . vinegar?'

'You didn't . . . *wash* anything,' Owen assured him.

'Oh, you say that but you don't really . . . Do I . . . do I . . . do I *know* you?' asked Mr Sparks. 'Wait, aren't you Algernon Flip? I mean, Reginald Blink? Er . . . Sidney, Arthur, Prendergast, Archibald, Cuthbert, Benedict, Montmorency, Marmaduke Moggins?'

Owen could only stand and stare. 'Mr Sparks, what are you talking about? You're not making any kind of—'

'Mr Sparks? Mr Sparks? Who do you think you are, calling me that? How *dare* you call me that? What do you, why do you, when do you think . . . when do you think? When? Do? You? Think?'

Gerard leaned closer and whispered the sequence of words into the dummy's ear again. Mr Sparks' body went limp and his eyes slid shut.

'Why did you do that?' Owen asked Gerard. 'We need to—'

'We don't need to do anything,' Gerard assured him. 'Not yet. He has to rest more. It's dangerous to try things too early. He needs longer to heal.' He pushed himself up from the stool. 'Come,' he said. 'I'll make us some coffee. We'll try again later.'

'But . . . has he been like this *before*?'

Gerard sighed. 'No,' he admitted. 'Not that I've ever seen. But he's never been so badly injured before. I think it makes sense to give him more time.' He placed a hand on Owen's shoulder. 'We must be patient,' he said. 'Come on. Coffee. And then I think we'll get a little fresh air.'

They walked away from the cottage, heading along a track that led deeper into the forest. The sun was gathering strength now, sending rays of light filtering down though the canopy of autumn leaves. Owen looked back at the building, reluctant to abandon Mr Sparks in his hour of need.

'He has you well trained,' observed Gerard, drily.

'I just . . . don't like leaving him on his own,' said Owen.

'I think it's the best thing we can do for him right now,' said Gerard. 'His head is . . .' He waved his hands in the air. '. . . all jumblied up?' he said. 'Is that what you say? Jumblied up?'

'Jumbled,' Owen corrected him. 'But he's alone. What if somebody came here looking for him?'

Gerard smiled. 'Not many people come here now,' he said. 'You are the first visitor I've had in weeks. I thought I'd show you the sights. That's what they used to call it in London, I think. The sights. Although in London, of course, it was the Houses of Parliament, Big Bill . . .'

'Big Ben?' suggested Owen. Gerard smiled.

'Yes,' he said. 'Big Ben. And Piccallily Surplus.'

Owen didn't bother to correct him on that one. They strolled on in silence for a while. They were moving deeper and deeper into the forest, the track becoming ever more narrow and winding as they walked. 'So . . . Charles . . . Charlie . . . he has told you about this place?' asked Gerard. He waved an arm to indicate the backdrop of red and gold trees all around them. 'About the Brocéliande?'

'Yes, a bit. He talked about it on the way here, on the boat. Well, he told it more like a story, really. But he was injured, so I wasn't sure how much was true and how much was made up.'

'This is one of those places,' said Gerard, 'where it is not possible to separate the truth from the fiction. It is . . . all the same thing. I thought perhaps you might like to

219

see the tree. You know, the one that Charlie came from?'

'It's still here?' gasped Owen. For some reason, he had thought that it would be long gone – that the gnarled hunks of wood in the corner of Gerard's workshop were all that remained of it.

'Oh yes, it is still alive. Trees last for many hundreds of years, you know, even thousands of years in some cases. Though I admit, this one has seen better times.'

Owen frowned. 'You believe it, then?' he asked. 'The story.'

'I have no choice. I am part of it.'

They passed a thick screen of bushes, and when they emerged on the far side of it, Owen saw, off to his right, a huge lake, the still water reflecting the trees that edged it. He turned his head to look in that direction and as they walked on, something else came into view . . . a high outcrop of rock, on the far side of the lake. It rose in a steep slope to a single shelf-like crag that overhung the edge of the water – and a shock of recognition went through Owen, making him stop in his tracks 'That's it,' he said, pointing. 'It has to be! The place where Charlie . . . I mean, Charles . . . the place where he dived in and broke his neck.'

Gerard turned to look and then he nodded. 'I believe

so,' he said. 'At least, it is where I have always thought it must have happened.'

'But that's . . . that's impossible,' cried Owen. 'That's like . . .'

'That's like reading *Pinocchio*,' said Gerard. 'And then finding the shop where Geppetto made him.'

They continued walking.

'I saw that book in your room,' said Owen. 'Do you keep it there because . . . because you think you're *like* Geppetto?'

'Of course. I am part of the man's family. Except that the family in my case is called Lacombe. But the story always makes me think of Charles. You see, part of his problem is, he believes he is a real boy.'

'He *is* real,' said Owen. 'He walks, talks . . . thinks . . .'

Gerard shook his head. 'Oh yes, he does all that. And he does it very well. And there is no doubt that, yes, somewhere back in time, he *was* a real boy. But now . . . now he is something that cannot be explained. He is . . . neither dead, nor alive. He is a monster.'

'No!' Owen reacted to the word. 'No, he's . . . he's just . . .'

Gerard shook his head. 'You see, you don't exactly know what he is. That's the problem. None of us do.' He seemed to ponder something for a moment. 'Owen,' he said. 'What will you do if he dies?'

'Dies?' Owen stared at the man, alarmed. 'Do you think he's going to?'

'Don't sound so surprised,' Gerard told him. 'We're all going to die one day. And many people would say that Charlie has already had more than his fair share of life.' He frowned. 'Let's say it *did* happen. Would you go back to how you were before you met him?'

'I don't know. I don't think so.'

'From what you've told me, it was not a good place.'

'No. It was horrible. Really bad.' Owen shook his head. 'But anyway, Charlie isn't going to die.'

Gerard seemed amused by this. 'You seem very sure of this.'

'There's something about him. What was it you called him last night? A survivor? I think he'll survive this too.'

'Well, let's hope so, eh?' Gerard stopped walking and nodded at something ahead of them. Owen had been concentrating on his own feet. Now he lifted his gaze and stared. The narrow path led to a tree – a gigantic tree. A great wide-trunked chestnut, its bark so pale that it was almost white against its darker brethren. It rose up from a collection of twisted roots that seemed to writhe around each other like a nest of intertwined serpents, and it was clear that it had once been lofty and imperious – but it was also evident that some mishap had recently befallen it. About twenty feet up, there was a great split in the trunk, an ugly jagged V-shape, as though a giant had hacked into it with an axe, causing the main body of the tree to almost split in two. Above this, there was very little in the way of branches, just broken black stumps. While most of its neighbours still had some of their autumn leaves, the Merlin tree's branches were completely bare.

'What happened to it?' asked Owen.

'Lightning happened,' said Gerard. 'About three months ago. I'm no expert, but I'd say the tree is dying.'

Owen moved closer. Now he could see that the branches were not entirely bare. Here and there, they were adorned with little items – strange, crudely made dolls, pieces of jewellery, bunches of withered flowers . . . all of them had been tied to the branches with lengths of twine. It was clear that some of the items were recent but others looked as though they had been there for many, many years.

'What are those things?' asked Owen.

Gerard shrugged. 'This tree has a local reputation,' he

said. 'People have been making sacrifices to it for centuries. Back in the old times, they made bigger ones. I have heard that farmers would kill a lamb and sprinkle the blood onto the roots to ensure a good harvest. These days, it is dolls and charms and whatever else people think will bring them luck.'

'And . . . does it work?'

'Who can say? I know the tree can make strange things happen, because I have seen the proof. The proof is back at the cottage lying on a bench. It shouldn't be alive but it is. So maybe the tree does have power. And maybe it works because people *believe* that it can. But I also think that not everything that comes from this tree is good. If you believe in magic, then you must believe in black magic, *oui*?'

Owen scowled. 'It sounds like you're trying to tell me that there's something evil about Mr Sparks.'

'I only say that the power that gave him life may not be a power of good.'

'But he's my friend.'

'Is he, Owen? Is he really? Or is he just using you. The way he uses everyone else who meets him?'

'He took me away from Aunt Gwen's hotel, a place I hated. He took me to see my mother, when nobody else would let me go. Even paid for a taxi to get there. And . . . it was my ma who injured him, you know?'

'Was it? I didn't know that.'

'Oh yes. I feel guilty about it. She . . . she didn't know what she was doing. She saw Charlie and she just seemed to go crazy. So it's kind of my fault that he's injured. And . . . he . . . he's been good to me. He's bought me meals . . . and he says he'll get me some new clothes the first chance he gets . . .'

'All things that he knows will make you feel like you owe him something. But that's not real friendship, Owen. You must realise that.'

They were close enough now for Owen to reach out an arm and touch his fingers against the ancient bark of the tree. He thought that he detected a low vibration in the wood, something that set his teeth on edge. He pulled his hand away and gazed around. He got the strangest feeling that the other trees were watching him, waiting to gauge his reaction.

'We should get back,' he said.

Gerard studied him. 'What is the big hurry?' he asked. 'I told you, the longer he rests, the better chance he has of recovering his mind.'

'I just want to get back,' Owen insisted. 'In case he wakes up and I'm not there.'

Gerard sighed. But he turned and began to retrace his steps along the path they had followed. Owen went with him, but as he walked, he experienced a strange sensation. The distinct feeling that danger wasn't far away and that it was steadily drawing closer.

18

The Inn

It was exactly where Mr Nail had said it would be, virtually the first building that Quinn and Wilkins encountered as they strolled into the outskirts of Erquy. It was still really early, the sun hardly above the horizon, but there was already a light on within and the aroma of fresh coffee spilling from the open doorway, so they went straight inside.

It was a small, gloomy place, rustic with dark wooden tables and far too many plants for Quinn's liking. The place had the lingering smell of grease and bad plumbing. Quinn ushered Wilkins to a table by the door and left the cases with him, then strolled over to the bar, where a thickset, middle-aged woman was half-heartedly wiping a damp cloth over the varnished wooden counter. She smiled welcomingly at Quinn as he approached, revealing two rows of teeth that would have kept a dental surgeon in constant employment for several months.

'*Bonjour, monsieur,*' she said.

'*Bonjour, madame.*' Quinn studied her for a moment, noting that she was wearing far too much makeup for a woman of her age and that her elaborately coiffed hair was dyed an improbable shade of red. He spoke to her in fluent French. 'Are we too early for breakfast?' he asked.

'No, not at all. What can I get for you?'

He ordered freshly baked croissants and coffee, realising how disappointed Wilkins would be that he hadn't asked for eggs and bacon, and taking a certain amount of pleasure in the thought. The woman moved to a doorway behind her and barked the order through to an unseen chef. Then she turned back to Quinn.

'It's very early,' she observed. 'Have you come far?'

'All the way from England,' he told her. 'Just to meet you.' He smiled charmingly.

'Oh, *monsieur*!' She rolled her eyes, which were framed by luxurious lashes that were caked with mascara.

'May I enquire if you work here every day?' he asked.

'Every day the Lord sends,' she assured him. 'Ever since I was a little girl.'

A very long time then, thought Quinn. But he maintained his smile.

'I wonder, *madame*, if you have seen a boy recently?'

'A boy?' She looked at him quizzically.

'Yes. An English boy of around twelve years of age. Travelling on his own with just a suitcase. I'm sure you'd remember seeing somebody like that. It would have been in the last few days . . .'

Her expression changed subtly and Quinn read her like an open book, just as he read everyone he met. Yes, she *had* seen the Dyer boy and she had thought it strange at the time, but Quinn sensed that she was reluctant to say anything about it now, just in case she got him into some kind of trouble . . .

He leaned over the counter and gave her a disarming look. 'Please don't worry,' he assured her, 'we're not the police and the boy isn't in any trouble . . . at least, not yet. He's run away from home, you see and his mother is naturally concerned about him. They had a silly argument and the boy packed a bag and ran away in the middle of the night. His mother has hired me and my partner to find him and fetch him back. She didn't want to involve the police, as I'm sure you can understand.' He made a big show of inhaling the smell of coffee issuing from the kitchen. 'Ah! Now that smells absolutely wonderful,' he told her.

He was lying. It actually smelled as though the percolator needed cleaning out, but he wanted to get into her good books.

She chuckled, enjoying his attention. 'Oh yes, it's the best coffee in town. Everyone says so. We have a very good supplier.' She arranged cups on a tray and filled an earthenware jug with milk from a container. 'There *was* a boy, actually. And I did think it was odd that he was on his own. He was travelling down to Paris to appear in some kind of variety show.'

'He . . . told you that?'

'Well, no, not exactly. As soon as he came in here, he got this dummy out of his case . . . you know, one of those talking creatures that are used by . . .' She waved a hand, unsure of the word.

'Ventriloquists?' suggested Quinn.

'Ah yes, that's the word I was looking for. So it was the dummy who told me they were going to Paris.' She smiled, recalling the moment. 'Now I come to think of it, the boy himself hardly said a word. English, you say? Who would believe it? His French accent was perfect! Anyway, he put on a little show for us. It was very funny. That dummy, what a character! The things he came out with!'

'There were others in the bar?'

She nodded. 'Oh yes, a few people came in while he was here. He got talking to each of them in turn . . . using the dummy, you understand, sort of like a little act he was doing and then of course, Henri came in and they got talking and he offered to give the boy a lift . . .'

'Henri?'

'Yes, just one of our regulars.'

'I see. So where did he take the boy?'

The woman shrugged her shoulders. 'I really couldn't say. Henri drives a delivery truck. He goes all over the place, sometimes as far as Paris . . .'

'Yes, but where was he going *that* day?'

'I'm sorry, *monsieur*, I really don't know.'

Quinn made a titanic effort to conceal his frustration. He smiled again. 'This . . . Henri, he'll be in today?'

'I don't know, *monsieur*. He calls by once or twice a week, depending where his work takes him. It varies, you know?'

'I see. Well, thank you, *madame*, you've been most helpful. If Henri should come in while we're here, would you be so kind as to introduce us?'

'Of course.' The door of the kitchen opened and a

surly-looking, moustachioed man appeared holding a plate of warm croissants. Quinn looked at him hopefully. 'Perhaps this gentleman might know where Henri was heading that day?' he ventured. But it soon became clear that the man, the woman's husband, didn't know very much at all. Indeed, judging by his dazed expression, he barely knew what day of the week it was.

Quinn gave the woman his thanks and carried the tray over to the table, noting as he did so the look of disappointment on Wilkins' potato-like face when he saw what his breakfast comprised.

'What's this?' he complained. 'No tea? No bacon?'

'Judging by your ever-expanding waistline, you'd do better to concentrate on a continental diet,' observed Quinn cuttingly. 'It'll be better for you.' He poured milk into his cup and stirred in a lump of sugar. 'And when in Rome . . .'

'But we're not in Rome, are we? We're in France.' Wilkins scowled, but he lifted a croissant to his mouth and took a generous bite. He chewed for a while, his expression blank. 'It's not so bad,' he muttered, unaware that shreds of pastry were now clinging to his lips and chin. 'Not like proper grub, though.' He took a noisy slurp of his coffee, grimaced and then added milk and sugar to the cup. 'Did you learn anything from your little chinwag?'

'Yes. The boy and his infernal companion were here. Somebody gave them a lift . . . the problem is that malodorous old mare at the counter doesn't know where to, so we're going to have to hang around in this dump of a town until the man in question puts in an appearance.'

Wilkins looked outraged. 'But that could take weeks!' he protested.

'Days,' Quinn corrected him. 'Our hostess claims that "Henri", as he's known, comes in several times a week. Who knows, we could get lucky.' He lifted his cup and took an experimental sip, then grimaced. 'If this is the best coffee in town, I'd hate to taste the worst,' he said.

Wilkins chuckled. 'You were doing pretty well with the old French lingo, just now,' he observed.

'That's because I know this part of the world well,' Quinn told him. 'My ancestors came from Brittany.'

'Is that a fact?' Wilkins took another bite of his croissant. 'I never knew that. Here, that painting back at your place. You know, the one of the bloke in armour, the one that's 'anging over the stairs . . .'

'What about it?' snapped Quinn irritably.

'Something tells me that bloke is French. There's some kind of flag in the background and I fancy that there's Frenchie writing on it.'

Quinn smiled. 'You're not quite as stupid as you look, are you?' he said. 'Well, yes, if you must know the gentleman in the portrait is one of my ancestors. He was one of the dukes of Penthievre.'

'Oh yeah? What were they when they was at home?'

'They were the rulers of the ancient kingdom of Brittany.'

This seemed to amuse Wilkins. He chortled, scattering crumbs of pastry in all directions. 'You mean to say that you're descended from royalty?'

'Does it seem so unlikely?'

Wilkins considered for a moment. 'No,' he said. 'No, actually it seems to make sense, now I think about it.' He took another mouthful of coffee. 'So what made you up sticks and move to England?'

'Oh, that's a rather long story,' said Quinn.

'Well, we need something to occupy us,' suggested Wilkins. 'We can't just sit here twiddling our thumbs.'

'Indeed, we cannot. Which is why as soon as you've finished eating, you're going to head out and find a garage.'

'A garage?' Wilkins looked puzzled. 'But . . . we ain't even got a car!'

'Precisely. Which is why you're going to find somebody who will let us hire one.'

'*Hire* one?'

Quinn tried not to lose his temper. 'Do you propose to repeat everything I say?' he snapped.

Wilkins reddened. 'Er . . . no, I just . . . I'm not sure how I'd—'

'It's a very straightforward arrangement, Wilkins. You find somebody with a decent automobile and then you offer them money to let you borrow it for a few days. Obviously, you allow them to hold onto a sizeable deposit to ensure that you return the car.'

'I know 'ow it works,' grumbled Quinn. 'But . . . I don't speak the lingo, do I? Wouldn't it be better if . . . well, with respect, if *you* went and sorted that?'

'And what if in the meantime, our Henri turns up and somebody needs to question him about where he took the boy? Are you suggesting that you would be a better candidate for *that* job?'

Wilkins looked crestfallen. 'Well . . . no,' he said. 'It's just . . .'

Quinn reached into the inside pocket of his coat and produced a notebook and pen. 'I will furnish you with a script,' he said. 'If in doubt, you can show it to whoever you're attempting to communicate with. And you never know . . . they might actually speak a little English.' He thought for a moment and began to scribble down a few lines. 'Look on it as a challenge,' he said.

'What about money?' asked Wilkins.

Quinn reached into another pocket and pulled out a thick roll of francs. Wilkins took it from him, looked at it for a moment, then transferred it to his own pocket. 'You ever stop to think how much you've already spent on this?' he asked.

'I beg your pardon?'

'Over the past two years. Travelling, staying in hotels . . . it must amount to a pretty penny, I'd say.'

'It's of no consequence,' said Quinn.

Wilkins shook his head. 'That's what you always say. But I don't get it. Why does it mean so much to you? I mean, supposing you do find this Henri geezer and supposing he does put us on to wherever the boy went? And let's say after all the chasing around we've done trying to find him, we finally get hold of that blasted dummy . . . corner him somewhere and grab hold of him. What are you gonna do with him then? Eh? What's the pay-off? You gonna take him back to your laboratory, are you? You going to study him, see what makes him tick?'

Quinn looked calmly across the table at Wilkins. Then he shook his head.

'I would have thought my intentions were obvious,' he murmured. 'I'm not interested in studying that abomination, Wilkins. No, I'm going to destroy him. I'm going to get rid of every last trace of him from this earth. And only when I've finally done that will I finally be able to rest.'

He smiled grimly. Then he lifted his coffee and took another sip.

19

Wake Up, Charlie!

Owen and Gerard got back to the cottage and went inside. Only now did Owen notice that, when they'd gone out earlier, Gerard hadn't even bothered to lock the door.

'Is that safe?' he asked. 'Leaving the place open?'

Gerard shrugged. 'I told you nobody ever comes here. And I don't have anything worth stealing.'

'What about all those lovely toys?'

'Those?' Gerard scoffed. 'Lately, I can't seem to give them away. They are like me . . . relics from the past.' He took off his jacket and hung it on a peg, then took Owen's coat from him and did the same. He led the way through to the kitchen. 'How about another cup of coffee?' he suggested, but Owen shook his head.

'No, let's try again,' he said. Gerard sighed but led the way into the workshop. Mr Sparks was just as they had left him, eyes closed, face turned up to the ceiling. Gerard regarded him for a moment.

'See how peaceful he looks,' he said. 'Aren't you a little bit tempted to leave him like that?'

'For another day?' asked Owen.

Gerard frowned. 'For ever,' he said wistfully.

'But . . . why? I don't understand, you're supposed to be the one who looks after him.'

Gerard shook his head. 'Forgive me, but I think that's y*our* job now.' He looked around the workshop. 'Oh, look at this place, Owen. It's finished. Nobody comes here any more and there's nobody to take my place when I'm gone. Supposing Charlie does recover and needs my help in ten or twenty years' time? Who's going to repair him then?'

'What about me?' asked Owen.

'You?'

'Well, why not? Maybe you could teach me to use the tools.'

'You'd do that? For *him*?'

'What else have I got?' Owen asked, and Gerard seemed to have no answer for that. After a few moments, he sighed again, bent over the dummy and whispered the sequence of words into his ear. This time, the results were dramatic. Mr Sparks' entire body jolted as though an electric current had passed through it and his eyes snapped open with a click. He began to sing in a loud, tuneless voice.

'Daisy, Daisy, give me your answer do.

I'm half crazy all for the love of you . . .'

His voice trailed away and he turned his head to look at the two people watching him. 'Oh, my giddy aunt, look who's here!' he exclaimed delightedly. 'My two closest friends in the whole world. It's Lucien . . .' He was looking at Gerard when he said this, then he swung his head to look at Owen. '. . . and Gerard!' he said. 'How are you both?'

'No, Charlie, *I* am Gerard. And this is your new friend, Owen. From Wales, you remember?'

'Owen? Owen?' For a moment, Mr Sparks' face remained blank. Then realisation seemed to dawn in his eyes. 'Owie!' he cried. 'Owie Bowie!'

'That's right.' Owen felt a sense of relief go through him. He took a step closer to the bench. 'You remember what happened, don't you? You came to the hotel in Llandudno with Otto and—'

'Otto?' Mr Sparks tried to crane his head around to take

in the rest of the room. 'Dear, dear Otto, where *is* he? Eh? Where's he hiding himself?'

'He . . .' Owen glanced at Gerard, seeking help, but received only a shrug in reply. 'Don't you know, Mr Sparks? Don't you know he's . . . dead.'

'Dead?' Mr Spark's mouth dropped open and his glass eyes welled with tears that trickled down his white face. 'Dead? How can he be . . . dead? I was only saying to him five minutes ago that he needed to have a shave.'

'Don't you remember?' insisted Owen. 'He was ill. He passed away back at my aunt's hotel.'

Mr Sparks' blue eyes narrowed, as though remembering. 'Oh yes, he did, didn't he? I remember now! Oh yes. It wasn't easy. He was old but he was still pretty strong. He struggled quite a bit . . .'

Owen felt his heart lurch in his chest. He actually took a step back. 'Are you . . . Charlie, are you saying . . . ?'

'Otto Schilling, what a man! Washed his face in a frying pan. Combed his hair with the leg of a chair . . . now he's gone and I'm still grieving. Took a lot to stop *him* breathing!'

Owen swallowed hard. He was finding it hard to catch his breath. 'Charlie. Are you saying . . . are you saying that you *killed* him?'

241

'Killed him? How dare you? I merely helped him on his way. He was old and tired, he wanted me to assist him, that's all. Don't you go pointing the thingy at me . . . er, the finger at me!' He moved his head restlessly from side to side. 'That's how rumours start. People hear other people saying things and that gets them stinking . . . I mean, thinking! And before you know it, the whole thing gets out of hand. So if anyone asks, Otto was old and tired.' He gave a sly wink. 'Got that? Good! Now, exactly where am I? Don't just stand there like a pair of lemons. One of you help me up!'

Gerard moved to assist him because Owen was still rooted to the spot with shock. He could barely believe what he had just been told. He watched, numbly, as Gerard lifted Mr Sparks into a sitting position. The dummy gazed around the workshop for a moment, taking it all in.

'I see you *still* haven't decorated, Lucien, ' he observed. 'What a mess!'

'It's *Gerard*!'

'I knew that. Didn't I say when I was here three weeks ago . . . ?'

'It was *years*,' Gerard corrected him.

'All right, no need to be picky! When I was last here, didn't I say that this place needed a lick of paint?'

'You did,' agreed Gerard. 'And I gave it one, the day after you left. But then the years went by and—'

'All right, all right, you don't have to go on and on about it!' Mr Sparks lifted a hand to touch the place where his head had broken. 'Feels like somebody did a good bob . . . er, a good slob . . . a good . . .'

'Job?' ventured Gerard.

'Exactly! That'll be you, Lucien . . . er, Owen . . . Er . . . Gerard! Always good with your hands, just like your dear old dad. And your dear old granddad. And . . . all the others.' He looked at Owen now. 'Ooh, I was well injured, I was. But I can't remember exactly how it . . .' His eyes narrowed and he glared at Owen. 'Oh yes I can, it was that mad mother of yours. She gave me a right kicking, she did. I hope she's not with us?' He stared at Owen, no doubt expecting some kind of reply. 'What's with you, Owie Bowie? You look like you've swallowed a horse.'

'Er . . . I'm still thinking . . . what you said about Otto?'

'What about it?'

'How could you *do* that to him?'

'Do what? I didn't do anything much. Just put a hand across his nose and mouth and gave a little squeeze.'

'Charlie!'

'Oh, come on, you saw how he was. He was old. He was slowing us down. And he'd had enough, Owie, he didn't want to be chased around any more. You saw how close those people were . . .'

'Who *are* these people who are chasing you?' asked Gerard.

'Oh, who knows? Bible-lovers, I expect. It's always Bible-lovers of one kind or another. People who think that I don't have any right to be on the same planet as them. Just because I'm a bit . . . different.'

Gerard couldn't resist a snort of laughter. 'Well, that's one word for what you are,' he admitted. He glanced at Owen. 'Are you all right?' he asked.

Owen nodded. He still didn't know what to think about what Mr Sparks had told him. He had confessed to a murder, but he seemed to think that Owen should accept the fact as readily as he might accept any of his other little 'confessions'. What's more, it was pretty obvious that he wouldn't have said anything about it at all, if he hadn't been so confused.

Gerard sighed and ran his hands through his long hair. 'So, it is just as I feared,' he said. He looked at the dummy. 'What are you going to do now?' he asked.

'Well, I'll need to rest up for a few days,' said Mr Sparks. 'My sports are still a bit mixed up . . .'

'Thoughts?' suggested Gerard.

'Exactly. But we can't stay here in Germany . . .'

'France?'

'Yes, because Owie doesn't speak any Chinese. So I was thinking London. Haven't been there for a long time, not since I worked with old . . . ooh, what was his name? Montague, that was the fellow! Montague Watts . . . and I was Lord William. The act we did, Lucien . . .'

'Gerard.'

'Yes, the act we did, I had to pretend to be slowly sizzled . . . I mean, slightly sozzled, every night. Went down a storm, we did! Did a show in front of Mean Dictoria herself. I mean, Bean Quicktoria . . . er . . .'

'Queen Victoria?' suggested Gerard.

'The very one! People reckoned she was a misery but she nearly laughed her knickers off at our act, I can tell you! Gave me a medal, she did. In fact, we've still got it in Otto's trunk . . .' His face fell. 'Oh!' He shook his head. 'Poor old Otto. Where *is* he, by the way?'

'He's dead!' snapped Owen. 'You killed him.'

'Who says that? Show me the man who says it and I'll knock his block off!'

'*You* said it,' cried Owen, and now he could feel the anger rising up within him. 'You lied to me. You told me he died of old age!'

'Well, he *was* knocking on a bit! I just . . . helped him along.' He lapsed into one of his little ditties. 'This is the tale of Otto Schilling. He always gave me second billing. He told me he was old and tired. So I said, "Otto, you are fired!"' He burst into a manic shriek of laughter, which faded quickly when he realised that nobody else was laughing. 'Oh, come on,' he said. 'What do you have to do to crack a smile around here?'

'Nobody's laughing!' cried Owen. 'You're talking about murder!'

'Well, I'll grant you, it's not the funniest material I've ever worked with . . .'

'You really think I want to go to London with you after what you just told me? That could be *me* one day!'

'Well, not for a very long time. I mean, seriously, you're only a kid.'

'That's not the point! Otto looked after you for all those years and that's how you repaid him?'

'You're taking this the wrong way,' muttered Mr Sparks.

'There's only one way I can take it. You're a killer. A murderer.'

'That's a very unpleasant word.' Mr Sparks looked at Gerard. 'Lucien, you tell the boy. He can't call me names like that.'

'It's Gerard! And yes, I'm afraid he can, because that is what you are. You just confessed to us.'

'Did I? That was a mistake. But you don't understand, Owie! Try and think for a moment what it's like to be me. Trying to survive in a world that doesn't understand you. Having to pretend that I'm just this stupid hunk of lead . . .'

'Wood,' said Gerard.

'Thank you. Yes, wood! A hunk of wood in a world where most of the people who find out your secret, think that you should be destroyed. That you're some kind of evil monster!'

'Maybe they've got that bit right,' snarled Owen.

'Oh, you're just overcome with emulsion . . . er, emotion! But if you think about it for a minute, you'll realise that I did what I had to do in order to survive. It's what I've been doing ever since I came into the world.'

'You didn't have to kill him. Couldn't you have just . . . put him into a trance or something?'

'Oh yeah, good idea. Let him slowly starve to death. Look, Owen, the man was finished anyway. He was already dying. I just . . . speeded things up a bit.'

Owen couldn't listen to any more of it. He motioned to Gerard. 'Put him back to sleep,' he said.

Gerard gave Owen a warning look and Mr Sparks reacted. 'You can put me to sleep?' he shrieked, glaring at Gerard. 'How long have you been able to do that?'

'It doesn't matter,' said Gerard.

'Oh, but it does. I bet Otto taught you that trick, didn't he? You know, I always wondered if that sly old devil had found a way to do it. It explains a lot.'

'Be quiet!' said Owen. 'I'm sick of the sound of your voice!'

'Oh now, Owie, don't be like that, please! I'm getting better now. I . . . I'll behave myself, I promise.'

Owen looked at Gerard. 'Sleep,' he said.

'You are sure?'

'Yes. I can't talk to him now.' Owen turned and began to walk away.

Mr Sparks shouted after him, 'Owie! Owie, don't let

him do it. Please! I'll be a good boy, I'll say my prayers every night, I won't kill anybody else, I promise, just let me—'

The voice cut off abruptly. When Owen glanced back, Mr Sparks was on his back again, gazing sightlessly up at the ceiling. Gerard was standing over him, looking thoughtfully down. Owen turned away and went through to the kitchen. He took a seat at the table and buried his face in the pillow of his crossed arms. After a little while, Gerard came into the room and stood behind him.

'It was what I was afraid of,' he said. 'He only spoke of it because he was . . . all mixed up. And you know something? I can't honestly say I believe it was the first time he's done something like that.'

Owen said something but his mouth was against the back of one arm and it came out unintelligible.

'Say it again?' suggested Gerard.

Owen lifted his head, his eyes wet with tears.

'Maybe we should have that cup of coffee now,' Gerard said.

20

The Trip

The day dragged on while they sat in the kitchen, drinking coffee and staring blankly out of the window. It was a pleasant autumn morning, the surrounding trees swaying in the breeze, but Owen wasn't in the right frame of mind to appreciate it. He didn't know what to do for the best. Part of him wanted to instruct Gerard to make sure that Mr Sparks never woke up again and he could tell from the Frenchman's grave features that, if given such an order, he wouldn't hesitate to carry it out. But, Owen told himself, if they did that, wouldn't it make the pair of them as bad as Mr Sparks? Wouldn't that make them murderers too?

Eventually, they could stand it no longer. 'I need to go into Paimpont for some provisions,' Gerard announced. 'Why don't you come with me?'

Owen nodded, telling himself that perhaps some fresh

air would help to clear his head. 'How will we get there?' he asked.

'I'll show you.'

They got their coats and Gerard led Owen outside and around the back of the building. There was a short track, which led to a clearing in the woods, where Owen was surprised to see a ramshackle old barn, that he hadn't even realised existed. Gerard pulled back the big wooden doors to reveal a brown horse, standing in a stall and alongside her, a simple four-wheeled carriage that looked to Owen like it must have been hundreds of years old.

'This is Mathilde,' said Gerard, slapping the horse on the rump. 'Like everything else around here, she's getting a little long in the tooth, but she gets me where I want to go, provided I don't need to be there in a hurry.' He took a bridle from a hook on the wall and fitted it into Mathilde's mouth, then led her out of the stall and began to hitch her to the carriage. Owen examined this in more detail. He could see that it once must have been rather grand, but now the black lacquered finish was scuffed in a dozen places and he could see where bits of wire and twine had been used to make temporary repairs. 'This thing has been in my family for many years,' explained Gerard. 'I can remember riding in it with my grandfather when I was your age. People keep telling me I should get a new one, but I say to them, "Why would I do that?" This suits me fine.' He smiled sympathetically at Owen, no doubt seeing the troubled expression on his face. 'But here am I, talking away and all you can think of is what to do about Charlie,' he said. 'You know, it doesn't have to be so difficult. It wouldn't be like we were killing him.'

'No?' Owen was unconvinced.

'No. If I don't say the sequence of words, he never wakes up again. I could just put him in a cupboard somewhere and . . . forget all about him.'

'But that wouldn't feel right either,' said Owen. 'That would be like . . . like we'd buried him alive or something.'

Gerard secured the leather yoke around Mathilde's neck. 'Well, what else are you going to do? Take him back to your country and inform the police that he's a murderer?' He chuckled. 'That's a trial I'd pay money to see,' he said. 'Can you imagine Charlie up in the dock answering questions?'

'It's not funny,' Owen told him. 'Not at all.'

'I appreciate that. It's not a decision I would like to have to make.'

'Why does it have to be *me* who decides, anyway?' protested Owen. 'You've known him a lot longer than I have.'

'True. But you are his operator now. Charlie chose you. When he did that, he gave you control of him. So it has to be your decision. But I will help in any way I can.' Gerard made a few last checks on the fastenings and then climbed up behind the reins and gestured to Owen to take the seat beside him. 'Come on,' he said. 'We will ride into Paimpont. Maybe a change of scenery will help you make up your mind.'

Owen clambered up beside him. Gerard clicked his tongue and Mathilde started walking, pulling the carriage out of the barn.

'Aren't you going to close the door behind us?' Owen asked him.

Gerard shook his head. 'I already told you . . .'

'Nobody comes here! Yes, you keep saying that. But what if somebody *did* come here? A thief or something. The door of the house isn't locked. Somebody could come in and take Mr Sparks away.'

Gerard considered for a moment. 'Which would save us both a lot of trouble,' he said drily. He slapped the reins against Mathilde's back and she broke into a trot, pulling the carriage along the narrow track that led to the main road.

Paimpont turned out to be a picturesque little village in the very heart of the forest, a few thatched-roof buildings, all made from the same grey stone, ranged on either side of a hard dirt road. As they drove in to its outskirts, Gerard chatted happily about the area and pointed out things of interest.

'You know, this village hasn't changed one bit in all the years I have been coming here,' he told Owen. 'There's the forge where I bring Mathilde, when she needs to have a new shoe. And over the back there is the church, where I go to pray . . . well, when I remember. But we stop here, at the épicerie – the village store.' He brought the carriage to a halt outside a grey stone building, with green wooden shutters and rust-coloured ivy clambering up the walls. 'Here they sell everything I need,' he explained. 'Bread, cheese, wine. I am a man of simple tastes.' He looked at Owen thoughtfully. 'Maybe you should wait here,' he suggested. 'Monsieur Rambroche, who runs the store, he is the long-nosed sort, you know? If he asks me questions about you, I don't know exactly what I would tell him. You don't mind waiting here a little while?'

Owen shook his head. 'It'll give me a chance to think,' he said.

Gerard smiled sympathetically. He climbed down from his seat and took a couple of hessian bags from the back of the carriage. 'I won't be long,' he promised.

Owen nodded and watched as Gerard walked to the entrance of the store and went inside. It was quiet in the village, just the soft sounds of birdsong from the surrounding forest. Owen looked around, but the place seemed deserted apart from three workmen who were crouched on the other side of the road, some fifty yards ahead of him. They appeared to be making repairs to the kerb. Two of the men wore blue overalls and flat caps, but the third man, taller and thinner than his companions, wore a heavy military-style greatcoat. He was helping the other two manoeuvre a heavy kerbstone into position at the side of the road and Owen thought that for some reason, the man looked vaguely familiar. A jolt of anxiety went through him as he thought about the two men who had pursued him back in Wales. Could it be one of them, the thin man who had chased him along the platform at Denbigh station? But no, he decided, this fellow wasn't quite as tall, or quite as thin and his hair was shorter and sandy-coloured.

And yet, for all that, there was *something* about the man that made Owen think that he had seen him before, that there was something maddeningly familiar about him. But how could that be? Owen had never been to France before, didn't know anyone that lived here. Unless . . .

Just at that moment, the workmen got the kerbing stone into position and the tall man straightened up and took a step back. For some reason, he turned to gaze down the street in Owen's direction. The face that looked at him was unmistakable, though there was not a sign of recognition in those dark brown eyes. Owen felt an abrupt shock ripple through him, a shock that seemed to momentarily stop his heart from beating in his chest. He gasped aloud, then couldn't seem to get his breath. It couldn't be, could it? Had he gone mad? Was he imagining things? Because the face was familiar for a very good reason.

Almost before he knew what he was doing, he was scrambling down from his seat, as though his arms and legs had taken on a life of their own. Now he was running along the street, his arms held out in front of him. The man saw him coming and his eyes narrowed quizzically.

He opened his mouth to say something but before he could speak, Owen flung himself the last few steps and wrapped his arms around the man's waist, almost knocking him off his feet.

'Da!' he cried. 'Da, what are you doing here?'

There was a silence then, a silence so deep that Owen thought he would fall into it, that he would go on falling for ever. It occurred to him that the man was not returning his hug, that the body beneath the greatcoat was stiff and unyielding. Owen pulled back a little and looked up into his father's face, only to see those familiar features staring blankly down at him as though he was a stranger. In that moment, Owen noticed something he hadn't been able to see from a distance – the long jagged streak of pale scar tissue that stretched from Gareth Dyer's left temple to the corner of his left eye.

'Da?' whispered Owen. 'Da, it's me. Owen. Don't you know me?'

But Da just looked down at him, his expression stern. Then he spoke in Welsh-accented English.

'Who the hell are you?' he asked.

21

Found

They rode slowly back from Paimpont, Owen sitting beside Gerard, Da hunched on a seat in the back, beside the sacks of groceries. He was staring straight ahead, his expression still blank. Owen was in shock and Gerard was clearly mystified by what had happened during his absence.

He had emerged from the general store to find Owen desperately trying to explain to the other two workmen that he was their assistant's son, and that he needed his father to go with him, so he could explain to him everything that had happened since they had last seen each other. But the men spoke hardly any English and Owen's jabbering had made them think he was some kind of maniac. Gerard had managed to explain the situation to them, and they told him that the Welshman was only with them because they had taken pity on him when he'd drifted into the area a couple of months ago. Yes, they knew he had no memory, he had managed to explain that much to them, and quite obviously his amnesia must have something to do with the scar on his temple, an injury they had assumed he'd sustained in the Great War. Of course they were happy to let him go. The problem was that Da didn't seem that happy to say goodbye to *them*.

'But these are my friends,' he kept saying, as Owen and Gerard led him to the carriage. 'I work for them. Why would I want to leave them?'

'Because . . . I'm your son and I . . . need to take you home to Ma.'

'Ma?'

'My ma . . . your wife. Megan?' But Da's expression had remained unchanged all through the conversation. If the name Megan meant anything to him, he didn't show it. Now he sat in the back of the carriage looking like a whipped dog, as though the last thing he wanted was to go anywhere with these two strangers who had accosted him in the street.

Gerard gave Owen a sidelong look. 'Well, I have to say that going shopping with you is full of surprises. I was expecting only to pick up bread, cheese and wine. But I come back with another mouth to feed.'

DANNY WESTON

Owen shook his head. 'I don't understand,' he said. 'How could he be *here*? He has the whole of France to choose from, and he just happens to be in the same little village that I'm in?'

'You are not glad to find him?'

'Of course I am! We thought he was dead. But . . . he doesn't *know* me. He doesn't know anything about me or Ma. How is that going to work?'

'Maybe his memory will come back,' suggested Gerard. 'Once he has got to know you again.'

'But those men said he'd been working with them for two months. And it's a year since the War ended.'

Gerard looked thoughtful. 'You know,' he said. 'Maybe it's not an accident that you came here. Maybe you were brought here for that very reason. To find your father.'

'What do you mean? Brought here . . . by who?'

'Don't you believe in fate, Owen? Don't you think that sometimes things happen that help people to find what they have lost?' He glanced briefly over his shoulder at the figure in the back of the carriage. 'Think about it! Think of all the little things that had to happen to make sure you met your father on the road by the store. What if he had gone to some other town to work? What if you had decided to stay

260

at home instead of coming to the store with me? What if I had told you to come inside and help me with the shopping? You would have missed seeing him. We could have got back in the carriage and rode home without even noticing that he was there. And think why you are here in the first place.'

'Well . . . because Mr Sparks made me come here.'

'Yes! So maybe that is why you met Charlie. Maybe something sent him to find you and bring you out here to meet with your father. Do you see what I am saying? Things happen for a reason, Owen! There is no such thing as chance. If Otto hadn't died, then you wouldn't even be here now. So . . . I suppose what I am saying is . . . maybe Otto *had* to die, in order for all these things to happen.'

'But that doesn't make it right!' protested Owen.

'I'm not saying it does. But I look back at the things that have happened in my life and I can see that it is like a set of er . . . how do you call them? The little black things. The game? Dom . . . dom . . .'

'Dominoes?' suggested Owen.

'*Oui*! You stand them in a line and you knock one over . . . and down they go, one after another, right to the very end of the line. Maybe our lives are like that. Take out one domino and the chain stops. You do not meet Mr

Sparks. Otto doesn't die. And you don't end up here! Maybe Charlie is one of the dominoes. Maybe we should not take him out of the line. Besides . . .' He glanced back at Da again. 'I have a feeling he could help your father.'

'Charlie? Help him? How?'

'There is something he has. A gift. It is called mesmerism.'

'Oh yes, I know all about that,' said Owen. 'I saw him use it on Mr Schilling once. He just . . . said some words that sort of put him to sleep. It's the same thing you do to Mr Sparks.'

'Yes, but that is just a little trick that Otto taught me, some words that he managed to plant at the back of Mr Sparks' mind, without him knowing. It's funny when you think about it, because I know that Charlie did the same to Otto. They could put each other to sleep, but neither of them ever knew that the other could do the same thing. So one time Otto told me the string of words he'd planted in Charlie's mind, in case I ever needed it. That is the full extent of my skills. But Mr Sparks, he is an expert. And there is another way he can use this gift of his. I have seen him do this once before. He makes a person go into a kind of . . . I don't know the English word for this, but it is as if they go back in time . . . in their heads. I saw him do it once with my father. Papa was very forgetful when he grew old and one time, when Charlie and Otto were visiting us, my father forgot where he had hidden something, the key to the safe. Charlie was able to take him back in his mind so he could remember where he had put it.'

Owen frowned. 'So . . . you're saying that maybe he could mesmerise Da and help him remember what happened to him?'

'It's just an idea. But it could work.'

'But . . .' Owen lowered his voice to a whisper. 'What's Da going to think when he sees Mr Sparks?'

Gerard made a face. 'That, I cannot say.' Gerard glanced back over his shoulder. 'You all right back there?' he asked.

Da glowered at him. 'Where are you taking me?' he asked.

'We're going to my cottage,' said Gerard. 'We'll have something to eat and a good cup of coffee. Then you'll feel better.'

'I don't like leaving Dominic and Claude,' he said. 'They need my help on that road.'

'They said it was fine,' Gerard assured him. 'They were happy to let you come with us. Don't you want to find out more about your son?'

'I don't have a son,' said Da.

'Of course you do! This boy is your son. You just don't remember him.' Gerard studied Da for a moment. 'What *do* you remember?' he asked.

'I don't remember anything.'

'Of course you do. There must be something.'

Da thought for a moment. 'The sea,' he said at last. 'Grey . . . rainy . . . and something sticking out into the sea. I dream about it sometimes.'

'The pier!' exclaimed Owen. 'Llandudno pier. It's where we lived. Before you went away to war.'

Da frowned, shook his head. 'I don't remember,' he said. 'Sorry.'

'That's all right,' said Owen, but he couldn't hide his disappointment. He turned to look at the way ahead.

'Don't worry,' Gerard assured him. 'We'll find a way to make him remember.'

But they didn't. Once back at the cottage, they sat at the table with bowls of stew and as they ate, they talked to Da, asked him questions, tried to come up with things that might possibly jog his memory. But he just sat there, looking miserable, answering monosyllabically, giving the impression that he'd rather be anywhere else but here. The day moved into afternoon and afternoon turned into evening and they felt they were getting precisely nowhere. Night-time came, and still Da could remember nothing but the sea. Finally, Gerard whispered to Owen that maybe they should try the idea he had put forward in the carriage on the way home. Owen didn't like the sound of it. He was worried that Mr Sparks' appearance might serve to tip Da over the edge into madness, just as it had with Ma. But he didn't know what else to try.

'You fetch him,' he whispered at last. 'Wake him up and tell him what we want him to do before you bring him in here. I don't want him messing about and frightening Da.'

Gerard nodded. He got up from his chair and went out of the room. Da looked at Owen suspiciously. 'Where's he going?' he muttered.

'He's just gone to get something,' Owen assured him. 'Something we think might help you remember.'

Da snorted. 'I think I should be going soon,' he said. 'It's getting late.'

'Why would you want to leave?' Owen asked him. 'It's warm here. There's a place where you can sleep.'

'I've got my own place,' Da assured him. He made a sound

of exasperation. 'Look, lad,' he said, 'I understand what you're trying to do here. You say you're my boy and I'm sure you have no reason to lie about it. But if I can't remember you, then what's the point of any of this? We may as well just say "Forget it" and let me move on with my life.'

'But we can't do that! What about Ma?'

'What about her? From what you've told me, she thinks I'm dead anyway.'

'But she never gave up hope that you'd come back one day. It's all she ever talks about. Why have you given up on it?'

Da shook his head. 'You have to understand,' he said. 'I've been living in a fog for over a year. Don't you think I've wanted to remember? Don't you think I've *tried*. But there's nothing there, nothing I can hang onto.'

'But you remember the pier at Llandudno. Doesn't that tell you something?'

'Who's to say that's what it is? It's just the sea . . . that could be anywhere.'

Just then the door opened and Gerard came in, carrying Mr Sparks.

'Hello, hello, hello!' said Mr Sparks. 'Who have we got here then?'

Da sat up in his chair. 'What the hell is that thing?'

'Oh, that's charming,' said Mr Sparks. 'Didn't they teach you anything at school? Like good manners?' He turned his head to look up at Gerard. 'Here, pop me on Owie Bowie's knee,' he suggested. 'I'm dying to have a chinwag with his dear old dad.'

'Whatever you say.' Gerard carried Mr Sparks across to Owen and sat him in the boy's lap. Then he stepped back and took a seat on the far side of the kitchen table.

Mr Sparks looked up at Owen for a moment. 'I knew you wouldn't leave me like that,' he said. 'You care too much about me.'

'Don't flatter yourself,' muttered Owen. 'It's only because we need your help.' He looked at Mr Sparks. 'Well?' he said. 'I'm waiting.'

'Ooh, you're a hard case!' Mr Sparks swivelled his head to look at Da. 'So,' he said. 'Gareth, I believe they call you. Another Welsh name. What's this I hear about you refusing to remember anything?'

Da allowed himself a thin smile. He looked at Owen. 'That's good,' he admitted grudgingly. 'Bit of a hobby, is it?'

'How dare you?' shrieked Mr Sparks. 'I'm not anybody's

hobby, I'm my own man entirely. Don't be looking at *him*, sunshine, I'm the one doing all the work! Now then, I want you to look into my eyes . . .'

'Why?' muttered Da.

'I'll tell you why, Gareth, and believe me, I don't say this to a lot of people. When I was made, the man who carved me, Lucien Lacombe, he made a tiny mistake. He made one of my eyes, a teeny weeny bit smaller than the other. Can you see which one it is?'

'The . . . the left one?' muttered Da. He was staring back at Mr Sparks now, his expression vacant.

'And . . . I don't know if you can see this, Gareth, but one of them is a slightly different colour to the other. One of them is clear blue, but the other is a kind of bluey green. Can you see which one that is?'

'I . . . er . . .'

Mr Sparks' voice seemed to getting lower in tone with each sentence he said. 'Now then, Gareth. You and me. Me and you. We're going to go on a little trip. Together. We're going to go back to before you had that scar on your head. Do you understand?'

'Yes,' said Da quietly.

'You're going to tell me what happened to you. You're

going to describe everything in detail, as it happens. Because it will be as though you're back there. You'll describe every little thing. Will you do that for me, Gareth?'

'Yes.'

'Good. Now, hold on just a moment. Will you wait right there for me?'

'Yes.' Da slumped slightly in his seat, his head drooping forward onto his chest.

Mr Sparks turned his head and waggled his eyelids at Owen. 'Piece of cake,' he said. 'We've got him right where we want him. He'll tell us everything we need to know.'

'Good.' Owen looked at Mr Sparks suspiciously. 'So . . . what are we waiting for?'

'I'll tell you.' Mr Sparks leaned closer. 'Are you planning to put me back to sleep after this?'

Owen scowled. 'I haven't decided,' he said.

'Well, decide *now*. I want you to promise me that you won't do it.'

'That's not fair!'

'Promise me.'

'All right. I promise I won't do it.'

Mr Sparks sniggered. 'You must think I was born yesterday!' he observed. 'Of course *you* won't do it. I doubt that you even know how! No, it's Gerard that knows the words.' He flung a mocking glance at Gerard and sneered. 'And I wouldn't even know that *he* could do it, if you hadn't given the game away, you nitwit. I'm guessing that Otto must have taught him that little trick.' He cackled. 'It's funny when you think about it. Otto didn't know I was doing it to him and I didn't know he could do it to *me*!'

Gerard started to get up from his chair. 'Charlie,' he said. 'The boy needs your help now. Don't . . .'

'You sit down and keep your mouth shut,' snapped Mr Sparks. 'This is between the boy and me.' Gerard glared back at him for a moment, but then did as he was told.

There was a long silence. Owen glanced at Mr Sparks impatiently. 'My da,' he whispered. 'He's waiting.'

'Let him wait. We need to get this sorted out before we can proceed. You have to promise me that you won't let Gerard put me back to sleep. Not ever.'

'But that's—'

'Say it. Or Gareth here stays in the land of Know-Nothing.'

Owen felt anger welling up inside him, and had to restrain himself from punching the dummy to the floor. 'You . . . you *are* evil,' he hissed.

'Flattery will get you nowhere! Just make the promise, Owen, and we can get on with the show.'

Owen spoke the words through gritted teeth. 'I . . . I promise I won't let Gerard put you back to sleep.'

'Good.' Mr Sparks looked again at Gerard. 'That's a promise from both of you now. Just remember, a person who breaks a promise is not an honourable one. So . . .' He turned to look at Da, who was still slumped in his chair. 'If we're all ready . . . I'll begin.' He took a deep breath. 'Gareth. We're setting off now, you and me. We're setting off on that day when you were injured. I want you to picture the scene, just as it happened, and I want you to tell me all about it. Like I said before. Every. Last. Detail. So, if you're ready . . . you can begin.'

There was a long silence, while Da sat there, staring into space. Then his eyes seemed to widen a little as though focusing on something that only he could see. He began to talk.

22

The Battle

'It's around midday and we're lying in a trench, eating our rations. There's me and Taffy Roberts and Billy Price and it's the same old bully beef they always serve us. Taffy says he'd give just about anything for a proper Sunday dinner, with roast potatoes, Yorkshire pudding and onion gravy, but I tell him to stop torturing himself. Everybody's trying to put a brave face on things, but the talk around the regiment is that we'll be going over the top soon and that it's going to be another big one, so as soon as I've finished eating, I go off by myself and I write a short letter that I can leave here, just in case anything bad happens to me.'

'That's good, Gareth. What do you say in the letter?'

'I tell Megan that I'm keeping my head down and that I got a food parcel last week and there was a lovely bit of bara brith in it, though it wasn't as nice as hers. I tell her the word is that now the Yanks have joined in, it's just a matter of time before this whole sorry business comes to an end. And I put a little note to Owen, telling him that when I get back, we'll buy him that bike he's been wanting. The two of us will cycle out along the promenade and we'll head out to the hills and take a packed lunch with us and we'll have ourselves a rare old time. And I tell myself that I won't think about the things I've seen since I came out here to fight, I'll just put them out of my mind and act like everything is fine.

'Anyhow, I finish the letter and I see the chaplain go by and I call to him and hand it over. I ask him to make sure it gets delivered and he tells me not to worry, he'll see to it. Just then, I hear shouting from up the line. I can see men getting to their feet and I know this is it, it's time, so I put on my pack and I check my rifle and I stand to attention with the others as Captain Jenkins comes down the line to give us our orders. I don't mind the captain, even though he's an Englishman and a bit la-di-dah with it. Billy always says it's easy for him, living the life of luxury while we eat bully beef, but I tell him that when the time comes, the captain will be out front with his pistol, leading us into No Man's Land and that takes guts, no matter where he comes from.'

'What happens next?'

'The captain gives us a little speech. He tells us that we're on the final push now, that the Boche are losing ground and it's only a matter of time before they throw in the towel. But he says that doesn't mean we can take it easy, because there's another trench that needs taking and we're the lucky lads who've been chosen to do it. But he promises us that he'll be with us every step of the way and I give Billy a sly look, that sort of says, "There you are then, what did I tell you?"

'Then we're ordered to about-turn and we're told to follow the captain and a sapper. They lead us along the maze of trenches and it *is* a maze, like a rabbit warren, Taffy always says, and as we march, you can't help but notice that the noises of explosions are getting louder and louder. We seem to walk for miles and after a while, we can feel the ground shaking under our feet and every time a shell passes overhead, we duck our heads, even though we're still below ground, because you could just be unlucky and catch a dose of shrapnel. Another troop of men pass us on the way, heading for where we came from I suppose, and I try not to stare at them, because they're filthy and some of them are covered in blood. Others have bandages around their eyes, blinded by mustard gas, and their friends are leading them along, helping them every step of the way. Every single man I pass has this haunted look in his eyes. I know exactly how they feel, because I've lost count of the battles I've been in, and even after all this time I couldn't tell you if I've killed a single one of the enemy, because it's madness out there, you just run forward and dive into trenches or shell holes full of muddy water and you shoot at shadows and when the shelling stops, if you're still alive, you sit where you are and wait for somebody to tell you what to do next . . .'

'So what *do* you do next?'

'Well, finally, we come to the Front Line and here, the force of the explosions seems to shake you like a rag doll. The noise is terrifying, shrieks and bangs and thuds, most of which you cannot identify. The captain stops walking and turns back to tell us to take up our positions. Ladders are brought and placed all along the sides of the trench and Captain Jenkins, fair play to him, he's the first to take up his position, so he can peep over the top with a periscope and take stock of the situation. A ladder is placed by us. Me and Taffy, we look at each other, as if wondering who should be the first to climb, but then Billy steps forward and climbs up the ladder. That's Billy for you, afraid of nothing.

'The noise goes on, the pounding, the shaking, but it's as though it's all suddenly happening miles away, because every part of you is waiting, waiting for the sound of the captain's whistle, our signal to go, and now I just want to get it over with, the longer I wait, the harder it will be to climb that ladder and step out into No Man's Land. I look at Taffy and he winks at me, gives me a grin, but I can see the fear in his eyes. He isn't fooling anyone. And then—'

'Go on, don't stop now!'

'Then . . . then we hear the sound of the whistle, so shrill that it nearly makes me jump out of my skin. In that instant, the captain goes up and over and ahead of me, Billy climbs and I take my place on the ladder behind him, but even as he sticks his head up over the parapet, something hits him with a force that throws him back against me and he goes somersaulting over my head and I see, briefly, that his face is a shattered mess that no doctor will ever be able to piece back together. I've known him since we were boys playing in the street and he's dead. In one instant his life has winked out like a candle flame, but there's no time to dwell on that.

I climb and I step out onto the muddy ground and I begin to run forward. For an instant, it seems to me that it's only me following the captain, he's just a few steps ahead of me, but then I'm aware of Taffy running alongside me and he isn't grinning any more, he must have seen better than I did what happened to Billy. I glance back and more men are streaming out of the trench, and with one voice they are yelling their defiance as they run towards the enemy. A machine-gun starts hammering and I feel rather than see the bullets whipping past me. A man to my left is hit and he drops in his tracks but I do not hesitate. Captain Jenkins turns his head to look over his shoulder and he shouts something, but I don't hear what it is and an instant later, he reels back and goes down, clutching his stomach. I drop to one knee beside him and I see he is grinning up at me, but there's blood spilling from his mouth and he waves me onwards. Pausing like that has allowed others to catch up, so when I get back to my feet, I am running amongst a crowd of men, we are all running blind and so far as I am aware, not one of us has fired a shot because we cannot even see the enemy, we can see nothing but a line of sandbags up ahead, which we know must mark the edge of the German trenches and it still looks such a long, long way off . . .'

'You can't stop there, sunshine. Keep talking!'

'The . . . the machine-gun chatters again and a man drops in front of me. I trip over him and almost fall on my face in the mud, but I recover and somehow I keep going, the rifle in my hands like a stupid, useless weight that I am almost tempted to throw away. There's an explosion from somewhere behind me, and a ragged figure catapults past me, his arms and legs flailing. And then I hear a long, whooshing sound and I know it's a shell, that it's going to be close, but even as I am thinking it, there's a flash of white light that blinds me and I feel a giant hand swat me aside like some troublesome insect. I am falling then and I wait for the impact of the ground against my shoulders but it doesn't come . . . it doesn't ever come . . .'

'It doesn't end there, though, does it?'

'No. When I open my eyes, it seems to me at first that only moments have passed but I realise very quickly that it's night. It's night and I was somehow expecting it to be day, though I can't say why. There's a terrible pain in my head, my face is wet and there's a ringing sound in my ears. I don't know who I am, or where I am, or what I'm doing lying in the mud, in the dark. With an effort, I manage to sit up. I look around me, but I can see nothing but heaps of men lying still in the dirt and I wonder how I came to be with them. They're wearing some kind of uniform. Soldiers, I tell myself. I know that much. But does that mean I'm a soldier too? I don't know. I don't know anything. My head feels like it's splitting open, like somebody has cut it open with an axe . . .'

'I know that feeling!'

'I manage to get to my feet and I look in all directions. There's a sliver of moon in the sky that gives a little light but I have no idea which way to walk. But I walk anyway. I pick my way between mounds of dead men, past heaps of discarded weapons. I'm parched with thirst. I keep walking, and after a while I leave the dead men behind and I come to a field and I walk across the field, then another one, and I feel weak and dizzy and when I finally come to a hedge, I drop to my knees and crawl into its cover and I sleep.'

'Do you dream?'

'Yes, but the dreams are just a confused jumble of things, none of which I recognise. Occasionally I wake and find myself wondering who I am, but I'm in such pain that I do not care much. I just want to sleep again and eventually, I do.

'Morning comes and it's cold and windy. I get myself to my feet and I begin to walk again, but I see no features to head for, no houses, no hills, only flat green land. I walk for most of the day. By now my feet are blistered and they shoot tongues of fire up my legs with every step. Finally, when I think I can walk no further, I see in a field ahead of me a man milking a cow. I stumble towards him and I beg him for milk. My voice isn't much more than a croak. He stares at me for a moment, then takes a metal ladle and scoops up some milk from the bucket, then hands it to me. I swallow it down and it's warm and creamy and I think it's the finest milk I've ever tasted, though I can't be sure, because I don't actually know if I've tasted milk before, I don't even understand how I *know* what milk is in the first place. But it tastes good. The man says something to me in a language I don't understand and I am trying to answer him when the world takes a sudden lurch to the right and I know nothing more.'

'So you sleep again?'

'Yes, I sleep until I open my eyes and I am lying on straw in some kind of barn. A woman sits over me. She is wiping my face with a warm, wet cloth and she smiles and the man appears, standing behind her, looking into the stall where I am lying and he says something in the language I don't understand and she nods and says something back to him and I sleep again.'

'My goodness, you *are* tired, aren't you?'

'Yes, very tired. I sleep again, until I open my eyes and now the same woman is pushing a spoon into my mouth, something warm and tasty. Whatever it is, it's good and I eat and I sleep and I wake and I eat and I sleep and I wake. This goes on for some time, I'm not sure how long, but one day I am able to stand and I find a mirror fixed to a wall of the stall and I look into it, thinking that now I will know something, but the face that stares back at me is that of a stranger, a stranger with a hideous scar on his head that somebody (the woman?) has sewn together with a needle and thread . . .'

'Ooh, that must smart!'

'It does. I am still looking at the reflection when the man arrives. He points to me and when I look down, I see I am not wearing the clothes I had before. He tells me in halting English that he has destroyed them, in case the Boche come here. He says that I can stay a few more days and then I should go. It's not safe for me here. I don't argue with him. I ask him if he knows who I am and he just gives me a strange look. He advises me to go west and I say I will, even though I don't know which way that is.

'After a few days, I am strong enough to leave. The man shakes my hand and the woman, who I think must be his wife, kisses my cheek and presses a parcel into my hands. When I look at it later, I see that it contains a piece of bread and some cheese, and as I am hungry I eat some of it but I keep the rest back for later. I walk for days, sleeping in hedges when it gets dark.

'One day, I find a road and I begin to walk along it. Then I hear noises coming from up ahead of me, so I run into a hedge to hide. A column of soldiers comes marching along the road, men in khaki uniforms. They wear steel helmets and they carry rifles. I think their uniforms look like the one I was wearing when I found myself lying in the mud, but I can't be sure. I don't want to reveal myself in case they aren't friendly (what if they're the Boche?). So when the column has finally moved on, I head back into the fields and I tell myself to stay off the roads, just in case more soldiers come.

'I travel for days, weeks perhaps. Sometimes I meet people in isolated homes and I indicate to them that I am hungry and they let me do work for them in exchange for something to eat. In one farm I work at, a man has good English and he asks me questions about myself, but when I can't answer any of them, he seems suspicious of me, so I'm glad when it's time to move on.

'In this way, I travel further and further away from where I started until finally, one day, I come to a forest and I see a road sign that says "Paimpont". Because I haven't seen any soldiers for a very long time, I decide to walk along the road. On the outskirts of the village, I see two men dressed in overalls who are struggling to move a heavy stone kerb, so I go over and give them a hand. They are surprised at first but then they seem grateful and when we have got the kerbstone into place, they offer to share their lunch with me. They watch as I wolf down the food, and in the end, they give me everything they have because I think they sense that I need it more than they do. They don't have much English, but I manage to make them understand that I'm willing to work for them on a regular basis in exchange for more food. They tell me that they are called Claude and Dominic. They ask me questions about myself in bad English and even though I cannot answer any of them, they don't seem suspicious. The one called Claude does most of the talking and he keeps looking at his friend and tapping his temple, the same place where my scar is. He tells me that they can't pay me anything but they *will* feed me and that he has a place where I can sleep, an old hut round the back of his house. I accept that. I am happy and for the first time in ages, I have some purpose in life and something to put in my belly.

'And then one day, I'm working with my two friends on the road and I look up and there's a boy sitting in a carriage in front of the general store and he's looking at me in a strange way, as though he recognises me, as though he knows who I am and before I know what's happening, he's running towards me, he's shouting that I'm his father and—'

'Wake up,' said Mr Sparks.

Da's eyes focused. He sat for a moment, blinking, as though he'd just woken from a deep sleep. Then he looked across the table and he smiled.

'Owen,' he said. 'I remember. I remember everything.'

Owen jumped up from his chair and ran around the table. He and his father hugged, the two of them crying.

'Don't mind me,' said a muffled voice and Owen looked back in surprise to see that he had forgotten all about Mr Sparks and that the dummy was sprawled across Owen's chair, his pink shiny face indignant. Gerard stood and picked up Mr Sparks. He carried him off towards the door.

'Let's give the two of them some time alone,' he suggested.

'Don't forget your promise,' said Mr Sparks slyly. 'No monkey business!'

'I wouldn't dream of it.' Gerard carried the dummy out of the room, closing the door behind them.

Da looked down at Owen, his eyes full of tears. Then a thought occurred to him. 'Oh my word,' he said. 'What about Megan?'

'Ah yes,' murmured Owen. 'Ma.'

He took a deep breath and told Da what had happened to her. It was the hardest thing he'd ever had to do in his life.

23

Lamballe

Quinn and Wilkins paced around Lamballe, looking for clues. They'd finally caught up with the elusive Henri late the previous evening back in Erquy and he'd told them that this was where he'd dropped the boy. So they'd set off in the hired car early that morning and now here they were, walking the cobbled streets of this pretty little town and asking every passer-by they met if they'd seen a young boy with a suitcase. But in each case they were met with indifferent shrugs and puzzled expressions. Wilkins was starting to lose patience with the whole enterprise. He was missing London and, more particularly, he was missing Ruby. What's more, he didn't appreciate some of the things that Quinn was making him a party to. Scaring the old woman back in Portsmouth, for instance. Wilkins was no angel, but he hadn't liked taking part in that. What's more, Quinn carried that heavy pistol with him everywhere, and though he claimed it was only there to scare people, Wilkins had no doubt that he would use it without hesitation if he had the least bit of provocation.

'I don't understand why we're wasting time hanging around here,' muttered Wilkins. 'That woman at the inn said the kid was heading for Paris.'

'That's what he *told* her,' admitted Quinn. 'It doesn't mean it's where he was actually going. And remember, it was Sparks that said that. We know the creature lies. It's his nature. Besides, if they really *were* going to Paris, they'd surely have taken a more direct route? Why come out here to the middle of nowhere?'

Wilkins shook his head. 'But surely it makes sense he'd go to Paris,' he insisted. 'It's where he started out all those years ago, ennit? At the theatre with Lucien Lacombe.'

'Yes, but you seem to have forgotten that we tried Paris last year and it was a dead end. And besides, it's not where Lacombe was originally from, is it? We know he originally came from somewhere in Brittany. We just don't know exactly where.'

'France is a ruddy big country,' said Wilkins.

'Oh well, thank you for that. Sometimes I wonder how we'd manage without your incisive eye for detail.'

'I'm only saying that this is like looking for a needle in a haystack.'

'And I'm only saying that we know the boy was dropped here, only a few days ago. We're on his trail. If we stay methodical and ask all the right questions, then sooner or later we're bound to get a lucky break and we'll find out where he was heading.'

'But that could take *weeks*.'

'I don't care if it takes *years*. We're not giving up on this. So you'd better get used to the idea.'

'I don't get it. All this, so you can destroy the dummy. Wouldn't it make more sense to take it back with us and study it? Find out what makes it tick?'

Quinn shook his head. 'There are some things, Wilkins, that are better left unknown. That thing is one of them.'

They were approaching what must have been the town square, where a bustling market was in progress. On the far side of it, there was an imposing-looking church with a tall spire. 'I'll ask around the market,' suggested Quinn. 'You go and enquire at the church.'

'The church? What would the kid go there for?'

'This may come as a surprise to a heathen like you, Wilkins, but to many people the church is the first place to go when you're in trouble. Now get your bloated carcass moving. Use the script if you have to.'

Wilkins knew better than to complain. Muttering to himself, he crossed the square and approached the church, in front of which stood a tall stone cross. He went past it, climbed the steps to the arched entrance, then pushed open the heavy wooden door and went inside. It was quiet in there and very cool. He stood for a moment, feeling distinctly uncomfortable. Churches always had that effect on him. It came from being brought up in a Godless family. Wilkins' parents had never had any time in their lives for prayer. Booze and gambling were his father's two pleasures and he had followed them religiously, right up to the end. Wilkins looked around. The place seemed deserted.

He took a few steps along the nave, his footsteps echoing in the silence. To his right, there was a huge stone font, elaborately decorated with mosaic designs. He was about to walk past it when something caught his eye, one of the images on the side of the font. For some reason it seemed oddly familiar to him. He stepped closer and had a proper look. The image was of two armoured men sitting astride a single horse. For a moment, he couldn't think for the life of him why it was so familiar. And then it came to him

– the little lapel badge that Quinn always wore. Wasn't this the very same image?

'*Bonjour, monsieur!*' The voice spoke from right beside him, making him jump. An elderly priest stood there, dressed in long robes. He was smiling at Wilkins, obviously keen to help, but all thoughts of Wilkins' real reason for being here were, for the moment, forgotten. He pointed a stubby forefinger to the image on the font. 'Er . . . *là?*' he muttered. '*Qu'est ce que c'est?*' It was one of the few French phrases that Wilkins had managed to pick up, but the priest looked puzzled to say the least.

'*Anglais?*' he enquired.

'*Oui.*'

'*Une minute.*' The priest waved a hand, indicating that Wilkins should stay exactly where he was. Then he turned on his heel and hurried away with a swish of his robes. Wilkins returned his attention to the image. He was convinced now that it was the same as Quinn's badge . . . and hadn't Quinn said something the other day about his ancestors coming from this part of the world? The dukes of . . . somewhere or other?

'May I help you?'

Wilkins turned in surprise to see that the elderly priest

had been replaced by a nun, a middle-aged lady with an angelic face, framed by a black wimple.

'Umm . . . yes, please. You obviously speak English, so . . .'

'I *am* English,' she assured him, with a smile. 'I came to live in France several years ago, but I haven't yet forgotten how to speak the language. I am Sister Anne.'

'Oh, delighted, I'm sure. Alfred Wilkins.' Wilkins doffed his bowler hat and then, thinking about it, refrained from putting it on again. Weren't you always supposed to keep your head uncovered in a Catholic church? He pointed again to the image on the font. 'I'm interested in this,' he said.

'Ah well, that font is very old, it dates from the—'

'Er no, not the font! I'm sure it's a very nice font and all that, but . . . it's this picture of the two geezers on the 'orse.'

Sister Anne moved a little closer and smiled. 'Ah yes. Well done for spotting that! That is a source of some controversy and a particular interest of mine, as it happens. You see, before the War, I studied French history. Of course, later on, I got the calling—'

'The calling, miss?'

'To become a nun.'

'Oh, right.'

'But I still continue to study in my spare time. A fascinating subject. Are you a scholar yourself, Mr Wilkins?'

'Er . . . not exactly,' he said. 'I'd just like to know a bit more.'

'Well, as I said, this little image is very interesting to somebody like myself. It's the seal of the Knights Templar. They were very active around this area when the church was built.'

Wilkins frowned. 'Knights Templar?' he echoed. It seemed to him that he had heard the title before, though he couldn't say exactly where. 'And who were they, exactly?'

'They were a religious order. A *secret* society, in many ways. Very powerful and wealthy people, in their day. They took part in the Crusades to the Holy Land . . . and it's said that they invented the whole concept of banking as we know it. They had secret initiation ceremonies and so forth . . . a bit like the Freemasons. You've heard of *them*, I suppose?'

Wilkins nodded. She didn't know how right she was. Back when he was in the police force, he'd often heard rumours that quite a few of the more successful officers belonged to that society, though he wasn't a member himself. You had to wait to be invited. It had long been his ambition to become a Freemason, because he'd been told that they always did rather well for themselves. Of course, it wasn't going to happen now, not since he'd been disgraced and kicked out of the police.

'So, these Templars . . . where would you find them now?'

'Oh, you wouldn't,' said Sister Anne. 'They were disbanded in the fourteenth century.'

'Really? That long ago? Why was that?'

Sister Anne frowned. 'Well, it's quite complicated . . .'

'Try me,' he suggested. 'But er . . . keep it simple.'

'Very well.' She seemed to consider for a moment. 'Well, when the Crusades to the Holy Land failed, the influence of the Templars began to weaken. Pope Clement had doubts about them and he voiced those doubts to Philip—'

'Philip?'

'King Philip of France? Because the King was already deeply in debt to the Templars, he saw an opportunity to wipe the slate clean. So he ordered that leading members should be arrested as "enemies of the faith" and their lands confiscated.'

'Strewth. That's a bit severe, ennit?'

'Oh, it got worse than that, I'm afraid. They were put

to torture and made to confess to all kinds of ridiculous things – that they worshipped idols, that they regularly spat upon the cross . . . all testimonies extracted under the most barbaric torture, you understand. Soon there were more arrests and many Templars were burned at the stake. The few who survived took whatever they could salvage and went into exile. Some to Scotland, some to Portugal . . .'

'And some to England?'

'Quite possibly.'

Wilkins thought for a moment. 'This one chap I was talking to, he said his ancestors came from around here.'

'Is that right?'

'Yeah. He said they was the Dukes of Pont . . . Pant-something?'

'Penthievre?' suggested Sister Anne.

'Yeah, that's it! Pont . . . what you said! French royalty, he reckoned he'd come from. Bit stuck-up to tell you the truth. I wasn't sure whether to believe him or not.'

'Well, it's quite possible,' said Sister Anne. 'And of course, there *is* a connection. To the Templars, I mean.'

'Is there really?'

'Oh yes, but it's quite obscure. Only somebody who has read up on the subject would know about it.'

'Hmm.' Wilkins looked at her impatiently. 'You er . . . gonna tell me what it is?' he asked hopefully.

'Oh yes, of course! You see, a man called . . . let me get the name right . . . Guillaume de l'Aigle was one of the dukes of Penthievre, back in the thirteenth century. He was also a Grand Master of the Knights Templar.'

'You don't say!' Wilkins scratched his chin. 'A Grand Master. That sounds quite important.'

'Oh, it was! It was the highest rank a member could achieve.'

'Right. And . . . what did he look like, this Gwilly . . . Guill . . . what you said?'

Sister Anne smiled. 'I really couldn't say,' she told him. 'There don't seem to be many portraits of him that have survived. Though I do seem to remember reading that his heraldic symbol was an eagle. An eagle with two heads.'

Wilkins experienced a vivid recollection. The painting in Quinn's house, the one that hung over the stairs. A knight in armour holding a flag – a flag that featured the image of a two-headed eagle. 'Well, I'll be jiggered!' he said.

'I beg your pardon?'

'Er . . . nothing, Sister. Sorry. But I was just thinking. If you was to see a man wearing a badge with that design

295

on it . . .' He pointed to the image on the font. 'I mean, in this day and age. What would that mean?'

She shrugged. 'Well, it's a long-dead society. But perhaps it would be a man who follows the beliefs of the Knights Templar. Perhaps it would mean that he was on some kind of a crusade,' she suggested. 'That was after all, their ultimate aim. To rid the world of evil and everything that challenged their belief in God.'

'I see.' Wilkins smiled thinly, recalling Quinn's experiment with the rats back in England. He couldn't help thinking that in many ways, Quinn was every bit as evil as the very thing he wanted to rid the world of. 'Well, thank you, Sister,' he said.

'I hope I've been of some help.'

'More than you could ever know. I'll bid you good day.'

He bowed his head to her and went out of the church, not even bothering to enquire about the boy and the dummy. Right now, he had other things on his mind. He studied the square and after a few moments, he spotted Quinn sitting at a wooden table in front of an inn, drinking a cup of coffee. Judging by the glum expression on his face, he hadn't found any answers to his questions. Unlike Wilkins, who thought he'd found more than he'd bargained for.

He crossed the square and took a seat opposite his employer. Quinn scowled at him. 'Any luck?'

'No, not really. Interesting church, though. Quite a history.'

Quinn regarded him suspiciously. 'Now why is that the last thing I'd expect to hear from you?' he muttered. He lifted his cup of coffee.

Wilkins ignored him. 'Got speaking to a nun in there. English lady.'

'Really. That was lucky.'

'Yeah. She told me that back in the day, this whole area was a hangout for er . . . a sort of secret society. The Knights Templars.'

That did it. Quinn nearly choked on his coffee. He glared at Wilkins across the table.

'And another coincidence,' continued Wilkins, enjoying this new-found power. 'It seems that one of your royal ancestors was one of their Grand Masters. Old Guilly-what's it.' He reached across the table and prodded the silver lapel badge on Quinn's coat. 'What do you reckon to that, then?'

Quinn's scowl deepened. 'I think you need to keep your nose out of my business,' he said quietly. 'I don't pay you to go snooping into my background.'

'Oh, I didn't,' Wilkins assured him. 'It's just something that came up. But it all makes sense now. *That's* why you're so intent on getting rid of old Sparky, ennit? See, all those things you've got in your collection back home, you know that they're fakes and you've proved it. But this dummy . . . this thing that goes against everything you believe in, he's something you can't explain. He's a . . . what was the word you used? Oh yes. An abomination.'

Quinn set down his coffee cup and gave Wilkins a look. 'You're feeling very pleased with yourself, aren't you?' he observed.

Wilkins shrugged. 'It's good to know that the old instincts haven't left me,' he admitted. 'Kind of reminds me why I wanted to be a detective in the first place.'

'That's all well and good,' snarled Quinn. 'But I'm warning you, Wilkins, if you even think about using this knowledge to your advantage, I—'

He broke off as he was interrupted by the sudden clamour of children's laughter. He and Wilkins looked up to see that an old man had just wandered into the square. He was dressed in an outlandish outfit of multi-coloured patches and a bright purple top hat. But what really caught their attention was what he was carrying in his arms – a rather splendid ventriloquist's dummy, dressed in a smart black suit. The old man took up a stance in the middle of the square and the children gathered eagerly around.

He began to perform. It was all in French so Wilkins didn't follow any of it but it soon became clear that the old man wasn't much of a ventriloquist. Whenever the dummy 'spoke', the operator's Adam's apple moved up and down and gave the game away. And there was something rather comical about the way the old man clenched his large, horse-like teeth when he produced the voice. The children didn't seem to mind though – they laughed delightedly at everything that the dummy said.

Wilkins couldn't help staring at the dummy. It was beautifully crafted, he thought, better than the average one you might see around the music halls of London, but wasn't there something terribly familiar about the pale pink face with its huge blue eyes? On impulse, Wilkins reached into his pocket and pulled out the folded poster he always carried with him. He opened it and looked at the face of the dummy in the illustration. It was remarkably similar to the one he was looking at now, not a complete copy, but in the same general style. He tilted the poster so Quinn could see it. Quinn nodded. He'd noticed the similarity too.

After a little while, the old man finished his act and pulled out a little felt bag so he could go around asking for coins. The children scattered in all directions. Clearly they had no money to give him, so he started working his way around the square. When he finally approached the table where Quinn and Wilkins were sitting, Quinn pulled out a bundle of francs and waved them enticingly. The old man was clearly interested. He moved nearer and Quinn said something in his perfect French and indicated that he should take a seat beside him.

The old man regarded him suspiciously. '*Anglais?*' he muttered.

Quinn nodded. He said something else and the old man smiled.

'*Oui, merci. Cognac, s'il vous plaît.*' Then he sat down, placing the dummy on his lap.

Quinn glanced at Wilkins. 'Go and buy our friend a glass of Cognac,' he said. 'The best they have.'

Wilkins sighed but got to his feet and went into the bar to get the drink. When he came out again, Quinn and the ventriloquist were deep in conversation. As Wilkins approached, he could see that Quinn was smiling excitedly. Wilkins set down the drink in front of the old man, who nodded his thanks, picked it up and took a generous gulp of the contents. Quinn excused himself for a moment, so he could speak to Wilkins in English.

'This is Monsieur Calvais,' he said. 'I complimented him on his wonderful ventriloquism skills.'

Wilkins grinned. 'Did you?' he muttered doubtfully.

Quinn nodded. 'Don't worry, he doesn't speak a word of English. And yes, I lied through my teeth.' He looked at the dummy, which was still slumped on Calvais' lap. 'I also said how superb his dummy was and mentioned that I was looking for somebody to make one for me. I asked him if he could recommend a place where I might buy one.' Quinn's smile stretched itself across his thin face. 'He told me that there's only one place to go to find that kind of workmanship. The same place *he* went. The shop of the celebrated toymaker, Gerard Lacombe.'

'Lacombe?' Wilkins gasped. 'But . . . that's . . .'

'Exactly. A toymaker with the same surname as Sparks' creator. And one who makes ventriloquist's dummies? Too much of a coincidence, I think.'

'So, this shop . . .'

'It's on the road to Paimpont, less than an hour's drive from here.' Quinn's smile became a triumphant grin. 'Well, don't you see, Wilkins? That has to be where they were headed. Sparks is injured. Where else would he go but to somebody who can repair him?'

'Well then, what are we waiting for?'

Quinn nodded. He got up from the table, thanked the old man profusely and bid him farewell. Just before he left, he paused to place one hand gently, almost lovingly on the head of the dummy in Calvais' lap.

Then he and Wilkins hurried away in the direction of their car.

24

Breaking the News

Owen stood by the back door of the cottage and watched as Da and Gerard climbed up into the carriage. 'We won't be long,' Gerard assured him. He was taking Da into Paimpont to meet a friend he had there, a man who Gerard thought could organise safe passage for Owen and his father back to England.

The three of them had sat up late the previous evening, discussing what they should do. Now that he had found Da, Owen had one intention uppermost in his mind. He wanted to get him home to Wales so he could take him to see Ma. He didn't know what would happen after that. He realised he couldn't expect a miracle cure for her, but at the same time, he was also aware that the main reason for her illness was Da's disappearance. If he brought him back to her, who knew what might happen?

But first, he had a difficult duty to perform. Mr Sparks

had been left in the shop overnight, far enough away so that he couldn't interrupt or overhear the conversation of his human companions. But having talked the situation through with Da and Gerard, there was now no doubt in Owen's mind. After Mr Sparks' recent confession, there was no way that Owen wanted to continue as his operator. The awkward bit was that Mr Sparks had yet to be told about the decision.

Gerard snapped the reins and the carriage moved away along the track.

'Help yourself to food,' he shouted. 'We'll only be an hour or so.' And Da looked back and waved, a warm smile on his face. It felt so good to see that smile. Owen instantly felt stronger, more in control. He turned and walked around the side of the house to the front of the shop. He took a deep breath. Then he opened the door and let himself in.

Mr Sparks was sitting in a chair, looking rather sorry for himself. When Owen came in, he gave him a sullen stare. 'Oh, here he is at last!' he exclaimed. 'They seek him here, they seek him there. They seek him blooming *everywhere*. Is he a saint or is he a liar? That darned elusive Owen Dyer!' He waited for a reaction, and when he didn't get one, he continued. 'Well, I hope you're pleased with yourself. I've been bored to tears sitting here all night. *All* night. Nothing to do, nobody to talk to.'

'I'm sorry,' Owen told him. 'We . . . that is, me and my da, we had some things to talk about'

'Oh did you now? And of course, you didn't want *me* there, spoiling it! Well, let me remind you, Owen Dyer, if it wasn't for me, your dad would still be sitting there looking like a great gormless nit. I'm the one who brought his memory back! And what thanks do I get? I get abandoned in this dump, that's what. Well, thanks a million!'

Owen frowned. He pulled over another chair and sat opposite Mr Sparks. For some reason, he didn't want to lift the dummy onto his lap. That would somehow have made it harder to say what he had to say.

'I should have thanked you before,' he admitted. 'I'm sorry I didn't. I was a little . . . confused. But I'm saying thank you now.'

'I should blooming well think so!' Mr Sparks fluttered his eyes. 'Oh well, let's not hold a grudge. I can see it must have been a very exciting time in your life. Blimey, I only wish I could see old Lucien again! I mean to say, Gerard's very nice, but nothing can beat your dear old dad, eh?'

Owen nodded. 'That's true,' he said.

'Well, come on, don't look so mournful! We need to draw up our plans.'

'Plans?' murmured Owen.

'Yes. Now, obviously you're going to want to go back to England.'

'Wales,' Owen corrected him.

'Well, no, not *Wales*, because those two blokes that were chasing us, they got a bit too close for comfort, didn't they? They could be waiting for us. So I was thinking London is a much bigger place to hide. We could—'

'They weren't chasing *us*,' Owen interrupted. 'They were chasing *you*.'

'Well, yes, I suppose they were, but . . . you and me are a team, Owie Bowie. We go together, don't we? Like peaches and cream. Fish and chips. Sausage and mash. *We belong*.'

'No.' Owen shook his head. 'No we don't. Not any more. I'm sorry, Charlie, but when me and Da leave here, you . . . you won't be coming with us.'

There was a deep silence then. Mr Sparks' expression froze, his mouth slammed shut, his eyes widened until they seemed to be popping out of his head. When he finally said something, his voice was barely more than a croak. 'Owie. You . . . you don't mean that. You can't . . .'

'I *do* mean it. I'm sorry, it's not something I feel good about but—'

Suddenly, the grin was back. 'Ooh, you devil, you! You really had me going for a minute there. Not taking me with you! That's a good 'un.'

'Mr Sparks, *please* . . .'

'Yeah, see, what I thought we'd do, we'll head straight for the old East End. There's still some cracking music halls there, and I'm sure if we can just get one audition, we'll soon have some bookings lined up and meanwhile—'

'Listen to me! I'm not going to London. I'm taking Da back to see Ma.'

'You are joking, I hope! That woman isn't safe. She'll most likely smash your da's head in, same as she did mine. And it will all be your fault. You'll probably go to jail.' He snapped into another poem. 'Owie Bowie isn't well. They've gone and put him in a cell. His mother cracked his father's head. He should have stayed with me instead!' He gave a shrill laugh, which faded quickly away when he saw Owen's grim expression.

'I'm sorry,' said Owen. 'I really am. But you'll be all right. You'll stay here with Gerard. He's promised me he'll look after you. You just have to promise to be good for him.'

'Here?' Mr Sparks looked around and Owen saw to his horror that once again, the dummy's eyes were filled with tears. '*Here*? I can't stay here. What will I do? Gerard won't even talk to me. He'll lock me in a cupboard all day long and he'll forget I'm even there. I hate being ignored! It's the worst thing in the world! Please, Owen, give me another chance. This is all because of Otto, isn't it? If I hadn't let that slip, you'd still want to take me with you, I know you would.'

Owen shook his head.

'It's not that. I just . . .'

'Look deep into my eyes, Owie. Have I ever told you that one of them is slightly bigger than the other?'

Owen turned his head away. 'I'm not falling for that again,' he said. 'I know that's how you got me to go along with you in the first place, but it's worn off now. And there's no point in going over this. My mind's made up. I've talked to Gerard, he's promised he'll keep things interesting for you . . .'

'But I'll be stuck here in the middle of nowhere. I need a life, Owie. I need something to keep me occupied. Listen, what about if you just take me as far as Portsmouth? I'll get Mr Nail to find me a—'

'That's enough,' said Owen. He got up from the chair. 'I'm not discussing this any more. Da and Gerard have gone to meet someone who reckons they can get us back to England, and from there we'll find our way home. But we can't take you with us. I'm sorry, but there it is. It'll take a day or so to sort things out, but then we're going and you'll be—'

He broke off as he heard an unexpected sound, something he hadn't heard since he'd arrived in the Brocéliande – the sound of an automobile engine. He turned and walked over to the window. A motorcar was pulling up outside. It wasn't the black Daimler and for a moment, he relaxed a little. But then he saw the two stern-faced men climbing out of the vehicle and panic jittered through him, making his heart thud in his chest.

'Oh no,' he whispered.

'Who is it?' asked Mr Sparks fearfully.

Owen backed away from the window. 'It's them,' he said.

'Them? You mean . . . ?'

Owen nodded. The men were heading towards the door now. There was no time to think. Owen span around, ran to the chair and swept Mr Sparks up in his arms. Then he went behind the counter, opened the door to the workroom and stepped inside. He turned back for a moment and examined the door. There was an ancient metal bolt on it, so he took a moment to slide it across. As he did so, he heard the shrill clamour of the bell at the front door. He turned away, went through to the kitchen and opened the back door.

He stood for a moment on the step, looking uncertainly around. He was aware of Mr Sparks shaking in his arms. For a moment, Owen was frozen in his tracks. He didn't know what to do. Then Mr Sparks looked up at him imploringly.

'Don't let them get me, Owie,' he whispered. 'Please!'

Owen didn't answer. The forest track lay ahead of him, the long ribbon of dirt unspooling as it led between the trees, deeper and deeper into the forest. There was nowhere else to go. Owen put his head down and ran.

Wilkins went to ring the bell a second time, but Quinn gave a snort of irritation and pushed him roughly aside. He reached out and turned the handle of the door, which opened easily. They found themselves in an empty shop, the shelves stacked with brightly painted wooden toys.

Quinn looked quickly around, his keen eyes taking in every detail. His gaze came to rest on a beautifully carved marionette, hanging in the window.

'This *has* to be the place,' he muttered. He spotted the door behind the counter and walked quickly around to it. He tried the handle, but it was clearly bolted from the other side. Without hesitation, he lifted one foot and kicked, hard, just beside the handle. There was a harsh splintering sound and the door flew back, the bolt shattered. They walked through into a workshop but that too was empty. An open door at the back of the room gave onto a small kitchen and there was a clear view of another open doorway and the track leading into the forest. At the far end of it was the figure of a boy, running for all he was worth.

Quinn cursed beneath his breath. He reached into his pocket and pulled out the pistol. He began to raise it to aim it at the fleeing figure.

'Wait,' said Wilkins. 'You're not going to—'

Quinn grunted. He lowered the pistol. 'You're right,' he admitted. 'He's well out of range. Come on.' And with that, he ran through the kitchen and out of the back door, his long legs covering the distance with ease. Wilkins stared after him for a moment. 'You . . . you aren't going to do anything daft are you?' he shouted after Quinn, but he got no reply. So with a groan, he followed his employer, his heavy frame lumbering in pursuit.

25

The Chase

Owen ran full pelt along the winding track. He had only been this way once before and then, only as far as the Merlin Tree. He had no idea what lay beyond it – more forest, he imagined, and hopefully places where he might hide. Mr Sparks had his arms up around Owen's neck and was gazing fearfully back over the boy's right shoulder.

'They're following us!' he gasped.

Owen didn't dare to look back, in case he tripped on a tree root, so he just kept going, while he tried to think of some kind of plan. Da and Gerard would be in Paimpont by now, he decided. He had no way of letting them know what was happening here and who knew when they would be back? He didn't know anyone else in this area or even where there were other homes where he might take refuge. It occurred to him that the two men weren't interested in him, that he could just leave Mr Sparks on the track and

313

carry on running and that would be the end of it. But the idea filled him with a sense of shame and though he knew that the dummy had done bad things, still it didn't seem right to just abandon him to his fate.

'They're gaining on us, Owie!' Mr Sparks' voice was hoarse with terror. 'You've got to run faster.'

'I'm going as fast as I can,' gasped Owen. 'I can't—'

He broke off in surprise as a section of tree trunk just ahead of him burst open in an explosion of splintered bark, flinging fragments of wood in all directions. 'What was that?' he cried.

'He's firing at us!' squealed Mr Sparks. 'He's a madman. He's got a gun!'

'Oh my . . .' Owen tried not to panic. It had never occurred to him that these men might be prepared to kill him.

'Get off the track,' said Mr Sparks. 'We're sitting ducks here.'

Even amidst his panic, Owen registered the command and when he glimpsed a narrow trail veering off to his right, he took it, plunging headlong through the under-growth, trying to ignore the twigs and dry leaves that scraped at his face and his clothing, as though attempting to hold him back. His heart thudded in his chest and a thick sweat trickled down his spine. But he didn't hesitate. He lifted one arm to shield his eyes as he blundered through a screen of thick foliage and then emerged suddenly into open air. Ahead of him, he saw a stretch of flat, open ground and beyond that, the still-mirrored surface of the lake he had seen last time he was here. It occurred to him that Mr Sparks probably wouldn't be so keen to be here, but the dummy was still gazing back the way they had come, so Owen kept going, telling himself that he'd run around the long curving edge of the lake to its far side, where thicker undergrowth seemed to offer more places to hide.

'Are they still coming after us?' he gasped.

'I don't . . . I can't . . . ah, yes, I can see them now! I think the trees have slowed them up a bit.'

'Good.' The muscles in Owen's legs felt like they were on fire, but he didn't dare slow down. He aimed for the easternmost edge of the lake and told himself if he could just get around it, then perhaps he had a chance.

Quinn burst through the undergrowth and came to a halt, gasping for breath. He studied the lake for a moment, thinking that he'd lost his quarry, but then he saw the boy, a distant figure, toiling around the far side of it. He lifted the gun and took aim, but instantly dismissed the idea. He was a decent shot but even an expert marksman wouldn't have a chance at this distance.

Just then, Wilkins came blundering out into the open, gasping and wheezing like a walrus. He nearly ran into Quinn, but managed to pull himself to a halt just in time. He leaned forward, hands on hips, as he tried to fill his lungs with air. He was looking at the gun in Quinn's hand.

'We . . . won't need that . . . surely?' he protested. 'He's only a . . . kid.'

'Thanks for the advice,' said Quinn. 'But he's fast, so if I have to use it, I will. He's not getting away from me this time.' He pointed off to his left. 'You go . . . around that way,' he suggested. 'We'll cut him off.'

'That way?' Wilkins stared off at the still-distant lake for a moment in sheer disbelief. 'But . . . that's miles.'

'Move your fat carcass!' snapped Quinn. 'If the boy eludes us again, I won't be responsible for my actions.'

'But—'

'Move!'

Wilkins straightened up and began to plod away.

'Faster!' bellowed Quinn and he waved the pistol, as

though suggesting that he might actually shoot Wilkins if he didn't pick up the pace. Wilkins took the hint and broke into an ungainly trot. Quinn turned back to look for his quarry. Now the boy was close to the edge of the lake and beginning to circle around it.

Quinn leaned over and spat onto the grass. Then he too began to run.

They were moving alongside the lake now, and for the first time Mr Sparks noticed where they were headed.

'Not here!' he hissed anxiously. 'Owie, I can't go here.'

'There's no other choice,' Owen told him, grimly. 'We have to.'

'But this . . . this is where—'

'I know. But . . . don't worry, we're only going . . . around it. There are more trees on the far side and . . . maybe we'll find somewhere to hide.'

Mr Sparks didn't reply to that but Owen noticed he was still trembling.

'Where . . . where are they now?' he gasped.

'I can only see one of them,' whispered Mr Sparks. 'The thin one.'

'Maybe the other one . . . dropped out?'

'Maybe. He was no stranger to a chip supper.'

The track around the lake began to curve to the left and Owen went with it, telling himself that there were many tall trees up ahead and that when he reached the cover of them, where the thin man couldn't see him, he'd angle sharp right and head into deeper undergrowth. He passed a pile of boulders, piled higgledy-piggledy one on top of another, leading steeply upwards. He realised that this was the diving place, the spot where young Charles had climbed up to his doom all those years ago. He wasn't sure if Mr Sparks had recognised it but he wasn't going to say anything. He rounded the bend, telling himself that soon he'd be able to make his break for deeper forest. But that was when he saw the figure straight ahead of him, the heavyset man with the bowler hat, who was lumbering around the western end of the lake and coming straight back towards him. Owen came to a halt, staring straight ahead, mouth open. The man had seen him now and was quickening his pace.

'Why have you stopped?' cried Mr Sparks. 'They'll catch us!'

Owen turned on his heel, began to retrace his steps, telling himself that if he broke for the deeper woods now, the second man would see him and would head him off before he ever got to them. He ran back past the pile of rocks, aware now that Mr Sparks was making a low whimpering sound. Owen ignored him, started towards the curve of the lake again. To his horror, he saw that the thin man was heading straight towards him. He was trapped. For a moment, he froze, not knowing what to do, but somehow he willed his feet to move and they obeyed him. He wheeled around, looking desperately left and right. There was only one possible escape. He ran back to the rocks and began to climb, telling himself that if he could get high enough, his pursuers might assume he'd headed into the trees and go that way.

'What are you doing?' shrieked Mr Sparks. 'No, Owen, not here, not here!'

'Quiet, they'll hear you,' snapped Owen. 'We're just going to—'

'No, no, no, no, no!' Mr Sparks was screaming, his voice echoing around the rocks. Owen pulled him away from his shoulder and clamped a hand tight across his mouth, continuing upwards as he did so, his feet straining to find purchase on the slippery grey rock. After a few moments, he had to release Mr Sparks and let him hang around his neck so he could use his arms, but thankfully, he'd gone quiet.

The rock face here was very steep. Owen spotted a shallow opening a short distance to his left and edging sideways, crammed himself into it, hoping against hope that he would not be visible from below. He stiffened as he heard voices.

'Where the hell is he?' snarled the thin man.

'He didn't pass me,' insisted the other one. 'I swear. He saw me and turned back. Then he went around the bend out of sight.'

'He didn't get past me either. Which means . . .' A long pause. Then a sly, mocking call. 'Hello, up there! My goodness, you are resourceful, aren't you? But that looks like a dead end, I'm afraid. My advice would be to come down from there and hand the dummy to us. That way, you won't get hurt.'

Owen pressed himself back hard against the rock. Mr Sparks' face was only inches from his and the dummy's eyes were closed, his lips moving as though he was muttering some kind of prayer.

'Hello? We know you're up there. Be a sensible boy and give the dummy to me. If you do that, I'll let you walk away unharmed. But if you make me come up there and get you, I won't be so forgiving.'

'Look, he's only a kid.' The other man's voice sounded worried. 'Let me talk to him, see if I can get him to come down.'

'Stay out of this, Wilkins.' A pause. 'Well, boy? What's it to be?'

Silence. Owen was aware of a breeze, blowing on his face. It ruffled Mr Sparks' red hair. The dummy opened his eyes and looked straight at Owen.

'Don't give me up,' he whispered. 'Please, Owie. He wants to hurt me.'

Owen nodded. He moved sideways, back out of the crevice and started to climb again.

'Right,' he heard the thin man say. 'You asked for it. Coming – ready or not!'

'You don't expect me to climb up there, do you?' The second man sounded nervous.

'Earn your money, Wilkins.'

'But—'

There was a brief silence and Owen could picture the scene, the thin man pointing the gun at his companion.

'All right, all right. I'm coming.'

Silence fell, the tense silence of fierce concentration as they all fell to the task of scaling the rock. Owen didn't have the first idea what he'd do when he got to the top. Hopefully there'd be some way of climbing down the far side. He knew only too well what might happen if he tried to dive off.

'Owen, this is ridiculous!' The thin man's voice echoed off the rocks. 'You might as well just accept it. It's over. We've come a long way to find you, you needn't think we're going to let a little thing like this deter us.'

Owen gritted his teeth, reached up to find another handhold.

'You think he's charming, do you? You think he's some kind of adorable jackanapes? Let me assure you, he's not. I don't suppose you know that he's had several owners before you. Well, he has. And I'd like to be able to tell you that all of them have died of natural causes. But . . . at least three of them, Owen . . . at least three, have suffered deaths that were highly suspicious. I'm including Otto Schilling in that. I believe you met Otto just before he died. Do you think he deserved what happened to him?'

Owen paused to look at Mr Sparks. The dummy was staring back at him, shaking his head from side to side.

'Shall I tell you what he is, Owen? He's pure evil. Unnaturally conceived, born out of madness and desperation. And a user, Owen, make no mistake about that. Like some kind of vampire, leeching the life out of innocent people. I swore when I first heard about him that I would eradicate him. I swore a solemn oath to do so. And you . . . you just think you're being noble. Protecting him. When really, the only person here who needs protecting . . . is you.'

Owen paused again. He looked at Mr Sparks, but the dummy was still shaking his head.

'Don't listen to him,' whispered Mr Sparks. 'He's mad.'

'You see, Owen, one day when you're old, like Otto was, that creature will realise that you've outlived your usefulness. That's when he'll decide to move on. It's happened many times. Ask yourself. Is that what you want? Is it?'

Owen continued upwards and quite suddenly, he was at the top, a great level slab of stone that overhung the lake. He clambered up the last few steps, got himself upright, then walked to the edge and looked over. Beside him, Mr Sparks gave a long, low moan. 'Don't jump,' he whispered.

'Don't worry, I'm just looking for a place to climb down,' hissed Owen.

323

But there was nowhere. He moved from left to right, peering over the edge, trying to spot a possible descent, but it all looked too steep, too precarious, impossible. And then he sensed movement behind him and he turned to see that the thin man was pulling himself over the edge. He straightened up and slid a hand into his pocket to pull out the gun. He strolled forward, smiling triumphantly, the pistol pointing at Owen's chest.

'Nowhere else to go,' he observed. He moved closer. 'What a shame. You're a plucky boy, there's no doubt of that. But I'm more than a match for you.' He made a gesture with his free hand. 'Now . . . hand the dummy over.'

Owen shook his head. 'No,' he said. 'You can't have him.'

The thin man laughed. 'You don't understand, boy. I'm not *asking* you. I'm merely telling you what's going to happen. Give him to me.'

Again, Owen shook his head. 'Why do you want him so badly?' he asked. 'What's he ever done to you?'

'To me? Nothing. This isn't a personal thing, Owen. You see, I belong to a society; a society that has pledged itself to preserving the natural order. That . . . *thing* you're holding. That's not natural. That's a twisted impersonation of humanity. Not so very long ago, people would have burned it alive in the town square. Now, they look and they think it's amusing . . . charming. They don't understand. They never will. I'm doing what I can do to cure a sickness in society. As long as that freak lives, there can be no rest for me. He must be destroyed.'

'You . . . you can't do that!' protested Owen.

'Oh, but I can. It's going to happen. You may as well accept that.' The thin man lifted the gun and pointed it at Owen's face. 'Now, for the last time, are you going to—'

He broke off at the sound of a grunt behind him. The other man was just hauling himself onto the platform. His face was grimy with sweat and his clothes torn in several places. He pulled himself over the edge and went down in an ungainly sprawl. He lay there for a moment, and then seeing what was going on, managed to get himself upright. He moved closer, wiping at his sweaty face with the sleeve of his jacket.

'Oh, now, Mr Quinn,' he said, pointing to the gun. 'There's no need for that, surely. Like I said, he's just a boy.'

'Wilkins, when I want your opinion, I'll tell you what it is,' growled Quinn. 'And the boy is frankly being very stubborn.'

'But he's got nowhere else to go.' Wilkins smiled at

Owen. 'You can see that, can't you?' he said. 'The jig's up, son. Time to throw in the towel.'

Owen stared defiantly back at him. 'Mr Sparks is my friend,' he said. 'I can't just walk away from him.'

'He's not the sort of friend a boy like you needs,' insisted Wilkins.

'How do you know?' snapped Mr Sparks, talking for the first time since they'd been cornered. 'How do you know what Owie wants?'

Wilkins' eyes got very big and his mouth opened in a grin. 'Blimey,' he said. 'I've heard so much about you over this last two years and finally, I hear you speak.' He looked at Quinn. 'He's just as you said!'

'What were you expecting?' sneered Quinn.

'But he's . . . almost human!'

'Don't be fooled, Wilkins. That's how he works.'

'I tell you what,' said Mr Sparks, concentrating all his attention on Wilkins now. 'There's something you don't know. We've got money. A great deal of money.' He glanced up at Owen. 'Isn't that right?' he said.

'Y . . . yes,' said Owen.

'What if we were to pay you to let us go?' asked Mr Sparks.

'We're not interested,' said Quinn.

There was a silence.

'No, 'ang on a minute, let him speak,' said Wilkins. 'How much money are we talking about?'

Mr Sparks' eyelids fluttered. 'How does a hundred thousand smackers sound?' he asked.

Wilkins' expression suggested that it sounded very interesting indeed.

'You see,' continued Mr Sparks, 'I know where I could lay my hands on that money today. I'd be happy to give it to you in exchange for my freedom.'

Wilkins licked his lips and looked at Quinn. 'A hundred thousand,' he muttered. 'That's a lot of money.'

'Don't be ridiculous,' said Quinn. 'You surely don't believe him? Can't you see what he's trying to do? He'll say anything if he thinks it'll get him off the hook.'

'Ooh, no, I'm telling the truth,' insisted Mr Sparks. 'You see, this is my home place. Back near the house, there's a fortune in gold and diamonds hidden away . . . stuff I've been accumulating over the years. A bit of a nest egg. It's all yours if you let us go.'

Quinn thumbed back the hammer of the pistol. 'That's enough,' he said. 'Now, boy, no more nonsense. I'm going to count to three and if you haven't handed over the dummy—'

'Wait,' interrupted Wilkins. 'Just a moment. We shouldn't be too hasty,' he said. 'Maybe . . . maybe he *has* got some treasure. And besides, I didn't sign on with you for *this*. Pointing a gun at a kid. I don't think that's right.'

'You don't *think*?' Quinn's mouth twisted into an ugly grimace. 'Let me remind you, Wilkins, you signed on for whatever I tell you to do.'

'Yes, but . . . with respect, Mr Quinn, it's all right for you with your millions in the bank. Maybe this is a chance to do myself some good. Maybe we should let him show us where this gold is hidden and then—'

Quinn took a step forward, raising the gun as he did so. Before Wilkins could move, Quinn brought the heavy barrel down hard against the side of his head, knocking him to the ground. Wilkins fell heavily, groaned once and then lay still.

Quinn gazed down at him for a moment and then looked up into Owen's appalled face. 'I think that proves that I mean what I say,' he murmured. 'So, let's go back to where we were, shall we? I'm going to count to three and if you haven't handed that dummy to me, I am going to shoot you where you stand. Do I make myself clear?'

Owen swallowed hard and nodded.

'Excellent. Right then, let's see if you come to your senses. One . . . two . . .'

'All right!' It was Mr Sparks who spoke and Owen looked down at him in surprise. 'It's no use, Owie. The game's up. I've had a good run, but it's time to face up to reality.'

'But . . . he's going to . . .'

'I know. But it's all right. Just hand me over to him. The last thing I want is for you to be hurt.' As he said the last line, he gave Owen a sly wink.

Owen nodded. Mr Sparks unhooked his arms from around Owen's neck. 'Turn me around,' he murmured. Owen did as he was told and, gripping Mr Sparks by the waist, he began to hand him over. Quinn reached out his free hand to take him. And in that instant, Owen felt the dummy's legs kick back against his chest with a power that Owen would never have credited – a power that propelled him forward through the air, his hands outstretched to claw at Quinn's face. Mr Sparks' gloved fingers tore at the thin man's eyes and Quinn shouted something. He dropped the gun and lifted his own hands to try and push the dummy away, but Mr Sparks was screaming now, screaming like a wild beast. His legs wrapped themselves around Quinn's neck in a powerful embrace as he punched and clawed and dug at the man's face. Quinn turned around, trying to fend his attacker off. As he reeled backwards, he stepped on the pistol, which slid on the smooth stone, carrying him to the very edge of the platform. Owen saw what was about to happen and he lunged forward. Quinn's heels teetered on the brink and he lost his balance, falling backwards towards the water. Mr Sparks threw out one hand and Owen managed to grasp it; just as Quinn, falling, grabbed hold of the dummy's other hand.

There was an instant, while everything seemed to freeze. Owen clung on, as Quinn clung on and Mr Sparks, torn between the two of them, looked up into Owen's face and said, 'Well, I didn't see this coming!' Then Owen felt himself being dragged forward, Quinn's weight pulling him towards destruction. He slid face-down across the smooth stone, until his head and shoulders crossed the edge of the drop. Then, unexpectedly, a pair of strong hands grabbed Owen's ankles, anchoring him. He glanced back in surprise to see Wilkins' bloody face, grinning at him.

Owen opened his mouth to shout something. But then he saw the look of agony on Mr Sparks' eyes, mingled with one of defeat. A fraction of a second later, the dummy's upraised arm tore away from his body with a hideous rending sound. Quinn started to fall again, still clutching his prize. Owen watched, horrified, as the two figures hurtled hand in hand to destruction. They seemed to fall for a very long time. Then they hit the water in a great splash of foam and went straight under. Owen lay there, staring down, holding his breath, waiting for one or the other of them to come back to the surface. But neither of them did.

There was a silence, a long deep silence, during which he heard a distant bird calling. Something moved in his hand. He looked in mute horror, to see that he was still clutching Mr Sparks' arm. It was twitching, the gloved hand opening and closing against Owen's, as though trying to find something that was now out of reach. Owen gave a grunt of disgust and let the arm go. It fell, spinning end over end, then hit the water with a small splash, and sank quickly out of sight. Owen lay there, staring down. He heard a grunt from beside him and when he looked up, he saw Wilkins trying to sit up, the deep gash in his head still pumping blood down his face. He said, 'Is either of 'em alive?'

Owen looked again and the water was nearly still now, the last ripples settling themselves on the green surface. Nothing had come up from the depths – nothing. He waited, thinking that if he counted to ten, something would appear. But he got to ten and there was still nothing. His vision blurred and something hot swelled like a balloon in his chest. His shoulders began to move rhythmically up and down and it was only after a few moments that he realised he was crying.

EPILOGUE

Wilkins steered the Daimler in through the entrance gates and cruised along the driveway towards the Denbigh Mental Asylum. It was good to be back behind the wheel of the beloved automobile. It had been waiting for him in Portsmouth, right where he'd left it. When he'd tried the engine, it had started first time. He'd pretty much decided to hang onto it, at least until somebody started asking awkward questions about it. He loved that Daimler.

He looked in the driving mirror at the boy and his father, sitting side by side in the back. Wilkins had no idea how the father had suddenly appeared on the scene. As he'd understood it, he was supposed to have died in the War. Wilkins would have loved to talk the matter through, ask a few questions in that policeman way he still had, but his two passengers had barely spoken a word on the long drive from Portsmouth and had made it clear that Wilkins was only travelling with them on sufferance. Oh, they'd accepted his offer of a lift across country to North Wales, but grudgingly, as though they were doing him the favour.

He could understand how they felt. He'd put the kid through a bad time, after all . . . but at the end there, he'd grabbed onto his ankles and stopped him going over the edge. He'd actually saved the boy's life. Surely that had to count for something?

Looking back over the last few days, Wilkins felt as though he was remembering some kind of bad dream. But he had to admit that being free of Quinn after so long in his employment did feel unexpectedly liberating, even if it also meant an end to his regular wage. No matter, he told himself. He'd find some other way to earn a crust. Something would turn up.

The last day or so at the cottage in the woods had been strange, to say the least. The French toymaker, Lacombe, had spent a lot of time splashing around in the shallows of the lake and eventually, he'd found Quinn's body, mired amongst the weeds on the lake bed and had managed to pull him to shore, so Wilkins could have a proper look at him. Quinn's head was lolling at a peculiar angle, and on his face there was still a look of indignation, as though even in death, he couldn't believe that the dummy had got the better of him.

As for Mr Sparks, there was no sign of him, not a scrap, though the Frenchman had spent the best part of two days searching. It was as though the dark, cold lake had swallowed him whole, as though it had been waiting all those hundreds of years for his return.

And that had been the end of it. Lacombe had promised to wait a day or so before informing the police of the 'accident' that he'd chanced upon, which would give Owen, his father and Wilkins time to make themselves scarce. Wilkins still had the hire car, which he could take back to Erquy. Lacombe's shady friend had organised safe passage across the channel, something that Wilkins felt obliged to pay for, though admittedly, he'd used what was left of Quinn's money. After everything that had happened, it seemed the least he could do.

And now here they were, the three of them, at their parting of the ways. Wilkins watched as the boy and his father climbed out of the back of the automobile and stood staring towards the big grey building with looks of apprehension on their faces.

Wilkins wound down the window and smiled out at

them, though he knew that the livid half-healed scar on the side of his head made him look like something out of *Frankenstein*. 'Will you two be all right from here?' he asked.

Owen turned back and managed a thin smile. 'Yes, thank you,' he said. He seemed to think for a moment. 'What will *you* do?' he asked.

'Me?' Wilkins shrugged. 'Something legal,' he said. 'For a change.' He chuckled. 'Tell you the truth, I can't wait to get home to my Ruby. Get a decent cup of tea and some kind words.' He sighed. 'Look kid, I want you to know . . . I was helping Quinn to get the dummy and all that, I can't pretend otherwise. But I never wanted anybody to get hurt. Specially not a kid. You do believe that, don't you?'

Owen shrugged. 'I suppose so,' he said.

Wilkins smiled. 'Well, I'll get going,' he said. He nodded towards the huge stone building. 'I hope everything goes all right in—'

But the boy had already turned away. He was standing with his father now, and as Wilkins watched the two of them began to walk purposefully towards the main entrance. Wilkins watched them for a few moments. He'd only managed to get the odd word out of the boy on the way over. As far as Wilkins could tell, he seemed like a decent enough kid, but he could only begin to guess at his story.

It was time to go. Wilkins wound the window back up and hit the starter motor. He grinned as, once again, the engine purred smoothly into life. Now he only had the long drive back to London to think about. He sincerely hoped that nobody would come looking for the Daimler for a very long time. There were still a lot of places he planned to take it to.

He slipped the automobile into gear and drove away.

Ma still had the same room. It seemed to Owen that it was months since he'd been here, though it was really only a matter of days.

'Please be careful what you say to her.' It was the same ruddy-faced orderly as last time and Owen thought to himself that, after the last visit the man had good reason to be nervous. He'd told Owen, rather crossly in the reception, that it had taken days to calm Ma down and it was really only because his father was accompanying Owen this time that he'd finally agreed to risk another visit.

Looking through the bars, Owen saw that Ma was in

her usual place, sitting on the wooden chair in front of the window, her face turned away.

The orderly unlocked the door and opened it. He seemed on the point of saying something else but the fierce look on Da's face must have made him decide to stay silent. Owen and Da walked into the bare room and the door clanged shut behind them.

'Remember now,' said the orderly, through the bars. 'Nice and calm.' He moved away.

There was a long silence. Da stood there, looking as though he didn't have the first idea what to say or do, so in the end, it was Owen who broke the silence. 'Ma,' he said. 'Ma, I've brought somebody to see you.'

No reaction.

'Ma, look! Look who's here. It's somebody you've been wanting to see for a long time.'

She turned in her seat then, and for a moment her expression was apprehensive, as though she was half expecting to see a malevolent dummy in Owen's arms, a creature with a pale pink face and wild red hair. But then she saw Da looking down at her and she relaxed into a delighted smile. 'Gareth,' she said. 'There you are!' She looked at Owen. 'See, didn't I tell you he'd be back?'

'You did,' said Owen gently. 'That's exactly what you said.' Impulsively, he took hold of Da's arm and pulled him closer to Ma. Then he put his father's hand against his mother's and watched as the two hands enclosed each other in a strong but tender grip.

Ma turned and looked back out of the window. 'I think it's going to be a lovely day,' she said. 'I've been sitting here looking at the world and thinking that it's not such a bad place. Shall we just stay here and watch for a while?'

'Yes, Megan,' said Da. He used his free hand to reach out and gently stroke her hair. 'I'd like that very much.'

Owen stepped back a little and looked at the scene, a scene he'd imagined in his head a hundred times or more. He smiled. It was everything he'd been hoping for. Everything.

For a moment, an image flashed into his head, the image of a pale pink face and piercing blue eyes, staring up through fathoms of cold, green water . . . but he shook his head and with an effort, pushed the image away. He didn't want to think about Mr Sparks or any of the things that had happened to him in France. He wanted to savour this moment, the one he'd longed for, and he didn't want anything to spoil it.

He didn't know what happened next. He only knew that for the first time in ages, there was the potential for something good to come along. Whatever form it chose to take, he was really looking forward to it.

THE PIPER

DANNY WESTON

He who pays the piper calls the tune

On the eve of World War Two, Peter and Daisy are
evacuated to a remote farmhouse. From the moment
they arrive, they are aware that something evil haunts
the place. Who plays the eerie music that can only be
heard at night? And why is Daisy so irresistibly drawn
to it? When Peter uncovers a dark family secret, he
begins to realise that his sister is in terrible danger,
and to save her he must face an
ancient curse...

'Wonderfully twisty chiller
that's sure to make you want to
keep all of the lights on'
Scotsman

9781783440511 £6.99

THE DOGS

ALLAN STRATTON

Cameron and his mom have been on the run for five years. His father is hunting them. At least, that's what Cameron's been told. When they settle in an isolated farmhouse, Cameron starts to see and hear things that aren't possible. Soon he's questioning everything he thought he knew – and his own mind.

Something is waiting for him, something from long ago. Cameron must uncover its dark secrets before it tears him apart.

'Brilliant, page-turning and eerie. Had me guessing to the very end'
Joseph Delaney

'Creepy, satisfying and exciting'
Bookseller

9781783442256 £7.99